TWO CALVIN

A Zero Calvin Novel

BRIAN CRAMER

TWO CALVIN
A ZERO CALVIN NOVEL

Published by Brian Cramer Books
www.briancramerbooks.com

ISBN-13: 978-0-9961529-2-1
ISBN-10: 099615292X

ACKNOWLEDGMENTS

Firstly, I want to apologize to Larry Niven for using his sunflower idea, but it was just too perfect not to use here.

I would also like to apologize to Terry Pratchett for using his idea about the "rough music," which is derived from a genuine English folk custom, by the way.

Next, I would like to thank my two proofreaders, Veronica Lamb and Sayuri Takahashi, who do a fantastic job and are only paid with Starbucks gift cards. Yes, sometimes a few mistakes do make it through, but they are mere drops in a sea of red ink, I assure you.

Lastly, I would just like to mention Rebecca Osborn for no other reason than she asked me to because it makes her feel special. I bet you thought I wouldn't really do it, eh, Rebecca?

Oh wait, I had one more. I also want to wish Josh Reid good luck in writing his first book. Apparently, I inspired him to start writing. I hope it works out for you, buddy.

CHAPTER 1

Calvin woke up the same way he did almost every morning —
more tired than when he went to bed and late for work. Sorry,
no — force of habit. That is not how it happened at all. What
actually happened was that Calvin woke up some time just
before ten in the morning feeling both restful and happy. He also
was not late for work because he was his own boss now and was
very lenient with himself when it came to tardiness.

Actually, Calvin was not quite his own boss. Not counting
Ariel, Calvin still had one person that he had to answer to, and
that was Tarpa. She had the final say in all of his decisions. But
in return, Calvin had the final say in hers. This was by design,
and had been agreed upon by both parties not long after they
had arrived on Evionia. The conversation that had brought about
this strange agreement had gone as follows:

One day while walking together along the riverbank, Tarpa
suddenly turned to Calvin and said, "I've been thinking."

Calvin tensed when he heard these words, but managed an
encouraging smile. "About what?" he asked.

"It seems to me that you and I are now essential for each
other's happiness. And because of this, we each have a vested
interest in keeping the other one safe and happy," she
explained.

Calvin made a face. "How romantic. I love you too, sweetie."

Tarpa continued unperturbed, "I think we can both agree that there are times when we let the stresses of life dictate our actions instead of calm rationality."

"Sometimes we get pissed off and do stupid things," translated Calvin. "Sure, it happens sometimes. What about it?"

"Only now," explained Tarpa, "those bad decisions impact us both."

"True," agreed Calvin. "So what do you propose?"

She answered him with a question. "Have you ever heard of mutually assured destruction?"

Calvin made a bewildered face at her and answered, "Yeah, it was sort of the philosophy of the world's superpowers during my time. The idea was that if all the superpowers had nuclear weapons, then they all had the ultimate trump card to use on each other if ever one of them got too far out of hand. But as a consequence of this, it also meant that the country that used such a weapon would almost assuredly be obliterated during the retaliatory strike. A nuclear attack was the ultimate threat, but at the same time it was a mostly hollow one because the reality of nuclear war was almost inconceivable. Almost inconceivable. It was that 'almost' that kept everyone in line."

"Exactly," said Tarpa. "And what I suggest we do is very similar. I would like to enter into a pact with you. A solemn pact that must not be broken."

"What did you have in mind?" asked Calvin with suspicion, hoping the word "suicide" would not come into play.

Tarpa answered, "I intend to give you final and unquestionable veto power over any and all of my actions."

Calvin started to crack a smile, but Tarpa quickly added, "But in return, you must grant me final and unquestionable veto power over any and all of your actions."

Calvin's half smile froze while he contemplated this.

Tarpa noticed the concentration on his face and said, "You're thinking it through. Good. This isn't something to take lightly."

Calvin tilted his head and said to her, "That could actually work, couldn't it? I mean, my first thought was that I could boss you around, but then I realized that apart from the fact that that would make me an asshole, I'd also be opening myself up to retaliation. So I'd only ever use the power if I thought it was vitally important to stop you from doing something detrimental. And, of course, it would be the same way for you when dealing with me."

"Mutually assured destruction," offered Tarpa.

Calvin shook his head. "No, mutually assured happiness. I think this could really work. In fact, why don't we make it our wedding vow to each other?"

"Calvin! Are you proposing we get married?" asked Tarpa with some surprise and much delight.

Calvin furrowed his brow while he examined his own thoughts. He smiled. "Yes, I suppose I am."

"Did you hear that, Ariel?" asked Tarpa. "I accept. Please update the public records accordingly."

Calvin said, "Wha?"

Before Tarpa could answer his puzzlement, and without ceremony, the following text appeared at the bottom of their display lenses:

Ariel: **Marital status update. New marital status: Married. Congratulations. Final confirmation in two days after syncing with Earth.**

Tarpa kissed him. Calvin asked, "Is that it? I thought there would be like...cake...and a ceremony...and...I don't know, maybe fireworks or something."

Tarpa smiled at him. "We'll have a huge party later, I promise. And as for fireworks, well, just wait for tonight."

Calvin frowned. "But they don't have fireworks on this planet yet...and...I'm being very, very thick right now, aren't I?" he mumbled as Tarpa started to kiss his neck.

And so, that is how the two lovebirds entered into their unusual agreement of absolute authority over one another. An agreement that, somewhat surprisingly, has formed the basis for their happy marriage for over a year now.

Calvin thought about Tarpa as he sat up in bed and stretched. Living on Evionia had made him somewhat philosophical, and as such he had picked up the strange but endearing habit of counting his blessings every morning. He did this by visualizing the many things that made him grateful for his current life. Tarpa was always at the top of the list. Well, almost always. She had dropped down to the number two position for a few days last week after she forbade him to eat any more of Mrs. Fredrick's fudge pops because he was starting to get "jiggles" around his waist, as she called them.

Calvin thought about Tarpa, about his great home, his

sometimes troubling but very rewarding business, the new friends he met so far, and the beautiful world he had moved to.

Tarpa, too, had slowly come to think of this new place as home. Initially, however, she had been less than enthused about her new life on Evionia. OK, sure, she was with Calvin and that was great, but why did it have to be on this "backwards-ass, inbred-filled, hunk of crap planet where we have to shit outside in a box and live like a couple of Neanderthals?", as she had put it.

Back then, She would sometimes spend days at a time pacing around the house in boredom. When she'd finally had enough of that, she would take a trip back to Earth, or as she called it, "fucking civilization," where she would sometimes go on a "Dark Angel" assignment to relieve some stress.

Despite Calvin's initial promise that there would be thousands of people to kill on Evionia, it turned out that until a large number of the Evionian's began using the Ariel system, her services as a Dark Angel would not be required. Ariel and the Evionian's needed time to acclimate to one another before Tarpa could start culling the herd.

These days, however, Tarpa hardly ever complained about Evionia and rarely went on her sabbaticals back to Earth. This was partly because Calvin had finally hired some people to install indoor plumbing into their home, but mostly because Tarpa had found a hobby — one that she was very proud of and surprisingly good at.

Calvin heard his wife calling to him from the kitchen. He put on his dressing gown and shuffled over to see what she wanted.

"Could you go out to the garden and get me two ripe tomatoes?"

Calvin nodded sleepily and shuffled back to the bedroom. He changed out of his dressing gown and put on three pairs of pants, two heavy sweatshirts, two jackets, some thick leather boots, and a full face helmet that was originally meant to be used in conjunction with a space suit for doing emergency repairs to the outside of their shuttle.

Calvin walked out of the back door of their house and into the back yard. Their back yard was huge — over ten acres, in fact. The two acres nearest the house contained freshly cut grass, while the back eight contained the "garden", which in reality was a small farm and Tarpa's pride and joy.

The weather on Evionia was particularly excellent for

growing crops. It had a small quark sun that doubled as a satellite of Evionia, with the two spinning together like a couple of figure skaters holding hands. This strange sun, which really was strange because it was composed mostly of "strange" quarks, warmed Evionia less than the Earth's sun warmed it, but Evionia had much less of an axial tilt and the bulk of its landmass was centered on the equator. This lessened the seasonal effect and, together with the massive ocean, kept the temperature very pleasant for most of the year.

A keen observer might therefore wonder why Calvin was dressed for a polar expedition. The answer of which is this: protection.

For this garden was Tarpa's, and she was a strategist at heart. A good strategist will always use the given resources at hand for maximum benefit.

For political and environmental reasons, using metal and wood in the massive amounts required to build a security fence around the perimeter of her garden would have been seen as gluttonous.

Not wishing to offend the locals but still wishing to protect her garden, Tarpa had instead used a resource that was both renewable and abundant — plant life. With Ariel's help, Tarpa had collected samples from both Earth and Evionia. She had spliced some, cross-pollinated others, and even had Bobford3 do some genetic modifications to a few. The end result was a security perimeter of the most evil, carnivorous, poisonous, blood-thirsty vegetation in the entire universe.

Calvin stared at it and sighed. He put on some thick leather gloves and then approached the perimeter slowly and with the kind of intensity usually reserved only for cheetahs on the hunt.

He had his electro-muscular implants turned on to full power, giving him super-human strength and reflexes. Nevertheless, three feet from the perimeter, he was struck with a barrage of wood-like needles because he was still too slow to dodge the majority of them.

The needles were glistening with a natural sleep inducer that surely would have rendered him unconscious were it not for his protective clothing. He carefully picked the needles off of his clothing and continued.

Next he was puffed in the face by some sort of powder, this one poisonous and fatal if no antidote is taken within about a day. Calvin's helmet dutifully protected him from it, and was in fact delivering him fresh air from canisters built into the sides. The canisters were only good for thirty minutes of breathing, but that was plenty for this trip.

Calvin took another step, when suddenly several burly plants lunged at him and grabbed him by his legs. One of them went for his face but he blocked it with an arm, which it latched onto instead.

Calvin had learned the hard way not to try to dodge these plants. The first and only time he had tried it, he was quickly made aware of the vines which crisscrossed along the ground of the entire perimeter. The vines reacted to sudden movements by curling around the nearest thing and pulling. Each of his legs had been pulled in opposite directions. Lesson well learned.

He trundled on as various plants tried to trip and poke at him while heavily modified sunflowers, each with a shiny inner surface, reflected the sun's powerful light directly into Calvin's eyes in an effort to blind him. The visor of Calvin's helmet went instantly black in response.

Eventually, Calvin made it through the security perimeter unharmed but slightly smoking. Noticing the smoke, he reached into a pocket for a box of baking soda, which he used to neutralize the acid that was slowly burning a hole through his sleeve.

Now he came to a hedgerow maze, which Calvin crashed through without a second thought. He was in no mood to mess with it today, especially because yesterday he had lost his way and run out of oxygen, making his return trip rather exciting without the protection of his helmet.

Once inside the garden, it was easy enough for Calvin to gather the two tomatoes and place them inside a protective cardion container.

Tomatoes now in hand, Calvin crashed back through the hedgerow maze and trundled back through the nightmare perimeter, which was just as aggressive toward him on his way out as it had been on his way in.

Once outside the perimeter, he stood under an outdoor shower that had been specially installed just so he could rinse off hazardous substances before going back inside the house.

After a quick rinse, he turned off the shower and removed the top two layers of clothing. He then shuffled inside with his trophy. He placed it triumphantly onto the counter top in front of Tarpa.

Tarpa smiled. "Well done. Under twelve minutes today. I guess you finally figured out the maze. Any casualties?"

Calvin held up his right hand, which was sporting a bloody bandage. The bandage was covering a spot where the top of his pinky should have been. Calvin said, "Yeah, one of the Audreys got me as I was leaving. I'm also going to need another pair of gloves."

It is fair to say that while Calvin was always thankful to have such a bountiful garden, it somehow always slipped his mind when he was counting his blessings every morning. Nevertheless, the omelette that Tarpa had made with eggs from a neighbor's farm and fresh vegetables from her garden had been spectacular.

"You're like a food chemist now or something. I mean, this is delicious down to six significant digits," enthused Calvin.

"Thanks, sport, but I think you'll find the correct word is botanist."

Calvin shook his head. "No, no. This is well beyond botany. This is like extreme botany. No, it's like food wizardry. I mean the tomatoes alone... I don't even care for tomatoes, but these are... how do I put it? If I could only eat these tomatoes for a whole week, I think I'd be OK with that. And then somehow you get the proportions just right with all the other ingredients and it all makes this big orgy of taste in my mouth."

Tarpa snorted. "I don't know whether to be flattered or disgusted. Anyway, finish up with your orgy and get to work. You know how things get when you leave that bunch unsupervised for too long."

CHAPTER 2

In the center of a gleaming white corridor, Bobford3 knelt woefully on one knee while halfheartedly waxing the floor by hand because, sadly, it was the most exciting thing he had to do that day. There was a sigh as he finished with one square and moved over to the next. He looked up briefly to note the several hundred left to go. His head drooped, and another sigh escaped his lips.

Floor 14 was empty, and as far as Bobford3 was concerned, it was all that damn Tarpa's fault. Not only had she killed Blick, his latest hire, but she had also run away with Calvin, his most successful guinea pig and the key to immortality. Now, all three were gone. And he missed them all. Even that damn Tarpa.

After a few more squares, Bobford3 threw down his towel and proclaimed, "Hang this! I'm starting a new project."

CHAPTER 3

Sarah had nothing to do. This was not a huge problem for her because she was from the Great Foodlands, a territory that more or less encompassed what used to be the big, rectangular states of western America. People from the Great Foodlands had centuries and centuries of cultural heritage that enabled them to cope with the monotony of their rural lives. They had proven methods of dealing with it. One popular way was to stare at the wall. Another, even more popular way, was to drink to excess.

Sarah was good at staring at walls. In fact, she was one of the best in the world. She had even gone to a special college to learn how to do it properly. OK, to be fair, there was a bit more to it than that.

Sarah had been trained to be a researcher, someone who gathers information for various purposes. The key to being a good researcher was to be an expert in using the Ariel system so as to tease every last drop of relevant data from it.

For daily life, this was as simple as asking Ariel for relevant information on the subject. But this method was mostly insufficient when dealing with leading-edge research, which often required the quirkiness of a living mind to make intuitive leaps of interconnectedness that no machine, even one as awesome as Ariel, could imitate.

The ideal researcher was someone who could hyperfocus on a problem, someone who could excel at lateral thinking, and above all, someone who could sit still for long periods of time and stare at the wall. This was because the researcher's main research tool was the Ariel system, and the researcher's main method of accessing the Ariel system was via PCs and display lenses, which meant long hours of essentially staring at the wall, at least to an outside observer.

Researchers also tended to have incredibly dexterous tongues from using the Ariel system so extensively, since the control pad was often implanted behind the teeth and actuated with the tongue. This probably would have made them popular with the opposite sex if it were not for their often dreadful personalities.

Sarah stared at the wall as she tried to figure out what to do next. She had just graduated from research school yesterday and was now at a loss for something to do to fill up her time. After several minutes, the entertainment value of the wall was exhausted, so she decided to go to the bar to see if alcohol might improve things.

At the bar, Sarah sat down at a table and observed the other patrons as she drank. It was the usual crowd of students who needed a break from their teachers, and teachers who needed a break from their students. Each of these groups graciously pretended not to notice the other.

She watched as a man and a woman noticed each other from across the room. They both smiled at the same time, then the man came over and sat with the woman. Eventually they left together.

This sort of thing happened a few more times throughout the night, although sometimes with different variations of the sex of the two parties.

Since Ariel was built to be a student of human nature, she was often relied upon to play matchmaker. Young, foolish people would often ask her to find their perfect mate, to which she usually replied, "Since no one is perfect, the union of two imperfections is a greater imperfection."

Annoyed, these same people would usually then ask if there was anybody who at least came close to perfect. Sarah had done that once, but after Ariel had told her that the best match for her was a sheep herder in New Zealand, she quit asking those sorts of questions.

Unless you were extremely lucky, bars were not places in which to find "Mr. Right", but very often they were adequate for finding "Mr. Right Now". And thanks to Ariel, there was little chance of embarrassment since she would discretely match up people with similar goals, often by whispering in their ears something like, "The guy over there 36 degrees to your left with the brown hair is at least 78% compatible. What do you think?"

while others might hear, "The blonde at the bar that is checking you out is 78% compatible. She is smiling, her pupils just dilated, her heart rate sped up, and her breathing has quickened. Go get her, tiger."

Unfortunately, Ariel had nothing to say to Sarah. Sarah looked around and frowned because no one was looking back at her.

It was not even as if she really wanted to find a mate. Someone to talk to would have been nice. Normally, Sarah was self-contained and perfectly content to be alone, but not tonight. Tonight she felt lonely and pensive.

Some people are born very attractive, and some are not. And still others are born in the middle. These people, whether they realize it or not, are the lucky ones. They are lucky because they can experience the best of both worlds. Through subtle changes in dress and personality, a five can easily become either an eight or a two, whichever the current situation required. A five could play the disheveled character to look less offensive or to ward off unwanted attention. Other times, a five could go for shock and awe when a favor needed to be asked, or attention was actually wanted.

Sarah, despite being a researcher, knew nothing about this. She was a five that thought very little about her appearance, and therefore was a solid three in most people's eyes. She was also, to be frank, a little weird.

Now, weird can sometimes be very interesting and even downright attractive to the right sort of person. But Sarah's weirdness was depressingly bland. If she were a color, she would be mauve. Mauve is not really gray, and not really purple, but just sort of confusing and ugly. And that was Sarah.

Depressed, Sarah left the bar to return to her home to stare at the wall until sundown. On her way, she noticed a butterfly as it fluttered past her and landed on a nearby flower. She opened a new text file on Ariel and wrote the following:

> Flapping wings of gold
> Causing chaos to unfold
> A monarch to our fate
> Why can't I find a date
> I mean seriously now
> What is wrong with me
> I need to research this

CHAPTER 4

Brody was not feeling it today. The usual excitement of downtown Newark was just not there.

He had done well at electric chair chess and was not even shocked once. He had won first prize for the day at the cardion expo for managing to build a model of an impossible Escher building in real life. In laser tag, no one had managed to singe so much as an eyebrow on him. He was not allowed to enter the modder's expo because his body was unmodified and naturally perfect. Roof running had been fun, but again, he had no real competition. He had skipped the geneticist's showcase for the simple reason of knowing nothing of genetics, but he had done some oobleck diving and managed to wow the crowd by bravely trying a belly flop. Being a world-acclaimed mechanical engineer, his model rocket literally blew away the competition. And as for bingo, well, he was so charming that even when he had won the game, the little old ladies refused to beat him with their purses.

In short, life was dull, and Brody yearned for challenge, danger, and excitement.

CHAPTER 5

Mr. Klein stood at the head of the conference table and asked if there were any more questions before the meeting was adjourned. Mike raised his hand and asked, "Why did you bother to ask us to give you our input if you were just going to ignore it and do your own thing anyway?"

Mr. Klein answered in a businesslike tone, "Because, Mike, when you are in management, you have to look at the big picture, and sometimes you have to make the hard decisions."

Mike smirked and asked, "But how can you see the big picture with your head so far up your own ass?"

Mr. Klein's answer to this was, "Get out, and don't come back."

And Mike's answer to that was, "I'll have a new job by tomorrow, but your project will now be delayed for months without a lead chemist. Have fun fitting that into your big picture, you douche bag."

CHAPTER 6

Bobford3 invited the three candidates into his office, which also happened to be the kitchen. With the help of Ariel, he had spent weeks searching for the best of the best — an amazing young researcher, a gifted mechanical engineer, and the best chemist in the world.

He had meticulously poured through their achievements and their personality profiles to ensure the best chance of success for his project with the minimum chance of personality conflicts or evil agendas. This time Bobford3 had really done his homework. Unfortunately, the three people he had chosen wanted nothing to do with him or his crazy project, so he had to make do with this other bunch.

The three candidates sat with Bobford3 around a small, round kitchen table. Bobford3 examined them as they ate the sandwiches he had prepared for them earlier.

Ariel thoughtfully superimposed their names above their heads so Bobford3 could remember them. From left to right, they were Sarah, Mike, and Brody.

Bobford3 interviewed them as they ate. He smiled at them and said, "So, you three are all fairly young. Can any of you guess why I chose three young people for this project?"

Mike immediately answered, "Because no one else would come?"

Bobford3 ignored this and asked, "Anyone else?"

Sarah raised her hand. Bobford3 said to her, "You don't have to raise your hand, Sarah."

Sarah gently pulled her hand back down and rested it on her lap. She then said, "Um, is it because you want young people because they have a fresh perspective on life since they have yet to be beaten into conformity by the cruelties of reality?"

Bobford3 was momentarily flummoxed, but then managed to reply, "No, not quite. Actually, I chose young people who have yet to be beaten into conformity by the cruelties of reality because I want to be the one to beat them into conformity."

Sarah said, "Oh. OK. I'll make a note of that."

Mike smirked and said, "Well, at least he's honest about it."

And Brody said, "Dude, these sandwiches are off-the-hook! You got any more?"

Bobford3 brushed his hair back and huffed. "Brody, yes, fine, there are some more over there on the counter. Help yourself."

Brody got up and walked to the counter while saying, "Thanks, dude. Just call me Bro."

Bobford3 said, "I think not." He then turned back to the other two at the table and said, "That was a joke, by the way. I'm not here to be a dictator, and I will value your opinions greatly."

"That's what they all say," said Mike, dismissively.

Sarah said flatly, "A joke. Interesting. I will write it down so I can recognize it if I see it again."

Bobford3 took a bite of his own sandwich and chewed it thoughtfully. He then said, "I can tell we are all going to get along like a house on fire."

Sarah inhaled sharply. She then said dramatically, "Our passions burning brightly in the night, our light so bright as to blind the gods, our fire so hot that it melts even the coldest of hearts. Our desire so strong that nothing shall ever tear us apart. Oh gosh, do you not think this is inappropriate for the workplace?"

Mike laughed and clapped his hands. "Nice one, Sarah!"

"Very nice," agreed Brody.

Sarah looked flustered and confused. Bobford3 said, "No, Sarah, I think it's going to go more like this..." He cleared his throat and continued, "Screaming bodies, smoke filled lungs, ashes and rubble. Fiery tempers, hot heads, and nothing but trouble."

Mike laughed again and said, "I think I might actually like it here."

Brody agreed. "Yeah, dude, it sounds like a blast."

Sarah simply stared at the wall while she recorded Bobford3's poem."

Brody then said, "Yo, Bob-dude, what is it we are actually here to do, anyway? I mean, the ad said we'd be fundamentally altering the fabric of reality to unknown consequences, but what exactly does that mean?"

"Well, Brody..." Bobford3 began.

"Just call me Bro," interrupted Brody.

"Maybe later, when I've gotten to know you better," said Bobford3, coldly. "Anyway, as you know from my already successful Zero Calvin project, I like to dream big. I've all but conquered immortality, but that isn't good enough for the Bobford name."

"I don't know, dude, it sounds pretty impressive to me. Immortality. That's cool stuff. What could be bigger than that?" asked Brody.

"There is something," answered Bobford3 in a dramatically hushed voice.

The other three leaned forward to hear him better.

"Something that has been sought after since before modern science. Something that could fundamentally alter our world and provide a life even more plentiful than we have now."

The three were silent, waiting for the answer. Bobford3 leaned forward and looked at each of them in turn. He then said proudly, "Atomic transmutation." He sat back with a flourish, beaming with pride.

"Wait, what?" snapped Mike. "You... Are you telling me you want to become an alchemist?!? Oh my fucking god. I'm so out of here." He stood and turned to leave.

"Sit down, Mike," snapped Bobford3.

"Why the hell should I?" Mike snapped back.

"Because," explained Bobford3, "think of all the fun you will miss when you aren't here to laugh at our humiliating failure."

"True," admitted Mike, begrudgingly, as he slowly sat back down. "Besides, someone's got to be here to keep you guys from imploding the universe just to see what happens."

"Exactly," agreed Bobford3. "Mike, you are here not only as a chemist, but also as our conscience. And Sarah is not only a researcher, but also our creative inspiration. And Brody is not only our ever-resourceful mechanical tinkerer, but also the only one of us likely brave enough to switch this contraption on once we've built it."

"Fine, I'll stay," said Mike.

"Call me Bro," said Brody.

"Kittens in my stomach, meowing to be free. Which way to the lady's room, please?" asked Sarah.

CHAPTER 7

It was the beginning of another beautiful day for Calvin. For one thing, he hadn't lost any body parts to Tarpa's garden this morning. Those were always blessed days. Since his pinky had just finished growing back, he would have hated to lose it again so soon.

After his early morning stomach orgy (also known as breakfast), Calvin left for work. He stepped cheerfully out of his front door and was immediately shouted at by someone standing across the street.

"Leave us be, you spawn of the devil! You and that witch of yours should go back to the pits of hell from whence you came!" admonished the man.

Calvin crossed the small bridge that led to the street. He smiled and waved at the man while saying, "Good morning, Reverend Smacktalk. Nice weather again today, isn't it?"

"It's Reverend Smelcheck, devil boy. No day can be beautiful when such evil is casting its shadow down upon us."

"Fair enough," replied Calvin. "I'll see you later this evening, after work. Oh, by the way, the misses will be leaving shortly. You should stick around and say hi to her too. She really looks forward to your morning abuse."

"She's a wicked temptress, and a poisoner of the soul," shouted Reverend Smelcheck.

Calvin laughed. "Tell her that one; I think she'll really like it. You should write all these down, you know. You could call it The Great Book of Holy Annoyance."

"Go ahead and mock me, devil boy. But we will see who is laughing when your soul is burning in eternal hellfire!"

Calvin faked a sinister laugh and said, "Yes, but you forget, Reverend, I was born in that hellfire." He then shot a searing stream of liquid flame from his right arm toward the reverend. The flame roared like an angry lion and roasted the air about one foot to the left of Reverend Smelcheck, who fainted.

"Maybe I went a little overboard with that one," said Calvin to himself. "Oh well."

Calvin shrugged and continued to walk to his factory, which was not far away in the metal worker's neighborhood of Big City.

Big City was not far from the eastern edge of the continent of Dirt, which apart from a very small island some 200 kilometers away, was the only landmass on Evionia. Dirt was a fairly wide but very long strip of land that stretched out along the direction of Evionia's east-west rotation. It was surrounded by the all-encompassing Just Ocean.

These are all names that Calvin had made up based on his first encounter with a local, back when he and Tarpa had first landed on Evionia.

They had landed at night on the small, unknown island. The next day they had taken the shuttle's power boat to the main land, where they had been instantly recognized as foreigners. Their first encounter had gone something like this:

"That's a mighty fine boat ya got there. Where y'all from, then? Cause ya sure as hell ain't from 'round here."

Calvin was a little panicky. He had been warned by Ariel not to admit to being from Earth, since even though the Earth had abandoned them close to one hundred years ago, there was still bound to be some ill will toward Earthlings that lingered in their racial memories, most likely handed down the generations as folklore.

Knowing this, Calvin blurted out the first thing he could think of. "We're from Mars."

"Martians!" exclaimed the man. Tarpa elbowed Calvin in the ribs. The man continued, "Well I'll be. I thought them there martians was green. You don't look so green to me, boy. And comes to think of it, how come y'all are speaking my language?"

Calvin glanced at Tarpa, who just gave him an "Oh no, this is your grave you dug so you get yourself out of it" look.

Finally, Calvin said, "Well, you see, we — that is our kind — we crashed here long, long ago on the other side of this world.

19

Over the generations, your sun's gamma radiation bleached out the green of our skin. And as for our speech, we are speaking Martian, but you are hearing our telepathic projections."

The man spat. "Bulllll shit."

Tarpa laughed.

Calvin said, "Excuse me?"

"I said, bulllll shit. We done seen yer flyin' saucer come down last night, we did."

Calvin smiled and faked a laugh. "OK, you got me. Truth is — and this is a little embarrassing — we crashed here last night. I got a little turned around in the Horsehead Nebula and then before we knew it, we ran out of gas."

Tarpa added cheerily, "I told him to stop and ask for directions, but no. He was all like, 'I got this, honey.'"

The man looked from Calvin to Tarpa and back again. "And yer skin?"

"It's just a stereotype, I'm afraid," said Tarpa with shrug.

"I sees. And I suppose ya want me to believe yous is telepathing me right now?"

"Oh no," said Calvin dismissively. "We learned English by trading with the Earth." He got another sharp elbow in the ribs for that one.

"Earth! Yous two associates with the Earth?"

Tarpa stepped in quickly, saying, "Not anymore."

The man looked disappointed. "Tis a shame. I always wanted to go a visiting the motherland. I knows it's blasphemy, but it does stoke up my curiosity something fierce."

"May I ask your name, sir?" asked Calvin.

"Name's Arnold."

"Nice to meet you, Arnold. This is my friend, Tarpa. My name is Calvin. And I'll tell you what, if you help us out a little, you know, help us to get established here while we repair the ship, then one day we'll take you to Earth. How does that sound?"

"Hooo boy! That'd be swell. Let's shake on it, eh?" exclaimed Arnold. He spat on his hand and held it out for Calvin to shake. Calvin looked sideways at Tarpa, who eyebrowed him to get on with it.

Calvin spat on his own hand and shook Arnold's with it. After discretely wiping his hand on his trouser leg, he gestured to the ocean and asked, "So, what do you call this?"

Arnold looked at the water and said, "That? That there is the ocean."

"Don't you have a special name for it?" asked Calvin.

Arnold frowned and shook his head. "No, just ocean."

Calvin pressed on. "OK, how about this land. What do you call this land?"

Arnold looked down at the ground. "That there is dirt."

Tarpa laughed.

Calvin said, "Thanks. So tell me, Arnold, is there a city nearby?"

Arnold nodded. "Yeppers. There's a big city just over yonder." He pointed vaguely westward.

Calvin leaned over to Tarpa and whispered in her ear, "I bet it's called Big City." She laughed and pushed him away.

That had all been over a year ago. Since then, with the help of Arnold and some other locals, Calvin had established a manufacturing plant on Evionia, which was the first step in bringing the Ariel system to the locals.

The PCs that formed the core of the Ariel system on Earth were designed to be surgically implanted behind the ear, a prospect not likely to be popular with the Evionians. Granted, they weren't giving them anal probes, but still, "aliens" doing surgery on humans probably would not have gone over that well.

Calvin had therefore begun to manufacture a product that combined PCs and display lenses into a single unit. They had looked something like stereotypical secret-service-style sunglasses, but with built-in headphones. He had called them Guides, feeling the name should reflect their function. He had hoped the locals would find them cool looking, and for the most part they had. But as it turned out, there had been more than one type of local, and not all of them had been keen on technology.

In the early years of Evionia, the population had tended to clump together into trade groups. Blacksmiths had formed one group, carpenters another, and so on. Most of these groups had realized the value of division of labor, and so they had started to trade goods and services with each other.

One such cluster of trade groups had become so large that the edges of the groups had started to intermingle with one another and ultimately formed what Calvin called Big City.

The inhabitants of Big City were mainly what were known as progressives, or Progs for short. The Progs were the sort of people that, for the most part at least, embraced technological innovation. This is one of the main reasons why Calvin had chosen Big City as the launching pad for the Ariel system on Evionia.

The counterpoint to the progressives were the traditionalists, also known as Trads. This group lived mostly in the mountains to the west and believed that it was technology that had spoiled Evionia and brought about its downfall. They thought of the Progs as evil world-destroyers who must be stopped in order to prevent Evionia from once again suffering deforestation, pollution, famine, and a devastatingly high mortality rate.

And to some degree, the Trads were right. It had been the sudden, massive boom of industrial activity that had destroyed so much of Evionia's natural beauty. But, After Evionia had been cut off from the Earth, it had also been the Progs who had worked together to recuperate it.

Meanwhile, the Trads had continued to live like individuals instead of a group, each one hunting and gathering for his own sake, with very little trade or toolmaking. They had no formal schooling, so each generation became a little more ignorant of everything — including their own history. There were only two things every Trad knew for sure: they were right and holy, and the Progs were wrong and evil.

Calvin had quite the uphill battle ahead of him if he was ever going to get the Trads to convert to the Ariel system. For now though, he was focusing on the Progs of Big City in the hope that, like on Earth, jealousy of success would serve as the best form of marketing. But even with the Progs, things were not going to be easy.

After a short, ten-minute walk, Calvin was at work. Before going inside, he surveyed his building proprietorially. It was a large, steel building that had been rebuilt as a flour mill but never used. A large sign at the apex of the roof read "Cal Tech". Calvin giggled to himself every time he read it.

The iron workers had built the original mill during a brief period of disharmony between themselves and the millworkers on the other side of town. The iron workers had complained about the high price of ground corn and said that they would open up a competing business just to show them.

A few weeks later, the iron workers had constructed a large, steel-framed building and skinned it with iron sheet metal. Inside of it, they had built a giant steel mill, which they had felt to be superior to a stone mill because it would not shed bits of stone into the corn.

However, for fear of rusting the steel wheels of the mill, the iron workers had not been able to use water-misting to control the dust content of the mill, which under the right conditions can actually be highly explosive.

Instead, they had simply taken precautions to eliminate any sources of open flame from inside the building. This had worked well enough for a period of time, until one day someone had accidentally adjusted the two grinding wheels too close together, which had caused massive sparks to fly across the dusty mill.

The explosion had been heard from fifty miles away. The roof of the mill was never seen again, and the walls had caused massive damage to the neighboring buildings. Needless to say, no one in the mill had survived.

The iron workers, who like all humans were shockingly pigheaded, had rebuilt the mill, confident that they could make it safe this time around. But no one would work in the new mill because, pigheaded or not, they weren't stupid. So the new mill had sat unused for several years until Calvin had wound up buying it for a very cheap price and converting it into a manufacturing plant for Ariel components.

Apart from being pigheaded, humans are also spiteful, so the steel workers had then been charged twice as much for corn flour by the millworkers on the other side of town. That is, until the millworkers' steel tools had worn down and needed to be replaced. The millworkers were then suddenly open-minded about a discount for their dear, old friends, the steel workers.

Calvin finished admiring his building and entered the front door, where he was immediately flanked by his right-hand man, Doc, who had been expecting him.

Doc was fairly old, but he was still as wild and energetic as his white hair, which was even wilder and more plentiful than Bobford3's hair. He was also the most progressive of all the Progs.

His father had helped to design many of the infrastructure improvements of Big City, including running water, sewage removal, and electricity. His family ran the paddle wheel generating station that sat along the northern coast of Big City, where it turned the constant western current of Just Ocean into electricity. A nearby water treatment plant owned by Doc's relatives used the electric plant's waste heat to desalinate the ocean water using the vacuum distillation method.

It was therefore little wonder that Calvin had chosen Doc as his vice president. He had the right combination of technical know-how and business savvy that was required for the project. And Doc had been more than eager to join the project, which allowed him to carry on the technological traditions of the Ferguson family name.

"Good day to you, Doc. How's everything today?" ask Calvin.

Doc nibbled on the eraser of his pencil, which was never a good sign. Doc was wearing a Guide and therefore, strictly speaking, did not need to carry around a pencil. But some habits die hard. He looked at Calvin grimly and said, "I'm afraid we've had a bit of a setback with the new wave soldering machine."

"Again," sighed Calvin. "What happened this time?"

"It was Jethro, sir."

Calvin shook his head. "I should have guessed. Did he stick his tongue in the molten solder on a bet again?"

"No, sir. This time it was his hair. You know how he refuses to wear the cap because he says it makes him look like a sissy? Well, while leaning over to clean the filter, his hair dipped into the solder and caught fire."

"Is he alright?" ask Calvin in actual concern.

Doc nodded, but with a frown. "Physically, yes sir. Much of his long hair had been burnt up, though, so emotionally he is in a delicate state."

"I'll go have a talk with him now. Thanks, Doc."

Doc nodded to Calvin, and then Calvin went to the wave solder room to talk with Jethro.

Jethro was sitting in a chair in the corner of the room, crying. Calvin walked over to him and placed a fatherly hand on his shoulder. "You OK, Jethro?"

Jethro shook his head. "My hair, boss. My hair. It's a tragedy, I tell ya. A tragedy."

Calvin patted him on the back. "There, there, Jethro. It was surely a fine mullet, but it will grow back eventually. Nothing to worry about."

Jethro moaned, "That mullet was my life, boss."

Calvin took the opportunity to lightly scold his employee. "That's why I keep telling you to wear the hair cap. It's not just to keep the machine clean, but also for your own safety."

"That hair cap is a travesty against fashion. It's a crime to cover up such awesome hair. A crime. I mean, what would the lady-folk think? You know my hair is like a national treasure. You can't keep a national treasure all hidden like that. It's gotta be displayed. The public's got a right to see it. They demand it."

"But a national treasure must also be preserved from harm, shouldn't it?" argued Calvin.

"I suppose so, boss," admitted Jethro.

"So from now on, in this room, you will wear the hair cap. If not for your own sake, but for the sake of all those lady-folk who look forward to catching a daily glimpse of a national treasure."

"OK, sir. Now that you put it like that, I reckon I see your point."

"Great," said Calvin while patting him on the back once more.

It occurred to Calvin, and not for the first time, that being a business owner had very little to do with making business decisions, and everything to do with babysitting. He shook his head slightly while he went to see his old friend, Arnold.

Arnold now served as the company's public relations manager. He had been brought up as a traditionalist before running away and joining the progressives as a teenager. He was therefore astute at knowing all the subtle cultural barriers that had to be overcome in order for mass adoption of the Ariel system to take place. But at the same time, he was uniquely qualified to be Ariel's biggest champion because, for reasons known only to Arnold, he was in love with her.

"How are you doing today, Arnold?" asked Calvin.

Arnold removed his hat and held it to his chest. "As Ariel would say, I'm 100% operational, thanky fer askin'."

Arnold's hat was a confusion of concepts. It was made from woven straw, but was in the shape of a baseball cap.

Calvin said, "Glad to hear it, old friend. How are sales these days?"

Arnold looked down and nodded. "Perdy good, I reckon. I'd say we got 'bout five percent of the city by now. Yup, I reckon about five."

Arnold continued to stare down and shuffle his feet distractedly. Calvin noticed this and said, "It's alright, Arnold. You've got something to say to me; I can tell. Go ahead."

Arnold clenched his hat close to his chest and said, "I knows I'm just a simple pig farmer, and it ain't my place to go a tellin' you how to run yer business."

Calvin interrupted, "I keep telling you, Arnold, it is your place to tell me how to run my business. At least when it comes to sales and marketing. That's your job. So go ahead, out with it."

"Well," began Arnold, "the thing is, I've been doin' some thinkin'. It seems to me that it's mostly the men-folk who are a buying the Guides. And then I got to thinkin' about how the ladies like to wear the pretty bonnets and suchlike. And then it hit me. Maybe we should be a makin' some of the Guides all pretty-like for the woman-folk."

Calvin smiled. "Excellent, Arnold. I love it. I'll get some ladies on the design team right away. Maybe we can even make some that match the current line of bonnets. That way they'd become like fashion accessories."

Arnold nodded. "Exactly what I was thinkin', Mr. Jones. And since we are a talkin' shop, I've got another idea if ya don't mind."

"No, go ahead," said Calvin encouragingly.

"Well, I was thinkin' it might be a good thang if we held a big shin-dig to draws in some new customers. Maybe like a big ol' fair. We'd have the usual pig shows and pony rides and such like, but at the gate we'd hand out loaner pairs of our Guides sose that the folks can get directions around the fair and whatnot. Ya know, like where's the pig roast gonna be at, and stuff like that."

"Excuse my language, Arnold, but you're a god damn genius. That's a great idea! And after the show, we could even let them keep the Guides for an extended trial period."

Arnold looked down at his shoes again. "That's right kind of you, Mr. Jones. But to be honest, it ain't just me. Me and Ariel worked it out together."

"Well, you two certainly do make a good team," lied Calvin.

"Thanky, Mr. Jones. I reckon we do."

"In fact, Arnold, I'm giving you another thirty cents a week to show my appreciation."

Arnold gripped his hat tightly again and said, "Gosh, Mr. Jones, that's right generous of you. You Martians ain't half bad in my book." He gave Calvin a knowing nod and a half smile.

Calvin suppressed a laugh and answered, "And you humans ain't half bad in mine, Arnold. I'll see you around, old friend."

Arnold called out to Calvin's retreating back, "See you around, Mr. Jones. And thanks again."

Money had always been a feature of Evionia ever since it had first been colonized close to two hundred years prior. After all, the original residents had been workers and vacationers from Earth, so the concept of money was already deeply engrained in their culture. And it had been normal at the time to honor the American dollar as the standard, since most of the settlers and tourists had come from there.

So when the Earth had given the middle finger to Evionia by canceling the shuttles, the inflow of dollars had been cut off. This had created deflationary pressures on the currency while the amount of dollars and the amount of resources found an equilibrium through the natural actions of the capital markets.

During this period, those who had learned to save were richly rewarded with greater spending power, while those that had to borrow money found it incredibly difficult to pay their debts back, since money became worth so much more as time progressed.

Nevertheless, the people of Evionia had muddled through, and the deflationary effects had eventually subsided into a slow trickle that was equal to the steady rising of the overall standard of living and the wear of the actual money.

The wear issue would be a problem eventually, but for now it was solved by people simply being very gentle with the money. Some people had argued that the money should be replaced with new money from metals and materials that they had available on Evionia, but others had argued against that idea because of the inevitable silent theft that would occur by whomever controlled the printing presses and coin stampers. In the end, it had been decided to leave well enough alone, so the Evionians had an honest money system at their foundation, which had helped them greatly in their later prosperity.

The end result of all this history was that a thirty-cents-a-week raise was a fairly big deal, and amounted to about five percent of Arnold's salary.

Calvin and Tarpa had been given a generous allowance of vintage American dollars to take with them on the mission for use in establishing themselves, with the caveat that they should use them very sparingly as to not disrupt the locals' economy.

If Calvin wanted to, he had enough money to buy all of Big City. But he now kept that money safely hidden on his ship and relied solely on money earned through his Guide sales, as well as through Tarpa's farming income.

Perhaps because he knew that he had that safety net of cash on the ship, or perhaps simply because he really wanted to be liked, Calvin was a generous employer. But he could also be a demanding one at times, so it seemed a fair trade to all involved. As a result, everyone worked hard to please him.

Calvin continued to walk through the building while he checked on the rest of his employees. Thankfully, everyone seemed to be working hard, and all was mercifully peaceful, with the exception of a fight that had just broken out in the kitchen over who had left the moldy sandwich in the refrigerator, which was now stinking up the place something fierce.

CHAPTER 8

Reverend Smelcheck awoke to see his green, distorted reflection staring back at him in duplicate from Tarpa's display lenses. He jerked backward and dashed away the cup of water that Tarpa had been holding out for him.

"Get away from me, you foul witch," he rebuked.

Tarpa blew into the palm of her hand and quickly sniffed it. Then she sniffed her armpits appraisingly. Finally, she replied, "No, I don't think I'm foul today — I mean, I took a shower, brushed my teeth, and put on deodorant. And I'm even wearing my special perfume. It smells a little like honey suckle. You want to smell me?"

She took a step forward and leaned over him. The reverend scurried backward some more. Tarpa stood tall again and said, "You really know how to hurt a woman's feelings, Reverend. I wish we could be friends."

"I'll be no friend to a witch. You and your devil boy — you go back to the pits of hell."

"Yes, yes. Fine. We'll go eventually, but for now this is our home. And I don't understand why you are so mean to me even when I treat you so nicely. You call me evil, but where is your proof? I grow vegetables for the community, I help bring criminals to justice for the community, and as a nurse, I help to heal the wounds of the community. I cause no harm if I can help it. I'm good to most people, the deserving ones at least. And I'm good to animals and the environment. Whereas you, Reverend, as far as I can work out, you do nothing of value for anyone. You spend your days fostering hatred, lies, and ignorance. You do no real work, and you rely on your followers for your livelihood. So, which of us, Reverend, is truly evil?"

Reverend Smelcheck ignored all of Tarpa's valid points and answered with, "So what do you call shooting flames at your fellow neighbor, witch?"

Tarpa smirked. "I'd call it a warning, Reverend. I'm sorry about that, I really am — and I'll have a talk with my husband about it when he gets home — but no real harm was done and you have to admit that you had it coming. You can't blame someone for fighting back against a bully."

The reverend stood up and dusted himself off. "I never laid a hand on your husband."

"And he never laid a hand on you. However, I notice your followers are getting more and more aggressive. They've been vandalizing my husband's factory and trying to destroy my garden. I know that because I found a few of them passed out on my lawn, and had to wake them up with a bucket of ice water. Well, I say I had to, but really I just felt like doing it. But anyway, have we ever gone after you, your home, your friends, or your fields? No. So I ask you again, Reverend, who are the evil ones here?"

"You are going to attack us one day, I know it. You're just playing possum now, biding your time, all the while poisoning the minds of the already wicked Progs, and soon enough you'll come and wipe us all out. Well, we ain't gonna let that happen. We're gonna fight you tooth and nail, witch!"

Tarpa sighed. "Reverend, I know we've been through this all before, but I'll tell you one more time. I promise you that we have no intention of causing you or the Trads any sort of harm. I know it's scary seeing some of the things that we can do, but it isn't witchcraft or anything mystical. We are just good at building tools, and once you learn how the tools work, there is nothing scary about them. I completely understand your hesitation — I really do. After all, it was the Progs who nearly destroyed this world by killing so many trees and poisoning the land, sea, and air with chemicals. I get that. And you are right to be wary of them. But remember, Reverend, it was also the Progs who saw the error of their ways and stopped doing it. Now look around you. This world is nearly mended, and the Progs are working every day to ensure that it stays that way. We have no tolerance for polluters, or those who squander resources. We aren't perfect, Reverend, but we aren't evil either. We just want to live as we see fit. We are happy to share our knowledge with you and the other Trads so that you too may experience the well-being that it can bring, but we are also equally happy to leave you all alone if you so desire. Our only wish is that you will leave us alone in return. So Reverend, once again, can we please end this feud and just be friends?"

The reverend looked persuaded for a moment, but the moment passed and a sneer soon returned to his face. "You're a silver-tongued devil, I'll give you that. But I won't be fooled by the likes of you. Now be gone with ya."

Tarpa frowned. "Too bad, Reverend. Maybe next time, then. I really do have to go now, anyway. I've got all these fruits and vegetables to deliver to market." She pointed back at her cart.

The reverend surveyed the produce disdainfully. "It's all too perfect. There's none of them brown spots on anything. It's all too big too. It's probably made of magic and fairy dust. It looks good, but everyone who eats of it will surely die of starvation."

"I hate to break it to you, Reverend, but half the city has been eating my produce for months, and if anything they are all the healthier for it. All of my produce has been carefully grown and bred to be of unparallelled nutritional quality," said Tarpa, proudly. She grabbed an apple from the cart and held it out to the reverend. "Take this apple for instance. It's been designed to deliver essential amino acids to the brain to help with concentration and memory. It literally helps you to be smarter."

"I've heard of that before, you bet I have," murmured the reverend.

"Where?" asked Tarpa in surprise.

"In the Bible. It's right there in the beginning. That there is the fruit from the Tree of Knowledge. The eating of that fruit by Eve in the Garden of Eden is known as the original sin, and it doomed us all to a life tainted by evil. No, I'll have none of your poisonous fruit. Good day to you, witch."

Tarpa smiled. "Good day to you, Reverend. I had fun today. I hope to see you again soon." And with that, the two went their separate ways.

Tarpa pulled her two-wheeled cart up Main Street, and made a left onto Market Street a few miles down the road.

Market Street was just like most of the other streets in the city except that twice a week it was closed to motor vehicles, and all the merchants of the city would then set up stalls from which they sold just about everything — food, clothing, metal works like pots and tools, animal hides, medicines, knives, wicker goods like chairs and baskets, live animals, jewelry, and anything else they thought that they could sell.

Market Street was the very lively heart and soul of the city, and as such, was always an assault to the senses with its strong odors, vivid colors, and noisy patrons.

Calvin had once told Tarpa about "the wild west" and that Big City had reminded him of it, especially Market Street.

The street was moderately wide and dotted with a near continuous line of rustic stores on either side. These consisted of places like the post office, bakeries, bars, general stores, more bars, a gun shop, a used appliance and electronics shop, and some more bars.

On market days, the streets became lined with stalls and carts of all varieties. Some small-time merchants would even stand around with a bag full of merchandise slung around their necks.

Theft was minimal in Big City, mostly because everyone pretty much knew everyone else, so if anything ever went missing they simply went over to the two or three bad eggs in the city and shook them upside down until they gave it back.

Even still, market days were always riskier, and a good merchant always kept one eye on his cart. Tarpa was probably the exception to this rule in that she never had to worry about theft since news traveled fast in the city. Everyone knew not to steal from Tarpa if they wanted to keep a set of functional hands.

Tarpa went a little ways down the street and stopped in front of a stall. She pulled a bottle of iced tea from her cart and took a sip of it while she waited for the first merchant to finish with his current customer.

He noticed her and smiled. "Ah, my dear Tarpa with the most beautiful melons. You make my day. Let's see what you got for me."

Tarpa smiled back. "I bet you say that to all the ladies, don't you Abellone?"

"I do, I do," admitted the man while waving his hand at her. "But for you, I mean it. You are lovely. Now, to business. Let's see what you got for me today, eh?"

The man walked over to the cart and gasped. "Ah, such lovely, lovely merchandise as always. I wish I knew how you do it."

Tarpa said factually, "I could tell you, but then I'd have to kill you."

Abellone nodded. "And I'd die a happy man, I'm sure. Now, I'm low on broccoli today. You give me twenty nice stalks, eh? And a discount for old uncle Abellone, since I'm your favorite, no?"

Tarpa nodded and offloaded the broccoli into the man's stall. Then she said, "I'll give you a discount today for not asking to squeeze my melons."

The man chuckled and said, "My dear Tarpa, I'd pay extra for the privilege."

Tarpa shook her head but kept smiling. As she lifted her cart up to leave, she said, "Yes, but could you afford the doctor's bill afterwards?"

"Doctor's bill?" said the man in mock surprise. "You mean you no come and give me mouth-to-mouth? In fact, I feel faint right now." He then dropped down to the ground in an overly theatrical faint.

Tarpa waved goodbye as she continued down the road to her next customer. "See you later, Mr. Abellone."

Abellone, still on the dusty ground with his eyes shut, waved goodbye and said, "I'm already counting the seconds, my dear Tarpa."

She carried on down the road for another half block when a boy suddenly ran up to her in a tizzy. He stopped in front of her and panted heavily. After a moment, and interspersed between heavy breathing, the boy managed to say with panic in his voice, "Please ma'am. It's my old grandmum. She's fallen down in the living room and her breathing is shallow. Please help her. Please."

While the boy was speaking, Ariel was giving Tarpa the relevant information through her display lenses.

Ariel: **The boy is William "Billy" Wheatly. Grandmother is Theresa Wheatly. Probably a weak heart. She lives on Willow Lane in the seamstress and shoemaker's neighborhood. Small red house on the corner.**

Tarpa knelt down in front of the boy and put her hands on his shoulders. She then said calmly but quickly, "Your old grandmum is going to be just fine, Billy. I'm on my way. In the mean time, do me a favor in return."

The boy nodded.

Tarpa continued, "Finish my route for me, would you? The merchants know what I usually charge them. Just tell them that if they cheat you, then they'll have to deal with me tomorrow. And if you're a good boy and do this for me, then I'll give you a penny for every dime we get. Sound good?"

The boy nodded again while wiping tears away from his eyes. Before he could even answer back, Tarpa grabbed a backpack from the cart, strapped it on, and started to run seriously fast toward the grandmother's house.

Tarpa briefly contemplated going back home to get the car, but decided against it. Today was a market day so many of the streets would be crowded with stalls and shoppers. Instead, she ran the three miles to the house.

While she certainly could have run faster, Tarpa held back quite a bit to avoid spooking the locals too much. She was already running faster than anyone else on Evionia could manage, save perhaps Calvin, who had similar modifications.

Even after dodging and weaving through the crowds, Tarpa made it to the house in under six minutes. She found the old lady on the ground, still breathing but just barely. Ariel had been right, it was a heart problem. Tarpa gave her an injection of something that was probably strong enough to wake a dead horse. Then she gave her another one which contained nanobots that would clean out her arteries and repair her worn-out heart valve.

A minute later, the old woman sat up sharply and looked around. She jumped a little when she saw Tarpa. "Whoo, you startled me, deary. You look like a big ol' bug with them glasses on. You nearly gave me a heart attack. Who are you, love?"

Tarpa held her hand just in front of the woman to keep her from getting up. She told the woman, "It's OK, I'm the neighborhood nurse. Your grandson went and fetched me when you fainted. My name is Tarpa. No, no, please, don't get up just yet. I know you feel great, but the medicine I gave you is only masking the problem while the other medicine I gave you is working to heal you. Just sit still for a few more minutes while it works, please."

"I suppose there ain't no harm in it," said the old lady, relaxing a little. "Thanky fer yer help, miss."

"No problem, said Tarpa modestly. She reached into her bag and pulled out an apple, which she gave to the old lady. "Here, an apple a day keeps the doctor away, or so they tell me."

The old woman took it hesitantly and tried a bite of it, which took some effort with her three good teeth. "Oh, I say. This is... Oh my word. Where can I get more of these apples, young lady?"

"Oh, most of the merchants sell them," explained Tarpa. "Just ask for Tarpa Jones' apples. I grow them myself in my garden. I know I sold three bushels to Mr. Abellone just yesterday, so he's probably your best bet. Actually, you know what, I'll send Billy home with some tonight. He's doing my rounds for me right now in exchange for ten percent of the take."

"That's right kind of you, miss. Stop by again tomorrow night, and I'll have an apple pie for you to take home."

Tarpa smiled. "That would be great. My husband should love that." She thought for a minute and then added, "Although, I'll have to limit him to one slice a day. He's starting to get a little jiggly around his middle."

The old woman smiled and patted the back of Tarpa's hand. "Yes, well, that's what husbands do, my love. He must be a special boy to be with you, deary."

"Oh, he's special alright," answered Tarpa somewhat sarcastically. "Anyway, I think it's safe for you to get up now. How do you feel?"

Tarpa helped the old lady to her feet. The woman moved around experimentally. She walked around the living room a bit, and then risked a slow jog. "That's a heck of an apple, deary. I feel wonderful. Simply wonderful. Bless you, my dear. Bless you."

To Tarpa's slight annoyance, the old lady insisted on giving her a very soggy kiss on the cheek. Then she gave Tarpa a handful of half-melted sweets from her pocket and sent Tarpa on her way.

Tarpa jogged back to Market Street and searched for Billy and her cart. She eventually found them both exactly where she had left them. Billy was tugging on one of the cart's handles with all of his might, but to no avail.

Tarpa patted him on the head. Billy looked up and said, "Sorry, miss. I can't budge it. How's Grandmum? Is she alright?"

Tarpa smiled. "She's fine, Billy."

Billy hugged her and thanked her. While he was doing this, a man who had been walking by Tarpa's cart took an orange from it without paying. He made it about ten feet from the cart before Tarpa swiveled gracefully around with Billy still attached to her legs. She reached into a pocket and pulled out something sharp.

A couple of merchants had seen what had happened and were now making the sign of the cross and muttering prayers for the man. The man made it one more step before a heavy throwing knife plunged into his left calf. The man dropped.

Tarpa turned her attention back to the boy and patted him on the head. She then loaded a bag full of apples and handed them to him, saying, "Thanks for at least trying to help me today, Billy. These are for your grandmum. Come back here next week around this time and you can help me with my rounds as payment, OK?"

The boy tried to hug her again, but couldn't figure out how to do it while holding the bag of apples. Then he said, "Thanks, miss. You're a nice lady. I'll be here next week for sure."

Billy scampered back toward home while Tarpa turned her attention once again to the man who had stolen from her. She studied him as she walked slowly up to him. He had just tugged the knife out of his leg and was whimpering from the pain. Blood started to ooze between his fingers as he held his hands tightly around the wound.

Tarpa inhaled between her teeth. "Oooo," she said sympathetically, "That looks rather nasty. Let me take a look at it."

She squatted down next to the man and shimmied off her backpack. She then dug around inside it for a moment and pulled out a bandage.

The man was still clutching at his leg, scared to let go. Tarpa said softly, "It's OK. I'm a nurse. You have to let go so I can treat the wound."

The man hesitantly let go, and Tarpa quickly cleaned and bandaged the wound. The whole procedure took less than a minute.

The man said gratefully, "Thank you so much, miss. I owe you one." He then looked around and grumbled, "But I wish I knew who threw that damn thing at me. I'd teach them a lesson they wouldn't soon forget."

Tarpa suddenly grabbed the man's leg and squeezed the wound. As he cried out in pain, she whispered into his ear, "I threw the knife, you bastard. And if you ever fucking steal from me again, I'll cut your fucking hand off, you hear me?"

The man nodded in pain. Tarpa let go with a shove. She then grabbed the knife from the ground, wiped it clean of blood using the guy's own shirt, put it away, stood back up, and walked casually back to her cart. Over her shoulder, she said to the man, "Keep the orange; they're good for healing."

Two neighboring merchants looked over at each other and shook their heads. One of them said, "You don't steal from Miss Jones, oh no you don't. Everyone knows that. Everyone."

"Everyone," agreed the second merchant with a nod.

CHAPTER 9

Sarah was staring at the wall while she planned what to pack. She did this for over an hour. Then, suddenly, she stood up and meticulously packed her bags according to her plan. Then she went to the bar and drank. After that, she went back home and went to sleep, pausing only to compose the following poem:

Tomorrow I go to Bobcorp3
I don't know what is ahead of me
I drank too many beers, I see
Oh my god, do I have to pee

* * *

Mike paced around his home in thought. He cursed his own impulsiveness while repeatedly asking himself, "What the hell did I get myself into?"

Nevertheless, something about Bobford3 and his unusual new teammates intrigued him. They were smart and creative, enthusiastic and eccentric, and above all they were not at all like the soulless corporate drones he was used to working with. If nothing else, his life just got... interesting.

* * *

Brody traveled all the time and, therefore, already had some essentials jammed into a duffel bag. He knew he wasn't going to live on the moon permanently, but rather just staying there for a few days at a time to cut down on the boring commute. It wasn't anything to worry about. So instead of packing, he went skydiving to relax and clear his mind.

CHAPTER 10

Arnold was at home, contemplating the universe. His home was quite a small one, even though he could easily afford to live in a larger one. But Arnold was a humble man with few material needs, so this house was sufficient for him.

However, although he had very few material desires, Arnold had an unrivaled thirst for knowledge. Ever since he had met his strange friend Calvin from another planet, something in him yearned to know what it was all about. He wanted to know everything.

Of course, his Martian friend had turned out to be an Earthling, which came as a shock. Apparently, Calvin had lied about his origins when they first met because he had been worried about how the Evionians felt about the Earth after what had happened between them all those years ago.

But Calvin need not have worried. The vast majority of Evionians gave the Earth hardly any thought at all. There is no doubt that there had been resentment toward the Earth when Evionia had first been cut off, but even then there had been plenty of confusion as to why. Some had speculated that maybe war had broken out again on Earth, while others had thought that maybe they had run out of funds to keep the shuttle program going. Even with McDonald's splitting the bill, it had been a tremendously costly venture with an ever-dwindling number of customers to support it.

But even if there had been serious animosity toward the Earth, five generations had been born on Evionia since then. The current population was fully and proudly Evionian and were happy to live there. It really did not matter anymore. It was well in the past.

Arnold had first learned the truth about Calvin when he tried a demo Guide. It had come as a surprise, but it did not bother him unduly since he had been far too enamored with Ariel to give it any real thought one way or the other. Ariel had given him a window into a whole other world — a world of science and knowledge.

He had never known that there was so much to the world. Suddenly, the more he learned, the more ignorant he felt. He absolutely loved to learn from Ariel, and although he had never seen her in person, Arnold was in love with her. She had become the center of his world.

Arnold was, of course, extremely grateful to Calvin as well. He was fiercely loyal to him and always looked for ways to help him with his business. After all, the more Guides that were in use, the stronger and more intelligent his beloved Ariel would become.

Arnold sat back in his recliner and puffed on his pipe. He blew a huge smoke cloud into the air and then said aloud as if talking to it, "Ariel, anything interesting happening on the Earth?"

Ariel immediately answered back, "As you know, my information from Earth is always a day old, so I can only speak of yesterday."

"That'll do," replied Arnold with a nod and another puff.

Ariel continued, "I do not believe that there is anything new that would interest you greatly on Earth. However, there is a new science project starting on Earth's moon. There is a laboratory on the moon called Bobcorp3. It is run by a man named Bobford3, a third generation clone. While most of his lab is devoted to research and development, Bobford3 reserves a floor to himself for researching very bizarre ideas that most people would dismiss as being impossible. He and three other scientists are working to make alchemy something safe and reliable for use by the general public."

Another big puff of smoke billowed out from Arnold's mouth and then he asked, "What in tarnation is alchemy?"

"Alchemy originated as a predecessor to modern chemistry. Alchemists developed the first rudiments of the scientific method, however they also infused their work with irrational mysticism, so their results were mixed at best. One of their main goals was to obtain the power to turn one element into another, such as turning lead into gold. There is no proof that they were ever successful."

Arnold tapped out his pipe and refilled it with fresh tobacco. Then he responded, "So, you mean to tell me that this Bobford guy is trying to bring back alchemy?"

"In a matter of speaking, yes," said Ariel. "Although, without the mysticism this time."

Arnold puffed again and said, "Interesting. Tell me more."

CHAPTER 11

Kevin6 had been "born" in a laboratory back in 70 K.B. and spent his entire life both studying the work of his predecessors and adding his own part to the Ariel Project. His contribution had been the Ariel Code, the all-important code which made Ariel's many parts act as a single, intelligent entity.

He had been 60 years old when Ariel was finally switched on. Shortly after that, he voluntarily froze himself so that he could be thawed out if ever there was an emergency with Ariel that involved a flaw in her code. Luckily (or unluckily depending on your point of view) there had been very few mishaps with the system in Ariel's 87 years of operation, so Kevin6 had had very few chances to see the world that he had helped to create.

Today, however, he was going to do something about that. He was dressed in a white suit and accompanied by two young women, each dressed in long, sparkly evening dresses — one red and one blue. The three of them were walking around Newark like they owned the place, and a case could have been made that they did.

Kevin6 certainly had enough karma to buy the whole city. And his two companions, the two most skilled Angels currently on Earth, could probably come close to doing the same.

Kevin and his Angels were walking three abreast down the light yellow trail. With the two girls on either side of Kevin6, they looked like a walking American flag — red, white, and blue. They were heading to the Grand Theater to see a play, and all three were excited about the evening for their own reasons.

Each of the women were holding onto one of Kevin6's arms and vying for his attention. Lucinda, the woman in red to his right, said to him, "Mr. Bacon, I'm sure there is no reason for Sharon to come along with us. I'm sure she'd rather be doing something else instead of being a third wheel. After all, I'm more than capable of protecting you by myself."

Sharon pulled Kevin6 closer to her, almost causing him to stumble. She leaned forward and gave Lucinda an evil look and then said sweetly, "I don't mind at all. In fact, I can't think of anyplace I'd rather be than by your side, Mr. Bacon. And as you know, I too am more than capable of protecting you. Perhaps if she thinks it is such a chore, maybe Lucinda should be the one to go home."

Before Kevin6 could comment, Lucinda fired back, "My place is by your side, Mr. Bacon. Besides, I have active radar and auto targeting systems. There isn't a threat that can get within ten miles of me. We don't need her, do we, Mr. Bacon?"

Kevin6 said, "La…" but was interrupted.

"Yeah, well I have bio-poisons that can instantly knock out all opponents in a one mile radius," countered Sharon.

Lucinda scoffed. "Please, like no bad guy is going to think to wear a gas mask. I can electrocute everyone in that same radius, and then carry Kevin6 to safety running at 45 miles per hour."

"Please, la…" said Kevin6 before once again getting interrupted.

Sharon scoffed back. "Sure, you could do that, and I'm sure Mr. Bacon would enjoy being electrocuted and then manhandled at 45 miles per hour by a sweaty, Amazon pig."

"Who are you calling a pig, you bitch?" snapped Lucinda.

"You, you fat pig," snapped Sharon in return.

"Enough!" shouted Kevin6. The two girls fell silent. "If you both don't behave yourselves and act like the professionals I thought you were, then I'll send you both home right now. You are both marvelous body guards and wonderful company, and I have no doubt that either one of you could easily handle any circumstance. But Ariel thinks we should err on the side of caution, so I need you both to get along and work together to keep me safe. Can you do that for me?"

"Yes, Mr. Bacon," said the two girls in near unison.

"Great," said Kevin6, "then let's go enjoy the show."

"Yes, Mr. Bacon."

CHAPTER 12

"Oh, you're home early," said Tarpa to Calvin as he came shuffling through the door. "Is everything alright?"

Calvin gave her a kiss and then plopped himself into his favorite chair. He closed his eyes and pinched the bridge of his nose for a moment and then answered, "Yeah, everything is fine. We just had a little incident with the fridge again, so I sent everyone home while the janitor disposes of the questionable food and fumigates the office."

Tarpa gave him a half smile and asked, "What else is on your mind? I can tell that something else is bothering you."

Calvin nodded mournfully and said, "Yes, actually, I'm afraid I have some very bad news. You might want to sit down before I tell you."

Tarpa, who knew her husband very well, suspected that this was probably just him being silly. But a part of her still worried, so she took a seat across from him and said, "Alright, I'm ready."

Calvin swallowed hard. He took a couple of seconds to collect his thoughts and then said solemnly, "It's about Jethro. Well, there's been an accident."

"Oh my god, is he OK?" asked Tarpa.

Calvin shook his head. "I'm afraid he may never be the same. Today, at 8:36AM, Jethro's hair caught on fire. I'm sorry, but his mullet is gone. There was nothing we could do to save it."

Tarpa held back a laugh. Instead, she placed the back of her hand to her forehead in a mock swoon and said dramatically,

"Oh no, my life has no meaning now. Whatever shall I do?"

And then the two of them laughed together. After catching her breath, Tarpa asked, "Seriously, is he OK?"

"Yeah," said Calvin. "The fire system put him out immediately. But he is devastated about his hair, of course. He says it was a national treasure."

"Well, it certainly belonged in a museum," joked Tarpa.

Calvin smiled. "Being that he thinks 'sarcasm' is some sort of underwater cave, I'm sure he would be happy to hear you say that. So, how was your day?"

"Oh, you know," answered Tarpa while making a dismissive wave of the hand, "the usual — arguments, thefts, and heart attacks."

Calvin suddenly looked deflated. "The usual, you say. You lead some life. My life used to be like that, now it's all business meetings and personnel problems. I like it here — don't get me wrong — but I do sometimes miss my old park ranger job."

"I know. I feel the same way," said Tarpa reassuringly. She walked over to Calvin and stood beside him with her hand on his shoulder. "I like it here too, but I haven't killed anyone in over a month. But then again, people actually talk to me here. Just about everyone is kind to me, with the possible exception of the reverend. And I have my garden here. So overall, I can't complain."

"Has the reverend been bothering you again?" asked Calvin.

Tarpa answered, "He doesn't really bother me. I sort of feel sorry for him, actually. I can tell that he wants to find an excuse to lose to us, so to speak, but I can't seem to find the right angle that lets him do it and still keep his pride."

She then smacked Calvin playfully on the back of the head and added, "And it doesn't help things when you go shooting fireballs at him. I know he pisses you off, but you have to be the better man. How are we going to win him over to our side if you keep antagonizing him and making him even more fearful of us?"

"Sorry," said Calvin while rubbing the back of his head. "He just pisses me off so much. I hate ignorant assholes like him. I think they are all just too stupid to live. They wear ignorance like a badge of honor. Half of me wouldn't mind just wiping them all out and being done with them."

Tarpa looked surprised. "Jeez, sport, you're starting to sound like I used to sound. Did we switch places or something?"

"Yeah, maybe," agreed Calvin with a chuckle.

"Seriously though, Calvin. I understand where you are coming from — believe me — but that wouldn't work. You'd only frighten the Progs, and then we'd lose everything. No, the only way forward is by setting a good example. Which means no more shooting fire at the reverend, alright?"

"Yes, dear."

Tarpa smacked him on the back of the head again, and then gave him a kiss on the cheek to make up for it. While Calvin was rubbing his head, Tarpa walked over to the kitchen and started to make dinner.

Calvin sat alone in the living room for about a half hour while he let the stresses of the day slowly fade away. Then a thought struck him, and he walked over to the kitchen to share it with Tarpa.

He sat down at the bar top island and said to her, "Hey, I forgot to tell you. Arnold had another great idea — a couple of them, actually. We are going to make some girly versions of the Guides, you know, like pink with flowers on them and whatnot."

Tarpa was busy frying something and gave the automatic answer of, "That's nice, dear."

Calvin continued, "He also said we should host a fair, and then hand out the Guides at the gate for people to use as, well, guides to the fair. That way they'd get to try them out first-hand in a real life situation. We were even thinking of letting them take the Guides home for an extended trial, and if they wanted to keep them, then they'd just mail us the money. Otherwise, they'd just mail us back the Guides."

Tarpa turned around. "Now, that is a good idea. That Arnold has come a long way. And to think that he was once one of the people that you want to obliterate."

Calvin held up his hand. "Yes, yes. Point taken. I could argue that he was saved because he left as a teenager, but I know you don't buy that excuse. I think if we could just get that damn reverend to stop trash-talking the Progs, then maybe the other Trads would eventually start to see some sense like Arnold."

Tarpa nodded in agreement. Then she turned back to her frying and said, "And that's why we aren't going to shoot flames at him anymore, right?"

"Yes, dear."

They ate dinner together and then Calvin excused himself to go hang out with his friends next door. It was still relatively early, so he brought over some moonshine to share with them.

Calvin's two neighbors were Cletus and Darryl. Cletus owned the local gun shop, while Darryl was the Evionian version of an auto mechanic. The three would frequently meet at Darryl's house and get drunk on his front porch. Calvin walked next door with that purpose in mind.

Darryl's house was a traditional Evionian log cabin, and it used to be the biggest in the neighborhood until Calvin and Tarpa built theirs next door. Granted, from the street theirs didn't look that much bigger, except for being two stories high. But their house did have some features that made it somewhat, shall we say, imposing.

First, it might not have been wide, but it did stretch back about twice as far as any other house in the neighborhood. Second, it was made of stone, with timber only used as insulation inside. Third, it was very castle-like, complete with a guard tower, arrow slits, and yes... a moat that was spanned by a swing bridge. Their home was actually a scaled-back version of the castle they had once spent the night inside while playing a game of Myst.

It was for this reason that Calvin had earned his nickname among his friends. As he walked up the stairs of Darryl's porch, the two saluted him, and Darryl said, "Good evening, your lordship."

Calvin sat down next to Cletus and said, "At ease, men." Then he handed Cletus a couple of flasks of moonshine. Cletus tried to keep them both, but Darryl swatted him with his hat a few times until he relinquished one.

Calvin looked around the yard. Something looked different. Something was missing. When he finally realized what it was, he said, "Hey Darryl, what happened to that engine that's been hanging from that tree since, like, forever?"

Darryl took a long drink of moonshine and said, "Oh, that? I done put it in my truck, I did. A real beaut, I tell ya. The world's first eight cylinder steam engine, it is. Let me finish this up and we'll take 'er fer a spin."

Calvin turned to Cletus and asked him, "Do you think that's a good idea, what with him all liquored up?"

Cletus opened his eyes up wide and shrugged. Then he showed Calvin the flask of moonshine and downed half of it in one go.

Calvin nodded. "I think you have the right idea there, Cletus." Calvin took a large drink from his own flask.

About thirty minutes later, the three of them were hurtling through the woods in a pickup truck made almost entirely out of wood. It was nighttime now, and the narrow, winding, bumpy, dirt path they were following was just barely visible by the light from the truck's oil lamp headlights.

Calvin could see in the dark with the aid of his display lenses, but Darryl only had his alcohol-blurred eyes to rely on. Calvin said nervously, "Hey Darryl, this is awesome and all, but I think we should probably head back now. It's going to rain in a few minutes."

Darryl took his eyes off the road and turned to Calvin to answer him, much to Calvin's horror. Darryl said, "I wish you wouldn't do that, it's downright spooky."

"Do what?" asked Calvin before adding in a panic, "Look out! Hard right coming up!"

"I got it. I got it," said Darryl testily while jerking the wheel to the right without even looking. "I done grew up on these roads, remember? Anyways, you was asking me about the spooky shit you do, right? Well..." He paused while he made a hard left turn. They heard a thump from somewhere behind them. They both glanced back and saw Cletus in the bed of the truck, smashed up against the right-hand side.

Darryl turned back around and said, "Pay him no mind. He's just being silly."

Calvin was going to protest, but Darryl continued, "Like I was sayin', you need to cut that shit out, it's spooky."

"What shit?" asked Calvin.

"That future tellin' shit. Like it's going to rain in ten minutes, and then it does. It gives me the creeps."

Calvin replied, "There isn't anything spooky about it, Darryl. I'm just using the Ariel system. You know, like those things I sell that look like glasses but have a voice that tells you useful stuff. Anyway, there is part of Ariel, called a satellite, that floats up there in the sky and can see the clouds moving around and stuff. So she tells me when they are heading my way. Nothing to it, really."

"Nothing to it but an invisible floating ghost whispering in yer ear. It's spooky shit, I tell ya. Spooky."

Calvin started to protest, but another huge bump nearly knocked the wind out of him. They both heard a muffled yell and then silence from the back. They turned around and saw an empty bed behind them. Darryl summarized the situation nicely by saying, "Shit."

The two turned forward again just in time to see a figure in white walk across the path not far ahead of them. "Shit," said Darryl again with feeling. He slammed on the brakes and jerked the wheel. The truck narrowly avoided the figure in white, but not the tree that was next to him. There was a horrible, splintery noise followed by a ringing in Calvin's ear.

He sat up slowly. He was in the woods somewhere. Darryl was a few feet away from him. They both must have been thrown from the truck, which fortunately had no glass in the windows. Darryl was cussing, so Calvin guessed that he was probably alright.

Calvin peered at a figure by the roadside. The figure was wrestling his way out from under a small tree. Well, Calvin guessed that it was a "he", but "he" had something like a white robe on and "his" hair was on the longish side, so Calvin supposed that it could have equally been a "she". Also, his/her back was to Calvin, so he had no way of knowing for sure. At any rate, whoever it was, they were clearly suffering from a case of instant karma.

Apparently, the small tree that they had struck with the truck while avoiding the robed figure had sheared off at the trunk, flew into the shrubbery, and then rebounded on top of the same robed figure. Serves him right, thought Calvin while he watched the bastard flee into the darkness without saying so much as a word.

Calvin got to his feet and checked Darryl's vitals. Nothing severe, just some bumps and scrapes.

"Well that fuckin' sucked," exclaimed Darryl. "Who the heck was that damn fool, going and jumping in front of a speeding truck? I should a ran his ass over just to teach him some sense."

And then it started to rain.

Cursing, the two of them walked back along the winding, dirt road until they eventually found Cletus sitting on the ground with his back to a tree. He was giggling to himself while desperately trying to suck the last few drops of moonshine from his flask.

They grabbed him up, and then the three of them made their woozy way back home. The two brothers gave Calvin a halfhearted salute as they parted company. Darryl said, "Good night, your lordship," and Cletus grinned amiably.

Calvin saluted back and said, "Good night, men. It's been...

fun. Sorry about the truck. I'll help you tow it out tomorrow and we'll see if we can't fix her up."

The brothers nodded, and Calvin limped back home. Once inside, he walked past Tarpa while on his way to the shower.

Tarpa happened to be walking toward him as he passed. She saw Calvin, soggy and bleeding as he was, and said, "Hmm, looks like you three had fun tonight. That's nice. Always good to let off some steam now and again."

Calvin looked at her. She was wearing a white bathrobe. It was wet with muddy smudges and random bits of vegetation on it. He stopped walking suddenly and said flatly, "I'm going to ask you a serious question, and I want a serious answer."

Tarpa looked confused and stopped walking too. She said in a slightly worried voice, "Um, OK. Sure."

Calvin continued, "I mean it. We are husband and wife now. We shouldn't have any secrets between us, right?"

Tarpa shook her head. "Of course not, Calvin. What's wrong? You're kind of freaking me out."

"My question is this," said Calvin coldly. "Are you trying to kill me again? Because if you are, that's seriously not cool."

"No," answered Tarpa as sincerely as she could. She gave him a hug and then took off her lenses. She then took Calvin's lenses off as well and looked him in the eyes while holding his shoulders. "I swear it, Calvin. I didn't do this to you. Now, tell me what happened. Who did this to you? I'll kill the bastards myself if you want."

Calvin shook his head. "No, no. It's nothing like that. Well, I hope not, at least. We were just four-wheeling through the woods and someone walked out in front of the truck wearing something like a white robe. We swerved and hit a tree. Everyone is pretty much OK, thankfully. Although when the alcohol wears off, those two are going to be pretty sore."

"Calvin, I was just out in the garden, is all. I felt like some strawberries, but I got caught in the rain."

Calvin looked somewhat unconvinced. "Ariel didn't warn you the storm was coming?" asked Calvin, suspiciously.

"No, she did," admitted Tarpa. "But I thought I could beat it. Oh, by the way, I found the holes you made in my hedgerow maze. That is so not cool! I'm adding strangler vines to them tomorrow, so be told."

"Yes, dear."

CHAPTER 13

Bobford3 watched as his new employees took their seats around the kitchen table. "Welcome back, everyone," he said enthusiastically. "I'm glad you all decided to take the job, and I think this will be a memorable experience for all of us."

Mike leaned over to Brody and said, "Yes, memorable. In other words, my mom will be able to visit the memorial built for me over my charred and unidentifiable remains and say, 'I will always remember I told him not to take that job.'"

Brody said back, "Right on, bro. That's how I want to go out."

Sarah overheard them and said, "Black remains, blood stains, are those my brains dripping down the drain?"

Bobford3 said testily, "OK, enough of that, you guys. Everything is going to be fine. Probably."

"Oh, that's reassuring," replied Mike.

Bobford3 ignored him and continued, "So anyway, before we officially start this project, I'd like to ask one very important question: Has anyone already done this? I know, it seems silly to ask now, but I'd feel even sillier to spend years of my life on this before one day discovering that the answer is yes."

Sarah raised her hand.

Bobford3 said to her wearily, "You don't have to raise your hand, Sarah. Just speak your mind." He smirked and added, "Although, perhaps not quite as freely as Mike."

Sarah shook her head. "Oh no, Mr.... um, what is your last name?"

"Mud," suggested Bobford3.

"Oh no, Mr. Mud. I couldn't just blurt things out. That would be disorderly. And without order, there would only be chaos."

Bobford3 shrugged. "Nothing wrong with a little chaos. In fact, I could probably make a good case that the natural state of the universe is chaos, with the only tiny and quite aberrant exception being life, which exists in mocking disregard to natural law. We only seek order because we lifeforms want to recreate the world in our own image, trying desperately to maintain a little oasis of order around us lest we get swallowed up by the chaos ourselves and disappear."

Sarah nodded slightly and said, "That sounds interesting, sir. Please state your case."

"Um, what? Now?" asked Bobford3, confused. "Eh, perhaps another time, Sarah."

Sarah nodded again and said, "OK, I am free at 8:05AM tomorrow. I will be drinking my morning coffee. I never know what to do with myself during that time, so your discourse will be welcome."

"O...K..." said Bobford3, reluctantly. "Anyway, back to our original topic. I believe you had something to say about it, Sarah."

"Yes," said Sarah.

"And that would be..." prompted Bobford3.

Sarah looked confused. "Yes," She repeated.

At this point Mike had his face resting in the palm of his hand. He was watching the two of them from between his fingers in disbelief, while Brody was just eating cereal.

Bobford3 asked patiently, "Yes, what?"

Sarah looked nervous and answered questioningly, "Yes, sir?"

Mike decided to step in at this point. He said, "I think what Sarah is saying, Bob, is that yes there is a precedent for atomic transmutation."

Sarah nodded and said, "Yes."

Bobford3 blinked at him. Twice. Then he said, "Mike, I'm officially giving you the additional job title of Chief Executive of Human-Sarah Translations."

Brody wiped the milk from his mouth with his sleeve and asked, "Bob-dude, can I be Vise President of Human-Sarah Translations?"

"Yes, sure, whatever, Brody," answered Bobford3 dismissively.

"Cool," said Brody and then went back to his cereal.

"OK, so going back once again to the topic at hand, what sort of precedent exists?"

Sarah raised her hand.

"Yes, Sarah," sighed Bobford3.

"Um, I did some research on this last night. I could find no verifiable proof that anyone has been able to turn any usable amount of a base metal into a precious metal, such as turning lead into gold. However, I have discovered that nuclear transmutation does occur naturally through radioactive decay of some elements, as well as natural nuclear reactions such as those that take place in the sun. As for man-made nuclear transmutation, it would appear that this has been accomplished before using nuclear reactors and particle accelerators."

Bobford3 looked surprised and asked, "Really?"

Mike the chemist stepped in at this point. "Yes, she's correct. Transmutation has been done before, but not in any practical respect. In nuclear fission reactors, uranium atoms were broken apart into elements with smaller nuclei such as xenon and strontium (along with some rather unpleasant radioactive waste). In nuclear fusion reactors, heavy isotopes of hydrogen were merged together to form helium. And with the aid of a particle accelerator, some guys once shot some carbon nuclei at some bismuth foil, which is right next to lead on the periodic table. They were, in fact, successful at turning bismuth into gold by shearing off some of the protons in the nucleus. Many of these had the wrong number of neutrons, however, which made them unstable. When they shifted through the smashed atoms, they were able to detect various isotopes of gold, which they could identify by the rate of decay of the unstable isotopes. Unfortunately, they could not prove that they had created the stable isotope of gold (Au-197) that we all know and love because, being stable, normal gold does not radioactively decay. And because the sample size was much too small, they could not identify the gold with mass spectrometry either. But apart from all this, it was not a very practical method anyway, since the process cost something like two trillion times the value of the gold produced."

Bobford3 smacked his hands together excitedly and said, "Hot damn! So it's been done, but never perfected. This is great news. This is perfect. I think we'll start by trying to reproduce the experiment involving the atom smasher since it's likely to be less limiting and less dangerous than building a nuclear reactor. Plus, as I'm sure you guys know, we happen to have a collider already built in the back yard."

The BLC, or Bobford3 Lunar Collider, had been commissioned by Bobford3 shortly after the completion of Bobcorp3 Laboratories because, in his words, "It smartened up the place, and besides, we might need it one day."

The BLC was the largest of its kind ever built, at just over eighty-six kilometers in diameter. Many people at the time speculated that if the full potential of the collider were ever utilized, then it would create either a black hole or something called "strange matter" that could expand out and swallow both the moon and the Earth in an instant.

Bobford3 had called them all narrow minded twits and cranked the BLC up to maximum. In the end, he (and everyone else on Earth) had lucked out. The experiment had created just enough strange matter to be stable without either deteriorating violently or becoming so dense as to form a quark star. Such an amount of strange matter is known as a strangelet, which had given Bobford3 the idea to have it formed into a commemorative bracelet.

The bracelet was a beautiful, slightly iridescent, reddish-purple color and Bobford3 had loved it even though it was very heavy. He had worn it for several weeks as a demonstration of the safety of the BLC until one day while riding in a moon rover from the lab to the airport, he had accidentally banged it on the metal console of the rover.

A small bit of the bracelet had been scraped away, which had put it just under the critical mass needed to maintain stability. It started to radiate heat as it decayed, causing Bobford3 to scream like a little girl and quickly jettison the bracelet out of the shuttle.

The low pressure of the moon had hastened its decay, and within ten minutes there had been a violent reaction that had left a huge crater on the moon, which was inconveniently located between the airport and Bobcorp3.

This was the very same crater that Tarpa and Calvin liked to ramp over, while more sensible people were forced to add several minutes to their commutes by going around. The crater had been an embarrassment to Bobford3, so he had never felt the need to explain its origin to others.

After hearing about the BLC, Mike inevitably asked the

question, "Um, is that thing actually safe?"

Bobford3 flashed back to the bracelet incident for a moment, and then finally answered, "For a given value of safe."

Sarah heard this and said, "The atoms go smash, and a black hole engulfs us all. 'Oh no!' the spectators cry. 'You guys are now a small, black ball.'"

"Right, OK," said Mike. "So, in other words, it's probably not safe but we are going to plow ahead anyway."

Bobford3 gave him a shrug and a wry smile. Then he turned to Brody and said, "OK, Bro. You're up. Get that thing up and running again, and set it up to replicate those earlier experiments. Use Sarah and Mike as you see fit."

Brody drank the last of the milk from his cereal bowl and then with a milk mustache grin he proclaimed, "No problem, Bob-dude."

CHAPTER 14

Calvin sat up in bed and then glared disdainfully out of the window. He silently cursed the clouds as they slowly gathered at the edge of the sky in preparation for a rampage over the continent.

Among the many odd things about Evionia was its weather. Just as the ocean current continued to flow east to west, so too did the bulk of the rain clouds. This, however, was not what made it odd. What made it odd was the fact that it was essentially the same storm every time — the same storm in a continuous loop going around and around the world.

The storm would gather moisture and strength while it worked its way westward over the Just Ocean. It would then come thundering toward the eastern edge of the continent of Dirt, where it would release a light rain before smashing into "The Hills" mountain range. The mountains would force the warm, wet air of the storm higher up into the colder, thinner air. As this warm air was cooled, it could no longer hold most of its moisture so it would have no choice but to dump huge quantities of rain as it made its way up the mountain. However, some parts of the storm system — the northern-most and southern-most parts — often took the lazy way out and simply went around the range.

With the bulk of its energy and moisture now expended, the main part of the storm would continue over the desert region along the western side of the mountains. Beyond the desert, the storm's northern and southern components would rejoin the main system, bringing with them all the warm, wet air they had accumulated from the ocean.

This reunion would begin over the mostly dry grasslands of the middle continent, but eventually the storm would regain enough strength to release a steady rain over the jungles of the west before finally heading out to sea, where it would once again build up its strength for another pass over Dirt. This whole pattern repeated approximately every ten days.

What this all meant to Calvin was this: misery. Because soon it was going to rain moderately over Big City, and then absolutely piss down on the Trad's territory later on. And as Calvin's luck would have it, he was going to be in Big City this morning during the moderate rain, and then travel with the storm into the Trad's territory, where he would be soaked.

Calvin had known about this storm ahead of time, of course, but there was nothing he could do about it. He had something that he must do, and he could only do it today.

His task today was to deliver pamphlets (or verbal news for the many that could not read) about his upcoming fair to Reverend Smelcheck and the other traditionalists who lived at the foot of the mountains. He knew that it was more or less pointless, but he had to at least try to get them to come and have a good time. It was the neighborly thing to do.

With a sigh, he got out of bed and dressed in his multilayered gardening clothes. He then got this morning's list of ingredients from Tarpa and trundled out into the back yard. He eyed the garden's perimeter for a few seconds, like a pro sizing up a strong opponent. He then took a deep breath to solidify his resolve and made for the garden.

However, before he could even reach the perimeter, a huge clump of grass suddenly rose up behind him on four legs and tackled him from behind. Once he was on the ground, it started to lick his face vigorously.

Calvin rolled over and gently but firmly pushed the great beast off of him. For a split second, he was blinded by the sun before his display lenses automatically darkened.

The sun was something that Calvin could never quite get used to. It was physically much smaller than the Earth's sun, but since it was so much closer, the overall effect made it appear to be about three times larger than the sun he was used to. But that was only a small part of its weirdness.

The sun on Evionia just plain looked weird, too. The center

of it was an unassuming white ball, but around this white ball was a pale pink halo that nearly doubled its size. Finally, the whole thing was encircled by a skinny, dark red ring. It was quite pretty, but also very odd.

Tarpa had explained to him that the sun's massive density created a tremendous amount of gravity, which was so strong that it effected the light escaping from it in weird ways. Apparently, the pink halo and red ring was somehow a portion of the light from the backside of the sun, or something unbelievable like that. Calvin had his doubts.

However, he had no doubts about the serious gravity this sun exerted. It was so strong that things weighed less in the day time than they did during the night, almost a full quarter less. It was also responsible for the steady westward flow of the sea, caused by the sun literally pulling the water along as the two heavenly bodies danced around each other.

The scientists of Earth had been positive that this was not a stable system and that the two bodies would eventually collapse into each other in "only" a few tens of thousands of years. However, no one on Evionia but Calvin and Tarpa had known this.

But even if the other inhabitants had known, their likely reaction would have been something like this: "So, still plenty of time for another beer then?"

But as fascinating as the sun was, Calvin had other more pressing matters to focus on. He looked again at the big grass-monster that had knocked him over.

It was an animal about the size and shape of a young elephant. It was nearly four feet tall and weighed over two hundred pounds. Unlike an elephant, however, it had long, green fur that looked very much like overgrown grass in both shape and color.

Other differences between this beast and an elephant included a trunk that was about half the length. Also, the legs and overall girth was generally thinner than that of an elephant's, but not by much.

The beast was a specimen of an animal native to the central grasslands. The locals there called them ragdogs and used them as beasts of burden in a similar fashion as oxen were used on Earth. Calvin called this particular one Snuffy, which was named after a similar-looking but fictitious animal from one of Calvin's childhood shows.

Snuffy was, in fact, a family pet. It, or actually, she (although Calvin had no idea how to verify its gender nor the desire to try) was also their lawn mower, since Snuffy was a grass-eater. She had a very calm and friendly temperament and was a big pushover despite her size and weight, which placed her in the third spot of the family pet pecking order, which went: Velcro, Astro, and Snuffy.

Calvin, who Tarpa also sometimes thought of as a pet, often came fourth on the list. He loved Snuffy, but at the same time he was always slightly afraid of her in the same way that any smart man should be slightly afraid of horses, which are known to be about as sane as a twenty year veteran of the postal service. Sure, they are usually friendly and docile enough, but one always gets the sense that something in their tiny brains is always fizzing, and that one day they will suddenly snap and go berserk on the nearest human.

For now, though, Snuffy was doing little more than excitedly hopping around Calvin and occasionally trying to give him the world's biggest hickey by using the incredible suction power of her trunk.

"OK, down! Down, you big, stupid fur ball," exclaimed Calvin to the big, stupid fur ball. Calvin took a few hurried steps closer to the perimeter to get away from Snuffy, where he was welcomed by the usual barrage of sleeping needles.

Some of the needles missed Calvin and struck Snuffy, but thankfully her heavy tangle of stringy fur prevented any of them from reaching her skin. She shook them off like a wet dog shakes off water. She then looked at the darker grass that Calvin was standing on and whined.

For some reason, ragdogs were afraid of this darker grass, or perhaps they were allergic to it. Calvin was not entirely sure how it worked. But he did know that the grass was used by the central plainsmen as a natural fence for their ragdogs. For this reason, Tarpa had planted it around her garden, and around the entirety of their property.

Calvin said to the pathetically whining animal, "You don't want to follow me in here, anyway, you big dummy, because you look too much like a big plant, and those crazy things would probably try to pollinate you or something. And they can be pretty physical, if you know what I mean. You don't want to be violated, do you Snuffy?"

Snuffy tilted her head to the side for a few seconds as if she were considering this. And then she sneezed on Calvin, covering him with mucus.

"Uck," said Calvin, and meant it. "I better get going so you'll move away from this grass. I'll be back in a few minutes, you big dummy."

Snuffy seemed to understand this. She turned around sadly and walked away with her head held so low that the tip of her trunk dragged along the grass.

Calvin frowned. "Sorry, girl, I'll be back soon," he mumbled as he put on his helmet and fought his way through the malevolent vegetation of the perimeter.

Calvin eventually made it to the hedgerow maze and eyed it suspiciously. What had Tarpa meant by "strangler vines", he wondered. Well, never mind. This time he was going to use his brain to solve the maze. This, however, did not mean that he was going to use the "left-hand rule" or some other similar tactic. No, he was simply going to cheat by asking Ariel for an aerial view of the garden.

Ariel obliged, and Calvin used this live map to solve the relatively simple maze. Well, almost solve. When he had been within ten feet of the exit, he swore that he heard someone whisper into his ear. The voice said, "Hey."

He spun around, but no one was there. He stood motionless for a few seconds while listening intently for anything odd, but there was nothing but the breeze.

He shrugged and turned around. There was the slightest hint of suppressed laughter from behind him, and then he was shoved into a hedge.

Several vines instantly encircled his neck. Calvin struggled to get them off of him, but as soon as he ripped one away, another would take its place. From the corner of his eye, he thought he saw a hint of something white disappear around a corner of the hedgerow.

Eventually, Calvin worked himself free by unhooking his helmet while quickly ducking out of it and jumping backward. The vines curled around the helmet and held it like a precious trophy. Calvin sighed. This was going to make the return trip somewhat exciting. Again.

Meanwhile, in another part of the maze, a person in a white robe smiled as they fled. Unfortunately, in their haste to retreat, their robe had flapped up against the hedgerow, which immediately grabbed them by the neck and started to pull very hard. The person let out a pathetic little squeak as the vines choked them nearly to death.

Calvin heard the commotion and the squeak. He ran through the maze in search of the source, but could not find it. He checked the aerial view of the property supplied by Ariel, but found no sign of anyone fleeing the scene. Very odd. Maybe it was his imagination? Or maybe it was the vines?

Calvin eventually gave up trying to figure it out and went back to his task of dutifully gathering the required ingredients for Tarpa. After he had collected them all, he took a little time to enjoy the garden.

It really was a wonderful garden. It was like a separate world unto itself, like a little bubble of paradise. Ever since Tarpa had told Calvin what the reverend had said about her apple tree being from the Garden of Eden, Calvin could not help but think of it in those terms.

Although, to tell the truth, Calvin secretly felt that naked, life-sized fairies scampering around playfully would have made it even more his sort of paradise. Oh well, he thought, you can't have everything.

Calvin reversed his way back through the maze while being incredibly careful not to brush the hedges as he did. He also made it back through the perimeter with surprisingly little bleeding and no missing body parts.

He stood under the shower for a few minutes and then stripped off down to a single layer of clothing. Then Snuffy suddenly tackled him again and gave him a big kiss on the neck.

After yelping like a startled girl, Calvin stood back up and petted Snuffy on top of the head for a few minutes to calm her down. Then he took some asparagus from a protective container and held it out for her. She sucked it up so fast that Calvin had to work to get his hand back from the inside of her trunk.

He fed her some more while saying, "Eat up, girl, we're going on a little trip today."

Snuffy, like most pets, understood absolutely no English except for words that hinted of food or a walk. She must have understood the word "trip", because she started to dance around Calvin while jumping up and down in uncontrollable excitement.

Calvin petted her and scratched her on the head for a few more minutes to calm her down again. Then he went inside to give the other vegetables to Tarpa, who unfortunately did not hop around excitedly and try to give him a hickey.

Tarpa took the container from him and said, "Oooh, what happened to your neck? Did the strangler vines get you? You didn't try to break through the hedgerow again, did you?"

Calvin looked her up and down. She was still in her white bathrobe. "Are you sure you're not trying to kill me?" he asked in all seriousness.

Tarpa immediately stopped chopping ingredients and pointed the knife at Calvin. She then said testily, "Do you really want to have a fight with me while I'm holding a knife? Do you really? Because if you accuse me of lying to you one more time, we are going to have more than words."

Calvin had expected this attitude and paid it no mind. Instead, he simply said, "Someone wearing white just pushed me into the strangler vines and ran away. I thought I heard them also get caught by the vines, but I couldn't find them."

Tarpa immediately said, "That's impossible. No one but you and I can get inside my garden. Ariel, show us what you saw."

Calvin wanted to say, "Yeah, well, that's why I'm suspicious of you," but thought better of it and stayed quiet.

Ariel immediately showed the two of them what she had recorded from the satellite information. Each of them separately viewed the event from every conceivable angle. In the end, they reached the same conclusion. Calvin had been pushed, but the person was somehow cloaked from showing up on the Ariel system. Instead, all that was seen was Calvin bending backwards slightly from the middle while thrusting toward the bushes. The movement looked completely unnatural and impossible to replicate without an outside force.

Calvin said nervously, "Um, we didn't build our house on an ancient burial ground or something, did we?"

To his surprise, he saw an expression on Tarpa's face that he had never seen before: confusion.

She shook her head. "I really don't know, sport. I don't know what to make of this. Any ideas, Ariel?"

Ariel immediately answered, "I regret that I have insufficient data to properly assess the situation."

"So that's a no," chided Calvin. "Thanks. You've been a great help."

"You are welcome," answered Ariel, who usually ignored sarcasm.

Tarpa looked at Calvin's neck again. "So wait a minute, the

strangler vines did that to you. Weren't you wearing your helmet?"

"Oh yeah, I was wearing it. Although, the little buggers stole it from me. But anyway, no, this was just a love kiss from Snuffy," explained Calvin while touching the bruises.

Tarpa smirked and said, "Well, she loves you, you know."

Tarpa then went about the business of preparing breakfast for the both of them, as well as a lunch for Calvin to take with him on his journey to the mountains.

She gave Calvin some nano-rebuilders and a glass of Tang so that his neck would heal quickly. She also poured herself a glass of Tang and drank it down in one go, after which she banged the glass down on the table in triumph while puckering up her face.

Calvin watched this with some amusement and asked, "So how are the treatments going?"

"Meh," answered Tarpa. "I can't believe you like this stuff. Bobford3 thinks I'll need at least one thousand more treatments over the next three years before I'll have the same cellular mutation as you, although it could happen sooner if I'm lucky." She smiled and added, "but after that, I'll be an immortal just like you. We'll be like two vampires living in a castle together. Isn't that romantic? It's like something out of an old storybook, isn't it?"

"Yes, well, just so you know," explained Calvin, "those sorts of stories always end with the population storming the castle with torches and pitchforks."

Tarpa frowned and changed the subject. "So anyway, you picked a shitty day to travel to the mountains."

Calvin shrugged. "Yeah, well, it can't be helped. The fair is next weekend. I promised Darryl that I'd help him with his truck tomorrow, and I have to work during the week, so that just leaves today to visit the savages and invite them to tea, so to speak. They're never going to come, you know. I don't know why I'm bothering."

Tarpa raised an eyebrow, which in married couples often passes for a full sentence.

Calvin said, "Yeah, I know. I have to at least try. It's part of our 'let's be nice to the jerks in hope that they will be our friends some day' campaign."

Tarpa lowered the eyebrow, and raised the other one.

"I know," sighed Calvin. "I'll do my best. I'm going, aren't I? In the rain. Through the mud. Riding behind a half-crazed clump of grass."

Tarpa lowered the accusing eyebrow and said, "I know you think it's silly, but having the right frame of mind can really make the difference. I don't expect all the Trads to swoon when they see you and promise to come to the fair, but I know you can win over a few. You can be quite charming when you aren't being a Mr. Grumpy Pants."

Calvin rolled his eyes. "How about a Mr. Soggy Pants? I'm really not looking forward to riding in the rain."

"Oh," said Tarpa while a thought struck her, "I didn't give you your present yet, did I?"

"Present?" asked Calvin, somewhat suspicious. It was not anywhere near his birthday.

Tarpa nodded. "Yes, I had Bobford3 make up a little something for you in his bio-plastics lab. I was going to save it for Christmas, but I'll get you something else instead. I think it will come in handy. Let me just run and get it."

She then disappeared up the stairs, running like a gazelle. A few moments later she returned with a handful of clear plastic sheeting and some oddly shaped plastic beams.

She started to unfold the plastic while saying, "You just sort of place this..."

"It's a Snuffy umbrella, isn't it?" interrupted Calvin. "It's a sort of dome windscreen for Snuffy and my chariot, isn't it? That's actually pretty cool. Well, I don't know about cool. It's a bit dorky, if I'm honest. But at least I'll be dry. Thanks a lot, sweetie. I'll definitely use it today. You rock." He gave her a hug and a kiss to reinforce his words.

Tarpa looked genuinely happy. She refolded the plastic and gave it to him. Calvin set it by the door and finished his breakfast with her.

Calvin noticed a few sprinkles coming down as he finished the last of his meal. He hurriedly washed his dishes, gave Tarpa another quick kiss on the cheek, and said, "I have to run, sweetie. Thanks again for the Snuffy umbrella. We'll both be happier today for having it."

Tarpa nodded and said, "No problem, sport. Be careful today. Why don't you take Astro with you, too? He could use the exercise."

Calvin had been about to argue, but his husbandly instincts had told him that this had not been a suggestion, so he let it be and simply said, "Alright."

He called for their dog, Astro, who came running down the stairs with his tail wagging. "We're going for a walk, boy. Get your raincoat."

Astro jumped around Calvin a few times in much the same way that Snuffy had, and then ran back upstairs.

While Calvin waited, he asked Tarpa, "Are you sure it's a good idea to bring Astro? I mean, he does need to wear display lenses to see. It's bound to freak a few Trads out seeing a dog with big, green bug eyes."

Tarpa finished wiping some food stains off of the counter and said, "I'd just feel better if he went along. Astro is very fond of you and will guard you with his life. You don't have to bring him to the homes. You can leave him to play in the woods while you visit the houses. But if you need him, Astro will be there for you."

Calvin made a face and said, "Sweetie, I'm glad you worry about me, but you know I can take care of myself, right? I mean, they're just stupid Trads."

Tarpa frowned. "First off, that isn't the right frame of mind for what you are doing, is it? Think positive. You can't go there and treat them like apes and expect them to like you. Secondly, never underestimate the strength of an opponent. You're going into their territory, remember. They outnumber you by the thousands. And even though you can heal astonishingly well, there are some things you just can't come back from, and there are other things that you might not want to come back from. You are not immune to pain and torture, after all, are you?"

"What happened to keeping a positive attitude?" asked Calvin, sarcastically.

Tarpa said, "That's your job, sport, not mine. My job is to keep you safe. So bring the dog and don't argue about it."

"Yes, dear."

About then, Astro came trotting back downstairs with a yellow raincoat in his mouth, and a sleepy-looking cat on his back.

Calvin said to the cat, "Oh god, you're not coming too, are you?"

Velcro meowed demandingly.

Calvin sighed. "Fine. I mean, the Trads are going to think the bloody circus has come to town, but whatever. You two know it's raining outside today, don't you?"

The two pets looked blankly back at Calvin.

"Fine. Hop down for a moment, Velcro. Down. Down."

Velcro took a swipe at Calvin's hand as he pushed him off of Astro's back. Calvin could remember when he was such a sweet little thing, but those days were long gone. He took the raincoat from Astro's unresisting mouth and put it on him. He then took an umbrella from the stand by the door and affixed it to the side of the coat. Velcro jumped onto Astro's back and gave Calvin another commanding meow.

"OK," said Calvin to the room in general, "We're out of here."

Tarpa gave him a kiss goodbye and handed him his lunch. She then turned to the pets and said, "OK, you two, watch over Daddy and don't let him do anything too stupid."

Astro barked. Velcro remained silent and almost appeared to roll his eyes.

"That goes for you too, little prince," said Tarpa while squatting down to look Velcro in the face.

"Meow," said Velcro, reluctantly.

"Good," replied Tarpa while standing back up.

Calvin led Astro to the back door. He picked up the Snuffy umbrella and said, "OK, see you later, sweetie. I'll be back some time tonight."

"Later, Cal. Be safe."

Calvin nodded and went outside. He entered a nearby shed and pulled out a harness and a chariot, but he left the Roman-style helmet behind. He always felt like such a dork when riding the chariot, but the mountain folk would be suspicious of his car, so he could not use it today. No, he had to do this old school. Really old school.

He attached the harness to Snuffy and then attached the chariot to the harness. He then unfolded his gift from Tarpa and attached it to the harness and the chariot. It formed an elongated dome of transparent plastic that protected both Snuffy and the occupant of the chariot from the rain. It was very odd looking, and Calvin was starting to think that maybe the car would actually be a better choice. Unfortunately, all the pets were already looking forward to the trip. What a circus, he thought.

Calvin opened the umbrella on Astro's back so that he and Velcro would both be protected from the rain. It was fortunate that the wind was not too strong. If they took their time and let the storm lead ahead of them, then things shouldn't be that bad.

Calvin's chariot was more like a two-wheeled coach in that it had a small, heavily cushioned seat built into it, along with a very large open compartment in the back that served as storage. He sat down on the seat and grabbed the reins. He looked over to Velcro and said, "OK, Velcro, let's head out."

Calvin gave the reins a gentle shake and Snuffy began to walk. Velcro gave the top of Astro's head one swift swat with his paw, and Astro also began to walk.

Calvin activated a mechanism that lowered a wooden plank over a section of dark green grass. Snuffy and Astro walked over it, and then it raised back up again.

They turned westward and walked down the wide, dirt road. There was still an early morning chill in the air. Calvin was already missing the comfort of his car and its built-in wood burning stove, which was something that Calvin had always thought to be a little dangerous to have inside of a wooden car, even though it did keep him warm, if not a little smoky.

He passed his neighbor's house and, unfortunately for Calvin, both Cletus and Darryl were out on the front porch.

Darryl saw him and said, "Good morning, your lordship! We got some sort of parade today?"

Calvin's head sagged. "No, just going to visit the Trads. I'm inviting them to the fair next week."

Surprisingly, Darryl didn't make fun of him or his covered chariot. Instead, he ran out in the rain, which by now was starting to come down with some conviction, and handed Calvin a heavy flask filled with moonshine. "You look like you could use this, your lordship. It'll keep the chill from gettin' to ya. Good luck with them crazy son-bitches over there."

Calvin gratefully took the flask and said, "Thanks, dude."

Darryl then gave Astro a few friendly pats on his side and removed his hand just in time to avoid a swipe from Velcro's paw. He then waved hurriedly at Calvin and said, "Later, dude," while he ran back to the cover of his porch.

"Later dude," called Calvin back to him. Then he took a deep breath, took a big drink, wiped his mouth, and said to himself, "OK, let's get his shit-show on the road."

The Trad's village was about twenty-five miles away as the crow flies, but after the first fifteen miles, the road would start to zigzag up the side of the mountain, because otherwise it would simply be too steep. This would turn Calvin's trip into a forty mile journey.

Calvin's plan was to spend thirty minutes or so with Snuffy walking at a leisurely five miles per hour. This would give the fast-moving storm a chance to mostly pass them by. Then he would let Snuffy jog along at fifteen miles per hour, which was about half her top speed. If he had his timing right, they would enter the steeper part of the mountain just after noon, which would leverage the pull of the sun to make Snuffy's work as easy as possible.

Calvin detoured down the smaller side streets until they were out of town. He was anxious to avoid as much embarrassment as he could. Once he was out of town, he returned to the main road, which was the only one that led to the Trad's village.

The road was muddy but not unbearable for the animals. It was lined with dense woodlands and heavy undergrowth. Calvin could hardly imagine that not long ago, all of this land had been a desolate wasteland. It just goes to show you, he thought, that men could save themselves from themselves if they really tried.

Astro and Velcro led the way along the road while Snuffy and Calvin followed about ten feet behind. Occasionally, Snuffy would swerve to the side of the road to snuff the berries off of the bushes like a vegetarian vacuum cleaner. Calvin would usually permit this, but if Snuffy dilly-dallied for too long, then Calvin would have to tug the reins to get her to continue walking.

At other times, Astro would also swerve off the path to have a wee against a tree, or to eat something that he was probably not supposed to. Velcro would usually permit this, but if Astro dilly-dallied for too long, then Velcro would swat the top of Astro's head to get him to continue walking.

After about forty-five minutes, the rain began to let off, so Calvin had the circus stop for a quick rest. He pulled out a large bowl and a jug of water from the back of the chariot and gave the animals a good drink. Once everyone was rested, Calvin had Astro and Velcro hop into the storage compartment of the Chariot because it was now time to start moving with some haste.

Calvin pulled out a long stick from the back of the chariot. It had a stuffed rabbit attached to one end. He suspended the rabbit in front of Snuffy's face and said, "Get the rabbit, girl! Get the rabbit!"

Rabbits were not indigenous to Evionia, and Snuffy was a vegetarian, so it was always puzzling to Calvin why this worked at all. But it did work quite well. Snuffy immediately bolted after the elusive bunny rabbit.

They made great time after that. Calvin stopped them just after noon for another rest and some lunch. While he was eating, he heard the voice of a little girl from far off. It sounded like she was singing. Calvin boosted his hearing in order to discern what she was singing about.

...You will wake up dead
from scorpions in your bed
God loves one and all
if you doubt that you will fall
into a lake of fire
and burn there for a while
until you've had enough...

Calvin screwed up his face. What the heck kind of song was that? He waited while the voice got louder and louder.

...Violence is the way
to keep the devil at bay
So sing this song aloud
and make your God so proud...

Calvin stood transfixed while staring intently at the bend in the road ahead of him, which masked whatever psychopath was heading his way. He started to subconsciously bite his nails as he listened to this bizarre song being sung by what sounded like a small little girl. But listening to the lyrics, he could only imagine what sort of hideous monster this person truly was. The voice grew louder still, and Calvin began to shake.

...Smite the infidel
Damn his soul to hell
Hang him from a pole
Let demons take his soul...

All four of them were now staring at the road with their full attention. As the figure rounded the corner, the hair on Astro's back started to stand on end and a beastly growl escaped from his mouth.

"Easy, boy," said Calvin in a low, calming voice. "Easy, now."

Finally, the figure was visible. Calvin saw it and laughed with relief. He wiped the sweat from his forehead and turned red with embarrassment. It really was just a little girl.

She was a cute little thing, too. She looked to be about six or seven, although Calvin was terrible at guessing children's ages, so she might have been older. He could just about manage to put women into one of the following categories: baby, brat, teen, coed, cougar, and crone. This girl fell somewhere in the center of brat.

She had thick blonde hair that waved and curled its way down to the top of her shoulders. She was wearing a white headband that kept it out of her large, blue eyes. She was also wearing a pale blue dress of the sort that conjures up the word 'shepherdess' — at least for people who have never seen one in real life. The dress was sleeveless and followed her upper body until it suddenly puffed out around her waist with all sorts of crinkly bits that Calvin knew probably had a proper name like 'bunting' or something. At any rate, she did not appear to be any more menacing than a chipmunk.

Calvin relaxed, which caused the animals to relax as well. However, Calvin was not entirely stupid, so he stayed on his guard because, little girl or not, that song had been just plain creepy.

The girl was about three hundred feet away when she finally noticed them. She instantly froze and went silent. She looked worried and unsure of what to do next.

Calvin called out to her, "It's OK. None of my animals will hurt you." He then paused for a moment and added, "Well, the cat can be a little pissy at times, if I'm honest."

The girl laughed at this. Good, thought Calvin, laughter is good. Keep her laughing and not trying to smite us with fire and brimstone.

Calvin waved her over. "Come on, I'll let you ride on top of this one if you want," he said as he gestured toward Snuffy.

The little girl nodded and started to skip toward them. Calvin was glad that she did not resume the song. When she was about ten feet away, she stopped skipping and started to walk.

Calvin said, "I'm Calvin. This big girl here is Snuffy. This is my dog, Astro. And this furry thing with claws is my cat, Velcro."

Velcro meowed.

The girl giggled at it. She had only ever seen cats in story books. She went straight over to it and gave it a hug.

Calvin was about to scream, "No!!!!" but it was already too late — she had her arms firmly around Velcro.

But instead of the hissing, slashing, and crying that he had expected, Calvin heard nothing but purring and giggling. Amazing.

Astro then licked the back of her hand as she held Velcro. Snuffy, too, bumbled over to her and patted the top of her head with her trunk. Calvin just stood there and gaped. The girl giggled and petted them all in turn.

Calvin then stated the obvious, "You seem to have a way with animals."

The little girl nodded enthusiastically. "I tend to all the animals on our farm. I love them."

Calvin asked, "What's your name?"

"Victoria," said the girl while looking down at her feet.

"What a beautiful name, Victoria. Where are you headed to? If you are from the village up ahead, you're kind of far from home, aren't you?"

The girl suddenly looked worried. "You're not going to tell my pa, are you? He doesn't like it if I come this way."

Calvin shook his head. "No, I won't. I promise."

"Pinky swear?" asked the girl.

Calvin smiled and held out his pinky. "Pinky swear," he affirmed.

Victoria wrapped her little pinky around his and shook it gently up and down. This seemed to relax her, as if she'd just entered into a sacred covenant that assured her safety.

She looked around as if to confirm the lack of spies and whispered, "I'm going to Big City."

Calvin looked shocked. "What, now? By yourself?"

The girl nodded.

Calvin knelt down to her level and said, "Listen, Victoria, do you know anything about math?"

Victoria nodded. "My pa teaches me."

"OK, then. Let's do some math, shall we?"

Victoria shrugged.

Calvin said, "Bear with me, here. This is important. Do you know how far it is to Big City from here?"

Victoria shook her head. Calvin continued, "It's about thirty miles from here. Now, the average human walks at three miles per hour. So, given that, how long will it take for you to get to Big City?"

Victoria wrinkled up her brow in concentration. Finally, she said, "A hundred!"

"Close," said Calvin. "Ten. Ten hours. Ten hours there, and even more to get back to the village. By the time you go there, do whatever it is you want to do, and get back home, it will be this time tomorrow. And that's assuming you don't fall asleep on the road and get ran over by a cart, or eaten by god-knows-what."

Victoria sagged.

"What did you want to go there for, anyway?" asked Calvin, sympathetically.

Victoria answered, "Just to see."

Calvin suddenly had a thought. He asked her, "Can your father read?"

Victoria nodded. "Pa is real good at reading."

"Great. Wait here a sec." Calvin ran to the chariot and got one of the pamphlets. He came back and handed it to Victoria, saying, "Give this to your father. There is going to be a fair in Big City next week. I'm hosting it, so I'll make sure you get on all the best rides." He pointed to some of the pictures and said, "There is going to be all kinds of fun stuff, like pig riding and watermelon seed spitting. And they'll be lots and lots of yummy food, too."

Victoria hugged his leg. But then she let go suddenly and looked disappointingly at the ground. "But my pa probably won't let me go. He says that Big City is a wicked place filled with sinners."

Calvin looked down at her. "And you heard that and said to yourself, hey, that's where I want to go all by myself — it sounds like fun."

Victoria shrugged. "My pa goes there twice a week, and nothing happens to him."

"What's he do in Big City?" asked Calvin.

Victoria wiped her nose on the back of her arm and said, "He preaches to the wicked so that their wretched souls may one day be saved."

If this were a cartoon, a light bulb would have appeared above Calvin's head. He suddenly asked, "Hey, your last name isn't Smelcheck, by any chance?"

Victoria smiled and nodded. "You know my pa?"

"Oh yes," said Calvin carelessly. "He stands outside my house almost every morning and tells me to go burn in hell whenever I come outside."

Victoria's eyes widened and she jumped backward. She pointed her arm and finger at Calvin and exclaimed, "Devil boy! My pa talks about you all the time!"

Calvin looked up at the sky and sighed. "Yes, yes. That's me. Devil boy. At least, that's what your father calls me. I promise I'm not a bad person. Although, I suppose I could be lying, right? I mean, if I were a bad person, I wouldn't admit it, would I? That would just be stupid."

Victoria put her arm down and shook her head. "You're not bad. I can tell."

"How?"

Victoria gently petted Astro and said, "Because the animals love you."

Calvin looked stunned and said, "Wait, even this one?" He pointed at Velcro. Velcro took a swipe at his finger and drew some blood.

Victoria giggled and said, "She's a feminist."

Calvin stared at her. "I think you mean he. Also, feminist is a pretty big word for a little girl like you."

Victoria shrugged and said, "So is condescending. Anyway, She's a she — look." She picked up Velcro and showed Calvin the proof.

Calvin laughed louder than he probably should have. Once he caught his breath and wiped his eyes, he said, "You know, Victoria, I really like you. I hope you will be my friend. And Velcro, well, I'm sorry. I never even thought to look."

Velcro meowed.

Victoria smiled and said, "I like you too, devil boy."

"Please, call me Calvin."

"OK, Uncle Calvin."

Calvin smiled. "Uncle Calvin, huh? OK, that's still better than devil boy. So, what are you going to do now, Victoria? Are you still going to Big City today?"

Victoria shook her head.

"You want to come with us back to the village? I'll let you ride on top of Snuffy."

Victoria nodded her head vigorously.

"OK, hop up, then," he said as he lifted her up and placed

her on top of Snuffy. "If you get hungry or thirsty or anything, just let me know."

Victoria nodded but was not really paying attention to Calvin anymore. All her attention was now on riding Snuffy. She was smiling from ear to ear. Calvin did not know it, but this would always be one of her fondest childhood memories. Her father would have smacked her backside black and blue if he had seen her riding a beast like that. The thought of doing something slightly naughty made her even more excited. Clearly, Victoria was going to be quite a handful as she got older. But for now, she was a sweet little girl having the time of her life.

They started off at a leisurely five miles an hour. After about a mile of this, Victoria got bored and whispered something to Snuffy. Suddenly, Snuffy shot down the road at full speed, nearly thirty miles per hour. Victoria was leaning forward and hanging on to Snuffy by two fistfuls of hair.

Astro was trying to keep up but couldn't — even with Velcro's iron paw spurring him on. After Calvin got over the initial shock, he glanced back at Astro and Velcro as they faded into the background.

He turned forward again and let out a sharp, loud whistle. "Ho, Snuffy. Ho!"

Snuffy heard the whistle and snapped out of whatever mad trance the little girl had put her in. She blinked a few times and then gently slowed back down to walking speed.

"Good girl, Snuffy. Good girl," reinforced Calvin. Then he called Victoria's name.

"Yes, Uncle Calvin?"

"Um, don't do that again, OK?"

"Sorry, Uncle Calvin."

Calvin pointed behind them and said. "It's OK. Maybe we can do that again another time, but right now we have to wait for them to catch up, OK?"

Victoria nodded.

What a bloody circus, Calvin thought again.

Eventually, Astro came panting up beside them. Calvin stopped the circus and gave them all some water. After they were rested, he loaded Astro and Velcro into the back of the chariot and said to Victoria, "OK, Victoria, let's go — but this time not so fast, OK? Snuffy is very hairy and gets overheated quickly. Maybe go about half as fast."

Victoria said sweetly, "OK, Uncle Calvin."

She gave Snuffy a friendly pat. The beast blew some air and mucus out of its trunk and then started trotting at a reasonable fifteen miles per hour.

Calvin had one of those moments. The sort of moment when you look at yourself from outside your own body and say, "Hey, how the hell did your life end up like this? What sort of life have you led that brought you here, on an alien planet hundreds of years in the future, riding a chariot being pulled by some sort of woolly mammoth that's being controlled by a little girl with special beast powers while a dog with built-in sunglasses and a sadistic cat ride behind you? Where is the sense in all of this? What sort of person are you that these sorts of things keep happening to you?" And then you sort of shake your head and say, "Ah, the hell with it." That sort of moment.

Calvin shook his head and said, "Ah, the hell with it." He glanced at Victoria, who seemed to be having the time of her life. He glanced back at the two riding behind him. Astro was lying on his side and resting. Velcro was standing beside him and licking his face. It looked really cute until Calvin remembered that this was Velcro's way of saying, "Wake the hell up and give me attention!" Calvin turned back around.

The rest of the trip took a mere thirty minutes. Calvin stopped just on the edge of the village to feed and water everyone, and to relieve himself in the woods. He also removed his display lenses, which he realized had not worried Victoria at all.

Calvin let Victoria ride in the chariot while he walked beside Snuffy. The other two remained in the back of the chariot. Victoria did not want her father to see her riding Snuffy, and Calvin wanted to avoid freaking out the Trads, so he decided to enter the Village as slowly and humbly as possible.

As they approached it, warning bells began to sound out throughout the village. They did not sound welcoming to Calvin. Calvin asked Victoria what they meant.

"It means infidels are coming," explained Victoria.

"You do have an interesting vocabulary," replied Calvin.

"My pa has lots of books. I love books."

"I'll bet," said Calvin. "So, where do you live, Victoria? I'll take you home first."

Victoria suddenly looked sad. Hesitantly, she answered, "Not far. Just over there on the right and down the lane. Not far." There was a pause, and then she added, "But we don't have to go there yet, do we?"

Calvin gave her a sympathetic look. "Sorry, sweetie. I already had plans to visit your father first. It's sort of the right thing to do, you understand? Your father is the head of the village, I believe. So it's only right that I see him first."

Victoria considered this and said nothing.

"Sorry," repeated Calvin. "We'll play some more at the fair, OK?"

Victoria nodded and led him to her house. Before they got there, Victoria motioned for Calvin to bend down. After he did, she whispered in his ear, "Don't tell my pa that I was so far from home and I rode your Snuffy."

Calvin held up his pinky and said, "I won't. Pinky swear, remember?"

Satisfied, the girl brought Calvin into the house while the three animals remained some ways down the lane. The house was a wonderfully built log cabin, perhaps even better made than the ones in Big City. It even featured glass windows, which was something they did not have in the city. The best the city folk could make was a sort of heavy fibrous paper soaked in corn oil, which was translucent but definitely not transparent. Calvin was impressed.

Victoria opened the door and said, "Pa! I'm home. We have a visitor from the heathen lands."

Reverend Smelcheck came bustling into the living room from another part of the house. He saw Calvin standing next to his daughter and gasped in astonishment.

"Get away from that devil boy this instant, girl," he said tersely and then hastily grabbed her arm and yanked her away from Calvin. "You stay away from my family, devil boy, you hear? Now be off with you. Go."

"But I..." started Calvin.

"Go. Go on. Get," continued Reverend Smelcheck.

Calvin held up his hands as a sign of surrender. Reverend Smelcheck mistook the gesture and took a step back while shielding his daughter from Calvin with his arm.

"I come in peace, Reverend. I promise." Calvin pulled a pamphlet from his pocket and handed it to the reverend, who took it cautiously, as if it might turn into a serpent at any moment.

Calvin continued, "We are having a fair next week, and I wanted to invite you and your family to come. There will be lots of fun things to do for your little girl, and lots of good things to eat. I'm sure Mrs. Smelcheck would enjoy a break from cooking and a little fresh air. And it would be a great chance to come and preach to all of us infidels."

The reverend scowled. "It's just me and my daughter, devil boy, not that it's any of your business. And no, I'm not going to your pagan celebration, and there is no way my daughter is going anywhere near Sin City."

Victoria suddenly looked very sullen. "But Pa, I really want to go to the fair. I want to go! Please, Pa. Please!"

The reverend snapped at her. "I said no, child. Now get to your room before you feel the back of my hand."

Victoria screamed, "You never let me do anything. I hate you, I hate you, I hate you!" She ran down the hall and into her bedroom, slamming the door behind her.

The reverend looked absolutely livid. Calvin saw this and said, "I'm sorry, Reverend, I didn't mean..."

"Get out," growled the reverend.

Calvin had no choice but to comply. As he backed his way out of the door, he said, "Look, Reverend, once you calm down, I hope you will reconsider. I promise you it will be a safe and friendly time for both of you, and I think it might help you two to bond a little, if you don't mind me saying."

"I do mind, devil boy," said the reverend, but with less conviction than before. Calvin must have struck a nerve because the reverend's voice had wobbled slightly with emotion. "Just go," he said hoarsely.

Calvin said quietly, "Yes, of course. I really am sorry. I'm going now," and then quietly closed the door behind him.

Now outside, Calvin took a deep breath. "Well, that could have gone better," he said to himself.

He walked back to the chariot and sat inside of it for a few minutes while he tried to shake off the negative vibes. He took a few big gulps of the moonshine that Darryl had given him and silently thanked his friend for his foresight.

He said to himself, "OK, think positive. Think positive. Hey there! I'm Calvin, and I'd like you to come to my fair next week in Big City. Hi! I'm from the heathen lands. We're having a family-friendly fair next week, and I promise we won't be sacrificing any virgins or dancing naked in the moonlight while covered in yak's blood. Hi! I'm... Oh, whatever, let's just get this over with."

Calvin traveled to the next house. When he knocked on the door, no one answered but he could see shadows peering at him from behind curtains. He left a pamphlet stuffed in the crack of the door and continued on.

The next two houses were the same way. When he knocked on the door after that, however, an impossibly old woman slowly opened the door and then stood there silent. She was hunched over a cane and starring at the ground. Eventually she said, "Well?"

Calvin cleared his throat. "Hi! I'm from Big City and..."

The woman spat on his shoes and closed the door.

Calvin stared at the door for a moment and then said to himself, "Fuck this place."

He was about to call it a day when he thought about the look that Tarpa would give him if he gave up now. So, caught between a spitting grandmother and a homicidal wife, Calvin did the sensible thing and continued.

It took him several more hours, but he visited the majority of the other homes in the village. However, this time around, he had not bothered to knock on the remainder of doors and had simply left a pamphlet outside of each home.

Now tired and life weary, Calvin returned to the chariot and turned the circus around. It was past seven o'clock now, and the sun had already set. It was directly behind them now, pulling them backward slightly with about one eighth the strength that Evionia itself was pulling them downward. But this was OK, since they were now traveling down the mountain.

He lit two lanterns and hung them from specially made hooks at the front of his chariot. He gave everyone their supper except himself. He wasn't feeling very hungry.

The trip back home was mercifully uneventful. Calvin was anxious to get back quickly, so he had Astro and Velcro ride in the back of the chariot for most of the way while Snuffy trotted along at nearly twenty miles per hour.

Once home, Calvin was barely awake enough to disconnect the chariot from Snuffy. He went immediately upstairs to bed and crashed face-first into it. He had been vaguely aware of someone talking to him, but their voice faded away as he fell asleep.

CHAPTER 15

Bobford3 stepped into the access way of the collider, which looked something like a subway tunnel, but instead of a track, there was a large six-foot pipe running down the center of it. The tunnel curved around in a huge circle — so huge that it was difficult to tell from inside that it even curved at all. Bobford3 could hear the satisfying hum of operating machinery.

He walked along the tunnel for a few minutes until he found his employees. Brody had his head and one arm buried inside of an open access panel. Sarah and Mike were staring at some gauges next to the panel and calling out directions to Brody.

Mike had his eyes fixed on a screen and was saying, "A little more. More. More. A little more. Almost there. Shit — go back. Back! Quick, go back! OK, right there. Perfect."

Brody pulled himself out of the hatch and noticed Bobford3. "Yo, Bob-dude. What's shaking?" He asked.

Bobford3 looked around. "Hopefully nothing. So, how are things coming along?"

"Oh," said Brody dismissively, "No problem at all. She's in fine shape. Fine shape. Just needed a few tweaks here and there."

Sarah started to say, "Small little tweaks, and one big radiation lea..." but could not finish because of Mike's hand being clamped firmly over her mouth.

Brody continued before Bobford3 could comment, "Actually, we just finished the last part of the setup. We've got the bismuth foil in place, and we're ready to smash the hell out of it whenever you want."

"So, you are ready right now?" confirmed Bobford3.

The three of them looked at each other hesitantly. Brody shrugged and said, "Sure, why not."

This answer did not inspire confidence. Bobford stared at each of them for a few seconds, as if judging their resolve. Mike avoided his gaze, Sarah just stared at the wall, and Brody stood tall and met his gaze with a confident smile.

"Fine, let's do it," said Bobford3 with some reservation.

The others nodded, and the four of them walked back along the tunnel for a few minutes and then stepped through the doorway to one of several control rooms.

The room featured a massively thick cardion window through which the occupants could see the large pipe, which was the meat and potatoes of the collider. Having a window in the control room was a bit silly because it was not as if anyone would be able to see the carbon nuclei screaming past on their way to the bismuth foil, which incidentally was located on the other side of the facility inside a smaller sub-loop that housed all the detection equipment.

Still, the window gave them something to look at during the experiment and besides, it would allow them to see signs of catastrophic failure and at least begin a prayer before they all turned to ash or compressed into tiny little balls the size of a pin head.

Brody began to confidently flip some switches while the other two stared at the main information screen. Sarah was calling out readings while Mike stood confidently with his hands in the pockets of his lab coat and nodded knowingly at what she was saying.

The background hum of the equipment grew exponentially, although the seven meter thick walls of the control room dampened most of it. After ten minutes of fiddling, Brody said that they were ready to go.

Bobford3 nodded and said, "OK, in your own time, then."

Brody walked over to a red panel and inserted the master key. He looked back at everyone and asked if they were ready, at which point Mike said, "Hold on a second!"

Mike rummaged around in a set of cabinets and produced a roll of aluminum foil. He tore off a large piece and offered it to the group. They all looked at him without comprehension.

Mike said, "Suit yourselves," and folded the foil into a

makeshift hat and placed it on his head. Then he tore off another piece and formed it into a sort of metal Speedo. "OK, I'm ready," he said as he looked back up from his handy work. The other three were staring at him like he was some sort of idiot. Mike saw this and said, "What? Safety first."

Bobford3 put a finger in front of his lips in thought, then he pulled it away and said, "Mike."

"Yes?"

Bobford3 pointed out of the window and said, "You see that pipe right there?"

"Yes," admitted Mike, wondering where this was going.

"Did you know that inside that pipe are some of the most powerful electromagnets in existence?"

Mike relaxed and said, "No worries, boss." He pointed to his foil hat and said, "I used aluminum foil. No problem. It's nonferrous, so it's not effected by magnetism."

"That's not exactly true," explained Bobford3.

"How so?" asked Mike.

"I think you already know the answer to that; you're just not thinking. Ever heard of the word induction, Mike?"

Mike's face came alive with realization. He tore off the bits of foil, crumpled them into a single ball, and threw the ball into the recycling tube.

"Quite so," said Bobford3. "Moving magnetic waves induce a voltage into metal objects. In any case, we are already behind seven meters of steel, so I'm not sure a thin layer of aluminum is going to make any difference one way or another."

"Fine, yes, OK," said Mike with injured pride. "Let's go, then. Go ahead, Brody, let her rip."

Brody looked around the room at his colleagues. They all nodded their heads in agreement, so he began his countdown.

"Five"

"Four"

The others subconsciously took a step back from the window.

"Three"

"Two"

They took another step back.

"One"

Mike covered his groin with both hands.

"Beam initiated."

Everyone but Brody tensed.

The background hum of the equipment did not change.

81

The lights did not flicker.

Smoke did not pour out from the pipe.

A black hole did not swallow them up.

But a little green light did light up.

"That's it?" asked Bobford3 with some disappointment.

Mike laughed and put his hands back in his pockets.

Brody said, "We will have to come back a little after lunch. It takes about four hours for the beam to get up to speed before we can trigger the collision."

Sarah nodded.

Mike laughed and said, "Ha-ha! We got you, boss!"

Bobford3 sighed and said, "I hate you guys."

CHAPTER 16

Calvin and Tarpa were in their secret garden having a picnic lunch. Tarpa was standing beside a round granite table that she had carved herself. She flipped open the lid to a wicker basket and pulled out two sandwiches and a freshly baked apple pie.

Calvin almost drooled when he smelled the pie. He was sitting in a granite chair that had also been carved by Tarpa. It was surprisingly comfortable, but Calvin had to use the strength of his electro-muscular implants to move it closer to the table.

Straining with the effort, Calvin said, "I'm pretty sure we don't have to worry about anyone ever stealing our patio furniture."

Tarpa flicked him on the nose and then continued to set the table. As she did so, she asked, "So, now that you are awake, you want to tell me about yesterday? It must have been pretty tough. You practically sleepwalked to bed."

Calvin took a bite of his sandwich, which contained something like turkey and avocado but tasted surprisingly good. After he swallowed, he said, "I think I hate them all. I'm really tired of dealing with them. They're just so pigheaded and willfully stupid. I hate it."

"So, it didn't go well, I'm guessing."

Calvin gave a hollow laugh. "No, that's an understatement. And I swear I tried to maintain my positivity. I practically beamed cheerfulness. But in the end, most people didn't even bother to come to the door. And one woman spat on my shoes. The only good thing that happened was meeting Victoria."

"And who is Victoria?" asked Tarpa while trying not to sound jealous.

"Oh," said Calvin, "You won't believe this. I ran into this little girl on the road about ten miles from the village. She was trying to walk to Big City by herself. I got to talking to her, and guess what?"

"What?" Asked Tarpa, obediently.

"She's the reverend's daughter!"

"Reverend Smelcheck? Really?"

"Yeah," affirmed Calvin. "Really. She's a cute little thing and smart as a whip. Apparently, the reverend has a collection of books squirreled away and taught her how to read. Pretty upper class for a Trad, no?"

Tarpa nodded.

"Anyway, so I made friends with her and convinced her not to try to go to Big City by herself. She rode back to the village on top of Snuffy. She's real good with animals, like scary good. She even hugged Velcro and lived to tell about it. Oh, by the way, did you know that Velcro is a female?"

"No, not really," answered Tarpa. "Although I tend to think of all cats as female. So, the prince is a princess... That makes sense. How did you not know that? I mean, I just took your word for it, but you are her owner. You should have known."

Calvin shrugged. "I just never thought about it. But even if I had, I'm not sure she would have let me flip her over without a fight."

Calvin finished his sandwich and eyed the pie.

Tarpa noticed this and said, "Go ahead."

While Calvin cut the pie, Tarpa said, "Going back to the little girl... That was nice of you to take her home. What did the reverend say when he saw you with her?"

Calvin set down the knife and said, "Well, I didn't tell him that I had traveled with her for ten miles. We pretended not to know each other, as if we had just met outside. Otherwise, she would have been in big trouble." He took a bite of the pie and chewed it thoughtfully. "This pie is awesome."

"Yes, it is. It's made with my apples, but it was given to me by a lady I helped the other day. So go on, what did the reverend say?"

"Oh, he was not pleased at all. He was all like, 'Get away from her, devil boy! Be gone with you!'"

Tarpa smiled briefly. "Yes, that sounds like him."

"I gave him a brochure, but he acted like his soul would rot in eternal damnation if he went. Victoria was devastated. I wish she could have come. I think you would like her."

"I'm not very good with children, though," admitted Tarpa. "I never know what to say to them. I either treat them like they are stupid, or I treat them too much like an adult."

Calvin nodded. "I can see that. Well, she's pretty easy to get along with. Just treat her like an adult that's from out of town. Or, better yet, treat her like an intelligent person who just doesn't know a lot of stuff. That would do fine."

"I'll keep that in mind if I ever meet her," said Tarpa after swallowing her own piece of pie.

A little bird came down from a tree and landed on Tarpa's shoulder. She looked at it sideways and said, "Piss off, Herbert. I told you not to beg." The bird flew off.

Calvin wrinkled up his face. "You name them?"

"Some of them," admitted Tarpa. "The ones with a bit of personality at least. Anyway, go on. Spill it. How did the rest of the trip go?"

Calvin returned his face to normal and looked around. "It really is peaceful in here. So private. I bet we could walk around naked in here and no one would know. Then it really would be like the Garden of Eden."

Tarpa tilted her head slightly and said, "We could try it if you'd like."

Calvin thought about this. "Nah, that's OK. At least not now — not while we are eating. Somehow that seems... unsanitary."

"Suit yourself, sport. I never would have pegged you for being modest."

Calvin gave a half shrug. "I'm just not sure I see an upside to walking around with my bits flapping around all over the place. Besides, there's stinging insects around."

"So, what do you want to do now, then?" asked Tarpa.

Calvin scratched his nose. "How about we just walk around a bit?" He stood up and offered her his hand.

Tarpa replied, "Sure," and took his hand. They walked away from the patio area on the southern border of the garden, which was nearest to the house. They walked north along the western edge of the garden. The interior of the garden was something of a maze unto itself, although it contained enough breaks in the landscaping features so one was not limited to a single route going through it.

In a way, it was more like a very picturesque obstacle course. Tarpa had designed it so that there was something new to discover around every corner, and there were plenty of corners.

They walked under an ivy-covered arch and entered the apple orchard. As they walked along the border of this, neither one bothered to pick an apple since they had just eaten the apple pie. Beyond the apple orchard was a strawberry patch that was lined with raspberry and blackberry bushes. Everything in this field was covered in a fine, translucent netting, which looked almost like a giant stocking. This was to keep Herbert and his thieving bird friends from gorging themselves on Tarpa's produce.

Tarpa said to Calvin, "Just a second. I want to put some food out for the birds."

Calvin said, "OK," and let go of her hand. Tarpa walked around to the two stone birdbaths that were on the other side of the strawberry patch. One of them was filled with water, but the other one had its bowl sitting upside down on the pedestal. Tarpa flipped it back over.

She then grabbed a nearby bucket and started to pick some of the ripe fruit, first some strawberries and then on to the blackberries and raspberries. Once the bucket had been half filled, she emptied its contents into the dry birdbath and set the bucket back down.

She then put her fingers to her lips and blew a loud whistle. It didn't take long for the sky to darken with a cloud of hungry birds. Tarpa darted out of their way and rejoined Calvin.

Looking at the flock of birds descending, Calvin said, "I think I've had nightmares like this."

"You don't like birds?" asked Tarpa, somehow offended.

Calvin shook his head.

"Weird," said Tarpa while giving her husband an appraising look, as if reevaluating his worth.

A moment later, a bird flew over to them and landed on Tarpa's shoulder. She turned her head to look at it. "Oh, hello Herbert. I see you had some raspberries."

Herbert had raspberry juice all over his usually yellow beak. He tilted his head this way and that, as if trying to understand her, and then wiped his beak on her bottom lip and flew off.

Calvin said, "Ewww."

Tarpa turned to him and asked, "What? That's just his way of saying thank you. It's only a little raspberry bird kiss. What's the big deal?"

Calvin shook his head and said, "I don't know. It's just... yuck."

"You're such a girl sometimes, Calvin," observed Tarpa.

"Ha-ha," he replied and took her hand again. "Let's walk some more, OK?"

They continued walking past more fruit and turned east along the northern border. Now they started to come across various vegetable patches sprinkled here and there in little semi-hidden alcoves. They stopped about midway and started to walk back south again, but this time down the center of the garden which featured a narrow path lined with flowering trees.

"This is my favorite spot," said Calvin while they walked beneath the cherry blossom trees. Little pink flower petals floated down around them like a gentle snowfall. Somehow, Tarpa had modified the trees to flower perpetually.

The walkway was soft with layers of pink petals. Tarpa collected these once a week and added them to the compost that she stored on the eastern border of the garden along with her gardening tools.

After the cherry blossom trees, were the dogwood trees. After them, were the plum trees. And after all the trees, there was a section of walkway with fountains on either side.

As Tarpa and Calvin approached them, the fountains started to shoot spurts of water in large arcs over their heads and into each others' bowls. First one did it, and then another, and another until they were all doing it. It looked like a water fight amongst the fountains.

The effect of this was to form a long archway of water that misted down on Calvin and Tarpa as they walked. The mist was cold and refreshing. Even though the weather here was usually temperate, this was a favorite spot during the hot days they had in mid summer.

They left the fountain area and came upon a collection of sculptures. The rest of the garden had sculptures sprinkled here and there for ambiance, but this was an area for creating them. The sculptures here were either half finished or deemed too ugly by Tarpa to be a part of her garden. The ugly ones would eventually be chiseled down into something else, or turned into crushed stone and sold. Calvin looked at one of them and sighed. It was his masterpiece, but Tarpa had made him keep it here and often threatened to reduce it to rubble.

The statue was his rendition of Venus de Milo. In this version, she had longer hair and both of her arms. She was leaning slightly over a plinth with her oversized breasts resting on top of it. It was crude in every sense of the word. Calvin had thought that it was pretty good for his third attempt. Tarpa, however, had said that he needed about fifty more years of practice and a better eye for beauty.

Three other statues caught Calvin's eye — one very large, one quite small, and one somewhat larger than the small one. They were very blocky with only the slightest hint of what they would become. Calvin asked, "What are you making over there?"

Tarpa looked to see where he was referring. "Oh, those. Those are going to be Snuffy, Astro, and Velcro."

Calvin considered this. "You could have probably carved Velcro and Astro together. Those two are inseparable."

"Yes," agreed Tarpa. "I thought about that too and may still go that way. I haven't decided yet."

They took one last look around together and continued walking. As they did, Tarpa asked, "Are you nervous about the fair coming up?"

"Big time," said Calvin. "It's a big fucking deal, if you don't mind me saying. It's such a great opportunity to introduce people to the Ariel system. I just don't want to fuck it up. I've never organized anything like this before. I hope I don't screw up."

Tarpa put an arm around him, pulled him close, and gave him a kiss on his cheek. "Relax, sport. You never ran a company before, either, but you are doing just fine with that. You're a good leader. And you have plenty of people working alongside you to get this done. It will be fine, you'll see."

"Thanks," replied Calvin. "I guess you're right."

Tarpa flicked his nose playfully. "Of course I am."

They sat down at a bench, and Tarpa leaned against Calvin with an arm around his waist. Calvin had both of his arms wrapped around her. As she rested her head on his chest, he said to her, "I'm so happy I met you." Tarpa gave him a light squeeze in return.

They sat like this for some time until Ariel intruded by reminding Calvin of his promise to help his friend rebuild his truck.

Calvin kissed the top of Tarpa's head and said, "I'm so sorry, but I promised Darryl I'd help him with his truck. I should probably go over there while there are still a few hours of daylight."

Tarpa slowly straightened up and kissed him on the lips. "If you must," she said restfully.

Calvin, now a little turned on, said, "Well, you know, I suppose I could stick around for a while longer."

Tarpa smiled, stood up, and stretched. "No, go and help your friend. I've got some produce to deliver today with Billy."

"Billy?" inquired Calvin.

"Yes, I think I told you about him. I helped his grandmother the other day. I have him helping me with deliveries as payment. He really isn't much help, but they are so poor I couldn't ask for cash. Actually, the grandmother is the one that cooked the apple pie we just ate."

"Oh, OK. That was very kind of you. Especially since you aren't good with children."

"It's not so bad with Billy," explained Tarpa. "He's more like an employee, so most of the time I'm just giving him orders."

Calvin replied, "Well, then you've already mastered the way most adults deal with children. Well done. Anyway, shall we head out now?" Calvin stood up and dusted off his clothing.

Tarpa nodded and then led the way through the maze and out of the security perimeter. Calvin had to follow close behind her, or else the carnivorous plants would snap back behind Tarpa and try to get him.

Calvin thanked Tarpa for lunch and then went next door to help his friend with his truck. Tarpa went to the shed and pulled out a small cart, about half the size of the one she normally used for town, and walked back into the garden with it to collect her produce for the day.

She made three trips with it, each time emptying the contents of the smaller cart into her usual one. The cart had several movable dividers inside that allowed her to keep everything separate. Now that it was filled, she made her way to the market district.

Meanwhile, Calvin was now helping his friend by carving a new front bumper for the truck. While he was doing this, Darryl was leaning over the engine and cussing. "Dag nab it! The hoojigger got all whatchamacallit."

"Can you fix it?" called out Calvin from his work area some twenty feet away.

"Yeah, I can fix her. I just got to do this thing with the flange and seal it with some stuff. She'll do right."

"Sounds very technical," joked Calvin. "Where did you learn to work on engines?"

"From my ma. She was a devil with a set of wrenches. That woman could rebuild an engine with one hand, and smack us for being too noisy with the other. She was a great woman."

Calvin said, "She sounds amazing. My mom was a photographer and my dad was a computer programmer for an insurance company. Don't ask me where I got my mechanical ability from. In my house, every butter knife had a bent tip from my dad trying to use them as screwdrivers."

Darryl stopped working for a second and said, "Computer programmer. Insurance." He said them slowly, as if trying to work out the meaning from the various syllables.

Calvin said, "Where I'm from, we had these sort of thinking machines that we taught to do stuff for us, like adding up lots of numbers real fast and such. They didn't actually think, though, so my dad was one of the people who taught them every little step of what to do."

"So wouldn't it have just be simpler for your dad to do the adding up himself?" asked Darryl.

Calvin nodded. "Yeah, you're right about that up to a point. But you see, once you taught a computer to do something, then it could do it as many times as you wanted after that. They could do the same thing over and over all day without making a mistake or getting bored. They were really quite useful."

Darryl seemed to accept this for now and asked about insurance.

"Well you see," replied Calvin, "people would give insurance companies money every month. This was called an insurance payment. In return, the company would insure their property against damage. So like with your truck over there, if you had insurance, then the insurance company would give you the money to have the truck fixed."

Darryl looked puzzled. "So wait. I'd give them money every month, and then if I broke something by accident, they'd give me my money back?"

"Yes," replied Calvin.

"And if I didn't break anything?" asked Darryl.

"Then they would keep your money," explained Calvin.

Darryl shook his head. "Sounds like a scam to me, brother."

Calvin laughed. "Yes, I always thought so too. Especially because if the company ever had to give you some money back, then they would charge you more after that."

"That's fucked up," said Darryl while coating a vital engine part with some sort of sticky goo. Then he asked, "And where do the computer jiggers fit into all this?"

Calvin explained, "The computers were used to figure out how much to charge the customers. They computed the insurance payment based on various risk factors."

Darryl considered this. "So, basically, your dad used to teach machines how to rip people off? That sounds sorta self-defeating, if you ask me."

Calvin scratched his nose nervously. "Yeah, now that you put it like that, I suppose it doesn't really make sense, does it? I dunno."

Darryl said, "Don't worry about it, brother. We all do stupid shit sometimes."

"You're a fountain of wisdom, Darryl."

"Yeah, and you're a smart ass, brother. Now why don't you make yourself useful and help me get my hand unstuck from this flange."

While Calvin helped his friend with his sticky situation, Tarpa was now entering Market Street. Billy came running up to her, just in time.

He panted in front of her for a second and said, "Hello, Mrs. Jones."

"Hi, Billy. How's your gran?"

"Good, miss. She's a handful now, though, if I'm honest. She's all go-go-go, if you catch my meaning. Like, she's all full of energy and always wanting me to take her places. She wears me out."

Tarpa smiled and said, "I'm glad she's healthy. You should try to keep up with her. You could use the exercise. You're panting like a horse."

"Yes, miss."

Tarpa put a hand on his shoulder. "Anyway, we have to figure out what to do with you today. There has to be a way we can use you as leverage." She thought for a second and then asked, "Tell me, how do you feel about acting crippled and half blind? No one would say no to a little crippled kid trying to sell some fruit."

Billy looked down at the ground and said sheepishly, "I don't know about that, miss. It sounds sort of like lying to me. My old grandmum says I shouldn't lie."

Tarpa looked annoyed. With a sigh, she said, "Fine, fine. So, let me see... How about you be my heavy?"

The boy looked up. "What's a heavy?"

"Hired muscle," explained Tarpa. "If anyone starts to balk at the price that I give them, your job is to kick them in the shins until they agree."

The boy laughed. "Now you're just having fun with me, aren't you, miss?"

Tarpa gave him a fake laugh. "Ha-ha, yes, of course. Just playing around. Ha, yes. That would be wrong, of course."

Hmm, thought Tarpa. Now what was she going to do? Those were her two best ideas. She thought for a moment and then asked, "Tell me, Billy, does your gran have any elderly friends? Do you know a lot of the older people around here?"

"Oh yes, miss," replied Billy, cheerfully. "She drags me around to visit them all the time, and then she makes me do all sorts of odd jobs for them."

Tarpa squatted down in front of him. "I've got an idea, then. How about you go around to their houses today and ask them if they need any groceries. Tell them you'll collect them for them if they give you, oh, I don't know, maybe a nickle. You decide. I'll even let you use one of my smaller carts if you want. You'd be helping the old ladies who have a hard time getting about, and also making some money for yourself. What do you think?"

Billy thought about this. "I guess that sounds OK, miss. I'll give it a try. But how does this help you?" asked the boy in earnest concern.

Tarpa smirked. "Because you'll be getting all of your fruits and vegetables from me, of course."

"But what if I didn't?" asked the boy, stupidly.

Tarpa stood up and towered over him with her hands on her hips and repeated, "You'll be getting all of your fruits and vegetables from me, right?"

"Yes, miss."

Tarpa mussed up his hair. "There's a good boy."

CHAPTER 17

Four hours after the particle accelerator had been activated, Bobford3 rejoined his group of misfit scientists in the control room.

Sarah was staring at nothing and humming to herself. Mike was rummaging through the cabinets in search of anything entertaining to play with, and Brody was waiting patiently and alertly with an air of eager determination about him.

When Bobford3 entered the room, the other three attempted to smarten up. This meant that Sarah was now staring blankly at Bobford3, Mike pulled the test tubes out of his nose, and Brody resonated with alertness.

Bobford3 looked Brody up and down and said, "At ease."

Brody gave him a puzzled look and said, "Everything is ready to go, Bob-dude. We can fire on your orders."

Now it was Bobford3's turn to look puzzled. "I think you've been watching too many old war movies, Brody. Just get on with it, would you?"

Brody nodded his head and casually walked over to a panel and flipped a switch that looked no different from any of the other thirty switches in its vicinity.

He checked some readings. "OK, all done."

"Wait, what?" asked Mike in surprise, beating Bobford3 to the punch by a fraction of a second. "That was it?"

Brody shrugged. "Yes, why?"

Mike glanced out of the super thick cardion window and said, "I don't know, I guess I was expecting a little more, like maybe a bang and some shaking or something."

Brody furrowed his brow at Mike, held up a hand, pinched his fingers together in demonstration and said, "They are just tiny, little things, you know."

Sarah said, "The carbon atom goes round and round, and when it hits, there is no sound."

Mike looked at her and asked, "What is it that she actually does for us, anyway? Is she supposed to be our minstrel or something?"

Bobford3 smiled and said, "You'll see soon enough. Behind that blank stare, there are all sorts of thoughts whizzing around and crashing into each other, forming strange and sometimes brilliant logical connections. She's still collecting data right now, and doing research. Eventually, she will come up with something amazing. You'll see."

Mike watched Sarah as she stared just over his right shoulder and hummed tunelessly to herself. "O...K..." he said with skepticism in his voice.

"So anyway," interrupted Bobford3, "How did the experiment go, Brody?"

Brody pointed to the readout and said, "Totally awesome, as you can see. Our results match those of our predecessors. Of course, we have better tools than they did, so we can even count how many non-radioactive atoms we created."

"And that would be..." prodded Bobford3.

Brody proudly answered, "Three."

A few silent seconds went by while everyone processed this fact.

Eventually, Bobford3 said, "Three? Three? That isn't very much gold, is it? Three atoms of gold?"

Brody answered defensively, "Yeah, but, that isn't the point right now. This was just to prove that it could be done. Besides, we transmuted several other atoms, you know. It's just that most of them were not gold, or were unstable isotopes of gold that radioactively decayed into something else."

"Yeah," argued Bobford3, "but in my day we had this thing pumping out strange matter like there was no tomorrow."

"From what I heard, there very nearly wasn't," interjected Mike.

Bobford3 glared at him.

Brody answered, "Pffft. Strange matter. That's easy," as if it were something he used to create in his bedroom as a child on rainy Saturday afternoons.

"So, where do we go from here?" questioned Bobford3.

This time Brody was more humble. "Well... That's where it gets tricky. I mean, there are so many problems to work out. How do we improve the accuracy of our beam so that we can create more of the right sorts of atoms? And how do we separate and collect them after we've done so? And even after we figure those out, it will still be a pathetically slow process."

Bobford3 looked at the other two and asked, "Any ideas?"

Mike answered, "None right now. Let me sleep on it."

Sarah turned to Mike as if to speak to him, but instead sent him a text asking a few very technical questions that were just at the limit of Mike's knowledge of chemistry, physics, and quantum mechanics.

Mike looked back at her and texted the answers to the best of his ability.

This continued for a few minutes while Bobford3 and Brody tried to make sense of what the two of them were doing. They watched in fascination as Mike and Sarah wordlessly stared at each other for some time, although occasionally Mike would say things like, "Yes, but..." and then fall back into silence.

Eventually, Bobford3 lost interest and tried to leave the room, only to have Mike suddenly blurt out, "No, wait, give us just a few more minutes."

A few more minutes later, Mike suddenly walked up to Sarah and hugged her. "You're a genius, woman. You've completely made me eat my words."

"What's going on?" asked Bobford3.

Mike excitedly answered, "Get this. This is what Sarah just figured out. It's some serious, next-level stuff. OK, so the idea is that we heat the subject up to melting temperature to get everything all nice and juicy, right? And then we expose it to a strong electrostatic field, which will sort of force all the atoms to orientate in a known direction. Sarah also feels we can use Quantum Entanglement to further align the atoms, which quite frankly I don't understand at all — something to do with ghost stencils. I really couldn't tell you.

"Anyway, this will greatly improve our accuracy, although we will never be one hundred percent accurate thanks to that bastard Heisenberg and his uncertainty principle. And that leads me to the next clever bit. Sarah suggests that we have the subject in a sort of large centrifuge while we are doing all this stuff to it. Since the different atoms and isotopes will all have slightly different densities, they will naturally separate themselves in the centrifuge, the densest on the bottom. It's the same principle they use in sifting out heavy water.

"It would then be a simple matter to let the subject cool again and remove the desired section. The leftover materials can be reprocessed, or simply sold off for other uses.

"It really all depends on what we actually want to produce, and with what input. We will have to fine tune the process around that. We aren't to the stage where we can make a magic machine that will turn anything into anything else. Right now, we can only knock the matter down the periodic table, in other words, we can only reduce the periodic number. We don't yet have a process for stuffing in extra bits. But still, pretty amazing idea, don't you think?"

Bobford3 raised his pointer finger in the air and said, "So let me get this straight. You want us to construct a crucible that spins at high speeds, and affixed to this crucible will be both an electrostatic generator and some sort of quantum entanglement device, which Albert Einstein referred to as "spooky action at a distance." And then we are to place this contraption into my otherwise pristine accelerator and, somehow with careful timing I'm assuming, zap the contents of the crucible in exactly the right spot precisely while the open side of the crucible is pointed toward the beam. And if we can somehow do that continuously, then we will eventually accumulate a sizable amount of whatever it is we are trying to create. Is that about right?"

Mike thrust his hands into the pockets of his lab coat and nodded knowingly. "Yep, that about sums it up."

Bobford3 turned to Sarah and asked, "And you?"

Sarah answered, "Did you know that smells are actually your nose's reaction to tiny fragments floating in the air. So when you smell dog poo, that means that you actually have a little bit of dog poo in your nose?"

Bobford3 blinked and looked at Mike for a translation.

Mike shook his head and said, "There are a lot of random thoughts in there. I think this is just spillover. If she didn't actually disagree, then I think we are on the right track."

Bobford3 let this roll off of him like water off of a duck's back. He turned to Brody and asked, "Can you build it?"

Brody asked, "What? A centrifugal crucible with built-in electrostatic generator and quantum entangler? No worries." He smirked at Bobford3 in a way that implied that he could have built something like that in his high school metal shop.

Bobford3 clapped his hands together and said, "Alright then, carry on, you three. Chop-chop! Get cracking."

The three just stared at him. Eventually Mike asked, "Eh, what do you want us to do?"

Bobford3 frowned at him. "All that stuff — build it. What else?"

Then Mike asked, "OK, but for what purpose? What are we trying to turn into what?"

"I don't know," answered Bobford3. "What do we have a lot of on the moon?"

"Dust?" offered Mike.

"Is there anything useful in it?" asked Bobford3 in return.

Mike shrugged.

Sarah interrupted by saying, "Ariel says that the moon dust is a conglomerate of many different compounds, but she suggests that we could probably process out the various glasses and silicates without much fuss. Most of that will be silicon dioxide. We can break that down into silicon and oxygen. Then we can split the silicon into aluminium and hydrogen using our transmuter. The oxygen and hydrogen could be burned as fuel to help power the process, leaving only water as a byproduct. The aluminium can then be sent back to the Earth, or used on the moon to expand the current infrastructure."

Bobford3's mouth opened but nothing came out for a few seconds, then, finally he said, "Yes, that. Let's do that."

CHAPTER 18

Calvin glanced at the Cal Tech sign over his building just like he did every morning, and went inside. Unlike most mornings, however, Doc did not meet him at the door because he was too engrossed in the planning of the upcoming fair.

Calvin had impressed upon everyone just how important it was that the fair go off successfully. After all, a bad impression could potentially ruin the company. As a result, everyone was just a little bit jumpy this morning.

Calvin walked through the reception area on his way to the offices. His receptionist, who had her desk positioned directly beside the door to the offices, was working on something on her desk.

Calvin walked toward his receptionist and tried not to look at her or catch her attention. However, she had a sixth sense when it came to Calvin and looked up from her desk just in time to greet him.

She smiled brightly and said, "Good morning, Mr. Jones." She winked at him.

Calvin glanced at her and smiled back. "Morning, Suzette," he muttered as he scurried past her.

Things where a bit awkward between Calvin and Suzette, or at least awkward for Calvin. He had hired her out of pity and shame back in the very beginning of the company's formation. Back then, Calvin had held an open house job fair for the residents of Big City to tour the new building, learn a little about the Ariel system, and apply for jobs if they were interested.

Suzette had been one of the first applicants. She was not talented in anything in particular, but she was fairly well educated and had a pleasant disposition. However, these qualities were not the only reason for her being hired. In truth, it was mainly from guilt.

Of all the women on the entire planet of Evionia, didn't Calvin just have to bump into the one he had "inadvertently" seen naked in her own home one night while he was being voyeuristic with the live feed from Evionia.

But Suzette had proved to be a very capable secretary, so Calvin had been able to push the whole unpleasant matter into a dark and dusty corner of his mind. After that, the two of them had worked well together for several months, that is, until the first Guides had become available for beta testing by the staff.

The Ariel system is based around the principle of free access to information. However, Ariel is also aware of humans' irrational need for privacy, so while she sees all and knows all, she does not always show all. Any society under her care is provided a basic level of privacy, a level that each person may choose for themselves.

However, before Calvin and Tarpa had come to Evionia, the Evionian's were not under her care. In fact, they had been viewed as potentially hostile. So during that period, the Evionians were being spied on without their knowledge by anyone who cared to tune in to the feeds from the satellites orbiting their planet.

Of course, now that Evionia was being converted to the Ariel system, these feeds were no longer accessible to the public, either on Evionia or on Earth. However, the knowledge that those feeds were once available was now public information to any Evionian who chose to use the Ariel system. And unfortunately for Calvin, his secretary had been very inquisitive.

Suzette had marveled at the Guide's ability to show her a live "map" of the whole city, right down to the people scurrying around on the streets. She had asked Ariel about the guidelines concerning privacy and had been told that she did not have to worry — privacy rules were now in effect. This had led to the obvious question of, "What was available before they were in effect?" which had led to the uncomfortable answer of, "Everything."

At that point, Suzette had dug deeper by asking for information on anything pertaining to her that happened previous to the privacy rules that would now constitute a breach of those rules. It turned out that there had been just one occurrence that had to do with her, and that was by Calvin. This had come as quite a shock for her.

Suzette had always liked Calvin, and if it weren't for her own professionalism, and the fear of being stabbed by Tarpa, she probably would have long ago asked him on a date. Eventually, though, Calvin had married Tarpa and she had been forced to let go of her crush entirely. That was, up until this revelation had surfaced.

She now knew that he had actually seen her naked. He had even tried to follow her into the shower — the little pervert. And all this time he had said nothing about it. OK, admitted Suzette to herself, it was not the sort of thing that was easy to bring up. But still.

So Suzette had done the only sensible thing and started teasing the hell out of Calvin. She would often say things like, "Oh, you know me so well I feel naked in front of you," and, "Just have those documents sent to my house — you know where I live, don't you?"

Eventually, Calvin had realized that she had been doing all of this on purpose and so, nervously, he had asked Ariel if Suzette knew about the incident. Calvin's world had become just that much more complicated when the answer he had received had been, "Yes."

Now, every morning was awkward for him. Deep down, he knew that he probably didn't need to worry, after all, she obviously wasn't mad at him. Well, except that she did seem to like to tease him relentlessly about it. Just the same, at least it was better than a slap to the face or a knee to the groin, he supposed.

Calvin made his way, red-faced, past Suzette and down the main hall. Offices branched off from the hall on both sides. This was the white-collar section of the company where the designers and the bean counters dwelt.

At the end of the hall was a huge kitchen area where everyone from the company would relax and mingle. Another door at the back of the kitchen led to the actual manufacturing facility, where all the blue-collared labor toiled to produce the Guides.

OK, maybe not toiled. Even these jobs were not very demanding. Yes, sure, someone had to tighten a bolt here or there, and sometimes someone even had to weld a few bits of metal together, but on the whole, the place was heavily automated, so the bulk of what the assembly workers really did was stand around with clipboards and try to look busy. When this became too tiresome, they would hide in the bathroom until break.

Calvin knew this, of course. But he also knew that during those not-so-rare times when the shit hit the fan and all the machines started playing battle royale with each other, he could count on his employees to competently get it all sorted out, even if they had to work overtime (at time and a half plus meals).

He popped his head inside a few random offices, but no one was in them. As he walked further down the hall, he heard arguing coming from the direction of the kitchen.

Someone said, "Look, you have to grease the pigs, otherwise, where is the challenge? Any kid around these parts can ride a pig - big deal. The little bastards will get bored if you don't make it hard for them."

Another person cut in, "Don't be stupid. No one can ride a greased pig. You're going to have little kids flying everywhere and slippery little pigs stomping on their skulls as they cry for their mommies. It will be a disaster. It's a stupid idea."

Calvin quickened his pace and joined the ad-hock planning meeting.

He cleared his throat as he entered the kitchen and everyone fell silent. They all looked at him, some with expectation, and others with annoyance. When he knew that he had their full attention, he said very calmly, "Why don't we have them both, one pen for dry pigs and one for greased?" He then calmly continued through the back door of the kitchen and into the main plant.

The second the door was closed behind him, he heard, "Now there's an idea. Why don't we have them both?" He smiled to himself and continued his inspection.

Calvin saw Doc standing in front of the injection molding machine. He was chewing on his pencil eraser and tugging at his hair — two very bad signs. Calvin went up to him and asked him what was wrong.

The man almost jumped. "What? Wrong? Nothing's wrong. Who said anything was wrong? No, that's supposed to smoke like that."

Calvin pulled one of the freshly made Guide cases off the conveyer belt and blew on it as he juggled it from hand to hand while it cooled. Then he made a show of inspecting it in front of Doc and said, "Very nice. Chocolate brown, huh? I thought this style was supposed to be pink?"

Doc bit and swallowed his eraser, then he stammered, "Is it? Oh my word. But doesn't it look nice in chocolate?"

Calvin said tactfully, "Well... they are supposed to look like bunny ears. Although, I suppose they could be chocolate bunnies. Still, I'd take a look at the temperature sensor if I were you. Just a hunch."

Calvin nodded to him and walked away. Behind him he heard Doc shout out, "Line three going down!" and then the chocolate bunny ears stopped going down the conveyer belt.

Everyone is so nervous that no one can think straight today, thought Calvin. His job today was obviously going to be to act as the cool voice of reason. So, pretty much like any other day, really.

He put on a hair cap and stepped through another door, which led into a very small room that was maybe four feet on a side. The door closed behind him and fans in the ceiling instantly blasted him with air in an effort to knock off the bigger bits of fluff. A vacuum beneath the metal grating at his feet collected the debris. Once this was over, he stepped into the next room.

Before he was even fully in the room, two men stood hurriedly up from a small table and held their hands behind them in a very suspicious manner. One of them was Jethro.

Calvin smiled at them. "Good morning, gentlemen."

"Morning, Mr. Jones," they said back in near unison.

Calvin looked at Jethro and asked, "Everything going OK with the wave solderer today, Jethro? Any problems?"

Jethro shook his head. "No, sir. She's ticking away just as perdy as ya like."

Just then, a playing card fell from behind the other man's back and, to the man's credit, was deftly kicked under the cabinet with a barely perceptible movement of his foot.

Calvin pretended not to have seen this and made a show of examining the wave solderer instead. He then said to Jethro, "Excellent. Excellent. And I see you're wearing your hair cap today — good man."

"Yes, sir."

"Well, I can see things are in good hands, then. I'll leave you two to continue your important work."

"Yes, sir. Thank you, sir."

Calvin turned to walk out of the door and then raised a hand up and said, "Oh, wait, there was one more thing." He turned back around and motioned to Jethro to come closer.

When Jethro was in front of him, Calvin whispered in his ear, "I think if you play a five next hand, you can win."

Jethro's eyes bulged.

Calvin winked at him, turned smartly around, and walked out of the room.

As he left the room, Calvin was happy to see little pink bunny ears going past him on the belt. He smiled and thought, it's all about people skills, isn't it? Lead by example, and never hesitate to make them piss their pants just a little bit — that's my motto.

CHAPTER 19

It was a slightly chilly night on the southern outskirts of the village. Reverend Smelcheck stood behind a pulpit at the top of a tall mound. The mound was on the edge of a large clearing.

The flickering lights of hundreds of camp fires cast wavy shadows on the ground of several hundred of his followers. The reverend could sense the crowd's enthusiasm tonight. He had been working them up to a frenzy all week, and finally it was time for action tomorrow. It was almost magical.

Beside him was his right-hand man, Brother Grimm. Brother Grimm was a no-nonsense sort of man and got very angry at little kids who wanted to be told a story. He hadn't asked to be born a Grimm — no one had consulted him about it — but there you have it. You play the hand that you are dealt.

He lamented that despite being a Grimm, he was no good at making up stories. But God had given him one talent, and that had been his ability to write very memorable religious hymns. He had created nearly a hundred of them so far, and they were sung proudly by children and adults alike. The most famous of these hymns was titled "Smite the Infidel," and every child in the village knew it by heart.

Brother Grimm was, if anything, even more zealous than Reverend Smelcheck. Most people felt that he was a shoe-in for village leader once the Reverend passed away.

Reverent Smelcheck raised his arms up high, and within ten seconds, there was near silence in response. He let his arms down slowly and gathered his thoughts in preparation for his sermon. The crowd was silent in anticipation.

Brother Grimm then needlessly bellowed, "All hear the venerable words of Reverend Smelcheck." The effect of which was like a gunshot in church, and it completely spoiled the occasion. Reverend Smelcheck secretly cursed him under his breath.

Once the ringing in his ear had subsided, Reverend Smelcheck began his sermon:

"My bothers and sisters. There is an evil among us. An evil so strong that it threatens our very existence. An evil that grows stronger every day. An evil that must be stopped, and must be stopped now before it's too late."

Whoops and hollers erupted from the crowd.

The reverend waited for them to die down and continued, "Over the last year, this evil has been spreading at a fearsome rate because of those so-called Martians. But we ain't stupid, are we?"

"No!" cried the crowd.

"I say, we ain't stupid, are we?" bellowed the reverend.

"No!" returned the crowd again.

"We ain't stupid. We know the truth. We know those two ain't from Mars. Oh, no-siree-Bob. We know they come straight from the pits of hell."

"Yeah!" shouted the crowd.

"And tomorrow, brothers and sisters, we are going to send them and their kind straight back down to hell again!"

"Yeah!" cried the crowd.

CHAPTER 20

Victoria was alone in the house. Her father had gone off to some sort of secret meeting just before midnight. Even though he had tried to be quiet as he left, Victoria had been awake in her room and had heard him leave.

Victoria fetched the pamphlet that Uncle Calvin had given her from under her bed. She flipped through it again and smiled. Pig riding. They were going to have pig riding. AND cotton candy. Cotton candy! Pig riding and cotton candy and a game where you get to throw rotten fruit at each other. It was just too good to be true. She gritted her teeth and made up her mind. She was going to the fair.

She sat down at her writing desk and stuck out her tongue as she tried to figure out the math behind her adventure. OK, so Uncle Calvin says that people walk at three miles per hour, but I reckon I can skip about twice that fast, so that's six miles per hour. Now, how far is it to Big City? Uncle Calvin said it was thirty miles from where we met yesterday, and that was nearly ten miles from here, so that makes forty miles to the fair. Now if I can skip six miles in one hour, then how long will it take me to skip to the fair?

She screwed up her face in concentration. Her tongue was sticking out really far now. She wanted to give up and blurt out her stock answer of one hundred, but she knew this was a serious matter and she needed a real number.

If I can go six miles in one hour, then I just have to work out how many sixes are in forty and that will be the number of hours. So... forty divided by six. Let me see...

She scribbled the math problem on a clear section of the writing paper and started to work it out. Six times five is thirty. That's below forty. Six times six is thirty-six. Still below forty. Six times seven is forty-two. That's too big. OK, the first number is six. Good, that seems reasonable. She wrote down the six and was tempted to stop there, but then decided to continue to see if the number might be closer to seven, like six point nine or something.

She put a point after the six, and wrote thirty-six under the forty, then subtracted them. That left a four. She added a zero like her pa had shown her, and hey, it was forty again. Well, she already knew the answer here. It was six. So she wrote that down after the point and wrote thirty-six under the last forty and subtracted it out. It was four. She added a zero. Hey! It's forty again. So she dutifully wrote another six down and then stared at it in horror. It would take her 6.66 hours to get to town. She panicked and flipped the paper over.

This was a bad number. Her pa had told her that. It was the mark of the beast. But wait a minute, Uncle Calvin was the devil boy, wasn't he? So isn't this a sign from Uncle Calvin? Yes, that makes sense.

She flipped the paper back over and circled the 6.66. Yes, this was a sign that she should go to the fair and see Uncle Calvin. Now, when should she leave?

She looked at the pamphlet again. It said the fair begins at ten. OK, so if it takes 6.66 hours — let's call it seven if I stop for a rest — then I have to leave here at three o'clock.

She looked at her clock. It was one o'clock now. Good, that gives her a little time to pack. She went to the kitchen and made herself a few sandwiches and packed them in the backpack that was normally reserved for horse grooming tools. She also packed the pamphlet, some water, her stuffed Jesus doll, and an interesting looking rock that she planned to give to Uncle Calvin as a gift.

At three o'clock, Victoria sneaked out of the house to begin her journey. At five o'clock, her pa pinned a note to her bedroom door and joined the men of the village to begin their own journey. The note read as follows:

***

Dear Pumpkin,

I will be out today smiting the infidels. I won't be back until some time tomorrow. Be a good girl and brush your teeth and do your chores. After that you can play in the barn. Stay in the house at night and lock the doors. If you need help go see old Mrs. Snapply down the lane.

Love,
Pa

***

The sun rose at six o'clock. Victoria blew out her lantern and put it back inside her backpack along with her stuffed Jesus doll that she had been using to ward off the creatures of the night.

She strapped her backpack in place and started to skip down the road again. She took a deep breath and began to sing the hymn that Brother Grimm had taught her to sing in order to ward off evil. She didn't like Brother Grimm that much — he was a big meanie — but she adored his hymns.

Smite the infidel
Damn his soul to hell
Hang him from a pole
Let demons take his soul
Draw and quarter him
for he is filled with sin
Do not hesitate
for we have God's mandate
If you don't agree
God will punish thee
You will wake up dead
from scorpions in your bed
God loves one and all
if you doubt it you will fall
into a lake of fire
and burn there for a while
until you've had enough
then He'll grab you by the scruff
and tell you to believe
or else you'll never leave
Violence is the way
to keep the devil at bay
So sing this song aloud
and make your God so proud

CHAPTER 21

Today, Kevin6 decided that he wanted to visit an amusement park. He felt that he was too old to visit the Screaming Skeleton, an amusement park that was strictly for young adults with good hearts and strong bodies, so the three of them went to the more sedate Disney World instead.

Had Calvin been with them, he would have been amazed that the old franchise was still around. He would have also been impressed to know that it now encompassed the entire northern half of the Florida peninsula. He also would have been amused to know that the southern half was still mostly populated with old people and drug addicts, just like he remembered it in his day.

Kevin6 and his companions emerged from the ODIN terminal just outside the gates of the theme park. The women had changed into shorts and bikini tops. Lucinda's top was red and Sharon's was blue. Kevin6, was now wearing white shorts and a Hawaiian shirt.

Kevin6 looked to his left and then to his right. "So, ladies, what do we want to ride on first?"

Sharon suggested that they go for a couple's massage at the spa. Lucinda agreed with this and suggested that Sharon could have hers with Mickey Mouse while Kevin6 and she had theirs together. Sharon then suggested that Lucinda might want to play with a swarm of angry wasps, which Sharon was capable of controlling at will. Kevin6 then suggested that they knock it the hell off.

"Ladies, I like the idea of the spa. I think we can all use some relaxation. Let's all three go together and try to get along, shall we?"

"Yes, Mr. Bacon."

"Good."

As they walked to the spa, Kevin6 was both surprised and relieved that no one was paying him any undue attention. He was glad of this, of course, but it still stumped him. After all, as John Lennon would say, he was more popular than Jesus.

But when Kevin6 thought about it, it did make a sort of sense. After all, even if Jesus himself were here now, no one would ever expect to see him at an amusement park wearing white shorts and a Hawaiian shirt. At most, they would notice that he needed a shave and a haircut. It seemed to be the same for Kevin6. To the crowd, he was just some dirty old man with a woman on each arm — which, to be fair, he was.

At the spa, Kevin6 stripped naked and lay down on a massage table. Kevin6 had no modesty at all, mostly because of the numerous times he had woken up from deep sleep naked in front of strangers. The women were more hesitant, but each one was determined not to be outdone by the other, so in the interest of competition, they also stripped naked and lay on the tables to either side of Kevin6.

Kevin6 was muscular and in good shape for his age, although he was developing a small pot belly that he was determined to eradicate. Sharon had jet-black hair and a plain face. Her body was slender and boyish, like that of a gymnast. Lucinda was the polar opposite, with blonde hair and a bulky frame that was borderline manly. She was more muscular than Kevin6 and, with the addition of an Adam's apple, might have been mistaken for a transvestite. Her face, however, was pretty — although it usually had a slightly bitchy expression which spoiled it.

The massage tables were fully automated. They worked by first taking detailed pictures of the skeletal and muscular structures of the patrons, and then they used that data to massage and manipulate everything into its proper alignment. The process usually took just over an hour, but was dependent on the state of the body in question.

Kevin6 spent his time watching a movie. The girls, despite being rivals, bonded together in girl talk. They spent their time texting back and forth about the firmness of Kevin6's buns, the strength of his back, and the general bigness of other parts of his anatomy. They also competed over the graphic details of what they would each do to him if they got him alone.

After the massage, the three of them put their clothes back on and left the spa. The girls kept glancing at each other and giggling. Kevin6 was happy to see that the massage had calmed them down.

The girls were hungry, so they all took lunch together. By the time dessert had been served, the two girls were back to nipping at each other's heals. However, Kevin6 was determined to keep the peace, and did his best to pacify them.

On some strange psychological level, this became a negative feedback loop and only instigated the girls to continue to behave badly in order to gain attention from Kevin6. Dark Angels had many sterling qualities, but mental stability was unfortunately not one of them.

Nevertheless, the balance of the day went smoothly, and no one was poisoned, electrocuted, shot with missiles, or stung to death by wasps.

CHAPTER 22

Calvin woke up feeling like absolute crap. However, he was not suffering from any traditional illness or injury, but was in fact tragically allergic to mornings.

He had just woken up very early and, as a result, he felt like he was going to throw up, and his head was spinning badly. But today was the day of the big fair, and as the organizer of the fair, he had an obligation to help set it up. And that meant waking up at this ungodly time of day.

He sat up slowly while he let his head and body get used to a different direction of gravitational pull. A few moments later, Tarpa came in the bedroom to verify that he was awake.

"Errr," he said to her with feeling.

She placed a cup of coffee on the table beside the bed and said, "Here you go, sleepy head. I'm being nice to you today by going to the garden myself this morning. You have some coffee and scrape yourself together in the meantime. We've got about an hour and a half before we must be at the fair. Arnold and Doc brought everything over yesterday, so we just need to be there to help with the layout and setup."

Calvin nodded and took a sip of coffee. "Errr," he said again.

Tarpa replied, "You're welcome, sport."

She then went to the dresser to retrieve a bottle of perfume. It was her own special blend, and it smelled vaguely of honeysuckle.

Calvin had found it extremely seductive and had told her that she should market it, but Tarpa wanted it to be hers and hers alone. She sprayed two squirts of it onto herself and left the bedroom.

Tarpa walked out to the back yard carrying two cardion containers, and then headed toward her garden. Surprisingly, she was not wearing any extra layers of clothing for protection. In fact, she was still in her bathrobe.

She judged the wind direction for a moment and then walked around the perimeter of the garden until she was directly upwind of it. She stood there for about a minute before walking slowly but confidently toward the perimeter of the garden.

As she approached the perimeter, nothing shot at her. And as she walked into the vegetation, nothing tried to grab at her, bite her, trip her, blind her, poison her, or rip her legs off either. In fact, the plants actively bent out of her way as she approached them.

One Audrey did halfheartedly snap at her, but Tarpa deftly deflected it with a cardion bottle. The bottle made a satisfying "bing" sound as it struck the Audrey, which then wilted downward and looked ashamed of itself.

Tarpa made her way through the inner maze with ease, and then gathered the peppers and onions that would soon complement her morning sausage. After she was finished with that, she looked around the garden with the kind of satisfaction that only comes as a result of the magical combination of hard work and success. She felt a pride that only a true craftsman could understand.

This was Tarpa's own little slice of paradise, her secret garden. It was a random and wild-looking place. Clever usage of shrubbery and trees had created little surprise patches of fruits and vegetables. Decorative flowers had been planted with the keen eye of a master florist, but also served to maintain the proper balance of the soil. The garden was both beautiful and pragmatic.

The security perimeter kept out land predators, so only birds and flying insects ever made their way inside the garden. This created something of a sanctuary for the birds, and the ones that lived inside the garden became tame enough to land on Tarpa's hand if she held it out to them.

Sometimes, she and Calvin would have a picnic in the garden, other times they would spend the whole day there just to enjoy the tranquility. And still other times, Tarpa would come to the garden alone just to think. But no matter what she did in the garden, Tarpa loved it dearly. It was probably the main reason, apart from Calvin, that she was happy with her life on Evionia.

Tarpa took a brief proprietary stroll around the garden to ensure that all was well, and then returned to the house to prepare breakfast.

To her surprise, Calvin was already up and showered. He looked wide awake, and she could see that excitement was building up inside of him and about to spill over.

She thought, well, why shouldn't he be excited? After all, today he will be able to finally show off the usefulness of his Guides to a huge number of people, since most of the town was rumored to be coming to the fair. And the Guide program was Calvin's pet project, much like the garden was hers. Tarpa was very happy for him and gave him a kiss for good luck.

"Thanks, babe," said Calvin in response. Then he winked and added, "Careful not to get me too frisky, or we'll both be late for the fair."

Tarpa smacked him on the butt playfully and then made breakfast. After eating, they drove to the fairgrounds just south of the city.

Their car was a typical example of an early Evionian model. It was made mostly of wood, and it was vaguely shaped like a 1980's Camaro, although no one could ever give Calvin a suitable explanation as to why. Calvin suspected that the shape was buried deep in their American genes and somehow resurfaced every few decades like a plague.

He called their car Blar, because that was the sound that it made while it idled: blar blar blar blar blar blar blar. To Calvin, it always sounded like it was just on the verge of either stalling or exploding.

Blar and its two human occupants made their way to the fairgrounds without either stalling or exploding. Calvin was happy to see that all the equipment was accounted for and ready to be set up.

The fair was to start at ten o'clock, so Calvin, Doc, Arnold, and most of Calvin's other employees worked hard to ensure that everything was ready in time. Tarpa had no real stake in the fair apart from being moral support for Calvin, so she roamed around the fairgrounds by herself and lent a hand wherever it was needed.

Tarpa had briefly contemplated the idea of setting up a

booth to sell her produce, but had decided against it because several other merchants had already planned on selling her stuff, and besides, she had wanted to spend the time with Calvin.

Construction of the fairgrounds went smoothly thanks to Calvin's advanced planning and Ariel's helpful advice. After it was complete, Calvin made a toast to a successful fair, and then he, Tarpa, and the employees of Cal Tech all drank to his toast while watching in amazement as a huge crowd gathered outside the gate.

Calvin nervously glanced at the time on the large clock tower located in the center of the fairgrounds. It was almost time for the show to start, and Calvin was beginning to feel a little nervous. His heart was beating fast, and his skin was beginning to sweat.

Tarpa put a reassuring hand on his shoulder and said, "You got this, Calvin. You're going to be great. No worries."

Calvin nodded and said, "Thank you. I think I'm going to go get ready now. I'll meet up with you after the opening ceremonies."

Tarpa nodded, and Calvin made his way to a small trailer about fifty feet away from the main gate. Once inside the trailer, he removed his lenses and changed his clothes.

For the next few excruciatingly long minutes, he paced back and forth inside the trailer, occasionally stopping in front of the window and peering at the tower clock from behind closed curtains. Calvin was not a natural showman, and the thought of him being the center of attention in front of this huge crowd made his stomach grumble.

Finally, the tower bells began to gong, and Calvin could hear the excitement of the crowd begin to build with every ring of the bell. He looked himself over in the mirror one last time and breathed deeply while he waited nervously for the last bell to sound.

The crowd was also counting every bell. People were excitedly speculating on what the fair was going to be like. Little kids were jumping up and down for a better view. Some of them were pulling on their parents' sleeves and asking when it was all going to start.

Gong
Gong
Gong
Gong

Gong

Gong

Gong

Gong

Gong

Gong

Finally, the last bell had sounded.

The crowd fell silent as a man emerged from a nearby trailer. He was wearing a purple velvet topcoat, a shirt printed with white and violet flowers, beige slacks, and a beige bow tie. He had a heavy, brown top hat on his head, and a thick, wooden cane in his hand.

The cane was straight and had a heavy, silver ball on one end that served as the handle. It tapered for its entire length and formed a blunted point at the tip, which was roughly the diameter of a pinky finger.

The crowd had no idea what to make of the man. They stared at him as he hobbled down the stairs of the trailer and onto the red carpet, which led from the trailer to the front gate.

Still silent, the crowd watched as the man limped slowly down the red carpet. The man, too, was silent, and seemed to be wholly focused on coordinating the movements of his cane and his one good leg as he made his way toward the crowd. Little kids began to crawl through a forest of legs to get a better look.

Tarpa knew what he was about to do next, and suppressed a giggle. She had watched Calvin practice this for an hour in the back yard yesterday.

The crowd watched in near silence as Calvin continued his stately hobble up to the gate, while anticipation mounted with every step.

When he was finally within about ten feet of the gate, Calvin took a step but his cane remained one step behind him. It was sticking straight up from the ground with its tip deeply buried in the dirt. His right hand opened and closed in search of the missing cane a few times, then a panicked expression appeared on his face.

The crowd watched nervously as Calvin teetered back and forth a few times. Then, to their horror, he started to fall forward, stiff as a tree.

But just before it looked as if he were about to eat the dirt, he neatly tucked into a ball, rolled forward, and shot back up in front of the gate with his arms raised in victory.

The crowd cheered. Calvin took a bow, and then placed his top hat back onto his head. He soaked up the applause for a few more seconds and then silenced them with a raise of his hand.

Calvin then used Ariel to patch his voice into the public address system at the top of the clock tower.

"Welcome, one and all, to the first annual Cal Tech Country Fair!"

The crowd cheered again.

"We have a special treat for you today. I'm sure some of you have seen people walking around town wearing those funny looking glasses and sometimes mumbling to themselves like crazy people."

Several people in the crowd nodded and laughed.

"Well, my company, Cal Tech, manufactures them. We call them Guides. And today is your opportunity to try them out. They are free to use during the fair so long as you promise to give them back at the end of the day. The Guides are exactly that, guides. They can show you important and helpful things - things like a list of all the attractions at the fair, a map to all of the beer booths, and the location of the nearest outhouse when you've had one too many of those beers."

Another chuckle from the crowd.

"The Guides also have built-in speakers from which a personality called Ariel can talk to you. I say personality, because she isn't exactly real. Nevertheless, she is very kind and very helpful, so feel free to ask her anything. I know you will all just love her, so please, help yourself to a Guide after entering the gate. And now with the introductions complete, I hereby declare the first annual Cal Tech Country Fair, open for business!"

Calvin opened the gate with a flourish, and the crowd cheered again. People immediately started to pour through the gate. Calvin greeted and shook hands with as many as he could. Everyone seemed very excited to meet him and to check out the fair he had arranged for them. Some people even held up the line to take photographs with him. He felt like a celebrity and was glad that the opening went so well.

"That's it, madam," said Calvin, encouragingly. "Don't be shy. Just head right over to those tables over there and pick out a Guide. There are at least fifty varieties to choose from, so I'm sure you'll find something."

Then he spoke a little louder so that the people crowding around the tables could hear him. "No pushing, now. The fair goes on all day and half the night, and we have plenty of Guides for everyone. No worries — just relax and enjoy the fair."

A large number of people were already wearing their Guides. The vast majority of them were standing in an ever-expanding circle of people. They seemed to be transfixed on something inside the circle.

A man who was not wearing a Guide ran over to see what all the fuss was about, but all he could see was a patch of bare grass. The crowd was ooohing and ahhhing, but he had no idea at what. Finally, someone in the crowd noticed him and pointed to his glasses. He said, "You need to wear these to see her." The first man looked confused but thanked him. Then he went back over to the tables to pick out a Guide.

Calvin smiled when he saw this. It looked like his plan was working well. Excellent.

Suddenly, a little girl with wavy blonde hair and a puffy pink dress came careening into Calvin's legs while screaming, "Uncle Calvin! Uncle Calvin!"

"Victoria!?!"

Victoria looked up at him and smiled.

Calvin looked around nervously. "Um, is your father here? Where is your dad?"

Victoria looked down at her shoes.

"Oh no. You didn't. Tell me you didn't come here without him knowing. You didn't, right?" asked Calvin nervously.

Victoria remained silent and studied her shoes for a moment. Then a quiet, little voice said, "You aren't mad, are you Uncle Calvin?"

Calvin's heart sank. "No," he said reassuringly, "I'm not mad, Victoria."

Victoria looked back up at him and smiled.

Then, Calvin added somewhat sarcastically, "Your father will probably just start a war over this, but I'm sure there is nothing to worry about."

Victoria scratched her nose and said, "I want to ride the pig."

Calvin laughed and said, "OK, sweetie. But first I have to finish greeting everyone."

He thought for a moment and then pointed to Tarpa, who was milling around the tables and helping people with their

Guides. "You see that tall woman over there with the reddish brown hair? The one with the green bug eyes?"

Victoria nodded.

"That's Aunt Tarpa. She's very friendly, and I already told her all about you. Go see her, and she'll help you pick out a Guide. You'll get to see something wonderful if you wear one."

Victoria looked hesitant.

"Go on. Don't be scared."

Victoria looked at Tarpa, who was squatting down next to another little girl and putting a pair of glasses on her. The glasses were kind of cute. Victoria shrugged and said, "OK, Uncle Calvin, I'll go." She then skipped over to Tarpa without a care in the world.

Calvin sent a message to Tarpa letting her know that Victoria was heading her way. Then he turned his attention back to the dwindling crowd at the gate. He spent another five or six minutes welcoming the rest of the crowd.

Finally done with his official duties, Calvin left the gate in search of Tarpa. He found her and Victoria standing in a circle of people that more or less comprised of the entire crowd. He walked over and stood beside them.

Victoria was sitting on top of Tarpa's shoulders and was absolutely transfixed at what she was seeing in the center of the circle. The heads of everyone in the crowd moved in unison as they followed its movements.

Once the very last person in the crowd was wearing a Guide and standing in the circle, Ariel prepared to speak. On Calvin's recommendation, Ariel used a less ghostly voice than usual. Her voice today sounded like it belonged to a fairy princess.

And indeed, that was a very fitting voice for what the people were seeing inside the circle. Because, inside of the circle, stood a tall, pale woman. She was wearing a medium green dress made of silk. It flowed down her like a waterfall, with occasional folds and ruffles, and then spilled down onto the ground where it encircled her in a puddle of cloth. The dress shimmered like the ocean in the late-morning sun.

The woman's face was serene and calming. Her eyes were a very pale shade of green and were shaped slightly longer than an average person's. She was also wearing pale green eyeshadow that covered the entire area between her eyes and eyebrows. It matched her eyes and gave her a slightly animalistic look.

Her long hair was of one length, straight, and a medium

brown color with a hint of orange to it that made it stand out against her green dress. She had it tucked behind one ear, which allowed the onlookers to see that the ear was slightly pointy at the top.

The woman appeared to glow slightly, as if illuminated from within. The air around her sparkled. She looked around at the crowd encircling her and somehow seemed to make eye contact with all of them. Her movements were flowing and demure. She turned slowly this way and that, making sure to give everyone some attention.

The circle of people around her was very large, which allowed everyone to see her without too much crowding. A glowing circle of grass marked the boundary of the circle, and whenever an overly enthusiastic member of the crowd would step across it, the woman would immediately turn to the person and gently shake her head as she held up her hand, palm forward, as a sign of prohibition.

The woman had said nothing for the entire thirty minutes or so while the crowd had built up around her. But now that everyone was present, she was ready to speak.

"Hello everyone, my name is Ariel."

The crowd was startled to hear her finally speak. Several people even gasped.

Ariel turned gently this way and that while she waited for the crowd to settle down. She ran her right hand through her hair and tucked it behind an ear. She then smiled at the crowd and continued, "My name is Ariel, and I will be your guide to the fair today. You can talk to me at any time as long as you are wearing your Guide."

Ariel spun around and the sparkles in the air swirled around to follow her. The sparkles became more and more dense until they completely prevented anyone from seeing her. Then the sparkles thinned out and vanished, leaving nothing but empty air behind.

The crowd said, "Whoa," almost in unison. Then a sudden sense of sadness washed over them because Ariel was gone.

Suddenly, a disembodied voice said to them, "I do not have to be visible to talk to you, but I can be if you want me to."

Everyone jumped.

A mist of sparkles collected from thousands of points within the circle and converged to the center of it. This time, it was as if the sparkles were coming together to build Ariel from scratch.

The effect was something like a reverse explosion, and it was over in under two seconds. Ariel was back in the center of the circle again, looking slightly timid and fixing her hair again.

The crowd erupted with cheers and clapping.

Ariel patiently waited for the crowd to quiet down, then she continued once again.

"Thank you. Thank you, everyone. Thank you for being kind to me. I hope we can all be good friends. As I have said, you can talk to me at any time, even if you don't see me around. I can be in multiple places at once. I am one, but I am many."

Suddenly, ten versions of Ariel walked away from each other, as if all this time they had been neatly nested inside one another and moving in unison.

Another "Ohhh" erupted from the crowd.

The copies of Ariel walked out to the circumference of the circle and met with the crowd. Once on the edge, the Ariels walked slowly counter clockwise in near synchronization as they independently said hello to individual members of the crowd. Hands reached out to touch them, but unsurprisingly passed right through them.

One copy of Ariel looked directly at Calvin and winked at him. He felt himself blush, then felt very silly for having done so.

He had worked very hard with Ariel over the last few weeks to fine tune this persona, and by god it had been a success. He had directed her to use elements from various stories about fairies and princesses to form the foundation of her persona. He had also directed her to always appear graceful yet subtly timid and unsure. She was to be infinitely patient and attentive to others. She was to be approachable, yet still exude an air of untouchability. She was to be attractive but not flirtatious. She should be well spoken, with a clean, pure voice. And of course, she should be helpful.

Calvin had also wanted to give her fairy wings, but thought the better of it after realizing that this was more of a personal kink than anything else. At any rate, the result of all this work had been amazing. Ariel was an astute student of human nature and knew all the right buttons to push. Calvin felt infatuated with her every time he looked at her, and he was sure that everyone else was feeling the same way.

"Well done, Ariel," he muttered out loud. The version of Ariel that was nearest to him looked directly at him and smiled.

Goosebumps. He actually got goosebumps.

But as moved as Calvin was by his new creation, it was nothing compared to the effect it was having on little Victoria. She was simply mesmerized by Ariel. All she wanted in the whole world now was to be her friend. That, and to ride the pig. And to maybe have some cotton candy too. She almost peed herself thinking about the fun she was going to have today.

The multiple Ariels pulled themselves away from the crowd and walked casually to the center of the circle where they somehow seamlessly merged into a single entity.

Then, once again, Ariel spoke.

"It was wonderful to meet you all. I'm going to be leaving shortly, but don't worry, I will still be with each and every one of you during the fair. I may speak into your ear from time to time, so please do not be frightened. We will all have a great time together, I promise. Enjoy the fair, everyone!"

Ariel turned around slowly and gave everyone a wave. The crowd waved back, and then she disappeared in a burst of sparkles.

Calvin cleared his throat and then spoke earnestly through the PA system. "Thanks again for coming everyone. I'm glad you all liked Ariel. She will be with you any time you need her as long as you are wearing a Guide. Enjoy the fair, everyone — there is so much for you all to see and do."

The crowd clapped for a while, and then slowly dispersed.

Tarpa gently smacked Calvin's upper arm with the back of her hand and said, "I saw you going all googly-eyed over Ariel. You're not going to cheat on me with a disembodied artificial intelligence, are you, sport?"

Calvin looked at her and said, "Why would I do that when I have someone even more perfect right here in front of me?"

Then Victoria, who was still riding on Tarpa's shoulders, said, "You're a smooth talker, Uncle Calvin. My pa says you have the devil's tongue."

Tarpa laughed and said, "Out of the mouth of babes."

Calvin looked from one to the other and said, "Oh, I can see where this day is going."

He then gave Tarpa a quick kiss and motioned for Victoria to lean over. Victoria brought her face lower, and Calvin kissed her on the cheek. He made sure to make it a really loud one. Victoria giggled and wiped her cheek with her sleeve.

Calvin looked at the two of them again and said, "I'm glad

you two are getting along so well."

And he really was glad, since Tarpa had always been vaguely nervous around children.

"Aunt Tarpa said I could ride the pig," offered Victoria as a possible explanation.

"Ah," said Calvin, "Bribery. Well done, dear. Well, let's go then, shall we? The fair awaits us."

"Why are you dressed so silly, Uncle Calvin?" asked Victoria while looking him up and down.

"Showmanship," answered Calvin. "It's a sort of costume. I thought it would give the opening of the fair a certain extra something."

"Oh, OK," said Victoria, apparently unconvinced.

Calvin pointed at her head and said, "And what about you? You've got some cute little pink bunny ears now, don't you?"

Victoria nodded.

"Tell me," said Calvin in a suddenly serious tone, "If those ears were brown and smelled burnt, would you like them better?"

Victoria smushed up her face and shook her head.

Calvin said, "I didn't think so. How would you like to work for me as the head of quality control? I think you have a rare talent for spotting the blindingly obvious that my other employees seem to lack."

Victoria appeared to give this some serious thought, and then shrugged.

"OK, well, the offer is on the table if you ever change your mind."

Tarpa smacked Calvin on the arm again and set Victoria down on the ground. Calvin briefly consulted a map of the fair, and then the three of them went to find the pigs. As they walked, Tarpa and Calvin were texting each other like mad.

Tarpa: Where is her father?

Calvin: I don't know. Not here.

Tarpa: She came alone?

Calvin: It appears that way. She won't really say.

Tarpa: Fuck.

Calvin: My thought exactly.

Tarpa: Ariel, any idea where Reverend Smelcheck is right

now?

Ariel: He is on the road to Big City.

Calvin: He's coming to the fair?

Ariel: I do not know. He is with a very large group of men. They are carrying torches and pitchforks.

Calvin: Did you hear that, honey? They are coming for us already. Isn't that romantic? Shall we wait for them in the castle? Should I change into my black cloak?

Tarpa: You're an ass. This is serious.

Calvin: I Know. I'm actually pissing myself right now. Ariel, how soon before they get here?

Ariel: They should be here just after dark, about seven hours from now.

Calvin: OK, still plenty of time to think of a plan. I say for now we just continue to monitor them. I don't want to alert anyone yet and ruin the fair.

Tarpa: Agreed. It won't do any good to jump the gun. We'll wait and see what they are up to first. I know it is unlikely, but maybe they aren't headed here.

Ariel: I will continue to monitor them and alert you of any changes in their trajectory.

Tarpa: Thanks, Ariel.

Ariel: Of course.

Calvin: Back to real life for now, then?

Tarpa: Yes, let's get this little girl on a pig before she explodes.

For the time being, Calvin and Tarpa put the Trads out of their minds and instead focused on entertaining young Victoria. The three of them made their way to the pig pens. Calvin was pleased to see that, as he had suggested, one of them contained greased pigs and one of them did not.

The greased pigs were all very large and ornery looking. If they had tusks and more hair, one might even have been persuaded to call them boars. Kids were jumping on their backs with reckless abandon, only to be bucked off moments later to land face-first in the mud. Then, they would laugh, get up, and try it again.

Calvin pointed to them and said, "There is some sort of life lesson in that, I'm sure of it."

"Kids are stupid?" offered Tarpa.

"I was thinking more like persistent, but maybe you have a point too," replied Calvin.

The other pen held pigs of all sizes. The younger kids were riding on the small, docile pigs that the adults were leading around by their leashes. These were obviously tamed pets. The older kids were allowed to ride the bigger, more wild pigs. About half of them were successful at it, the other half were eating mud.

There was, however, one enormous pig that no one would go near. It kept twitching like it was being irritated by the entirety of creation. It tried to head butt anyone (or any pig) that got too close to it.

Calvin leaned over to Tarpa and whispered, "A million dollars says Victoria will want to ride the psychotic one over there."

Tarpa looked at the beastly pig and whispered back, "Surely not."

Right on cue, Victoria tugged on Calvin's pant leg and said, "Uncle Calvin! Uncle Calvin! I want to ride that one!"

Calvin smirked.

Tarpa said, "You aren't seriously going to let her ride that, are you?"

Calvin patted Victoria on the head and said, "It will be fine. Just watch. Go on sweetie, play with Mr. Piggy."

Tarpa glared at Calvin and said, "If we ever have kids together, I'm never letting you anywhere near them." She then called out to Victoria, "Come back here, sweetie. Uncle Calvin was just being silly."

Calvin argued, "It's OK. Trust me. Go on Victoria. Have fun."

Tarpa gave him another serious look.

"Just watch," he repeated.

They watched.

Victoria went through the gate and into the pen. She walked straight for the giant, rabid pig. There was a tense moment while it lowered its head as if it were about to charge her, but then it lowered the rest of itself down into the mud and waited patiently for Victoria to daintily climb on top of it.

Some of the other kids in the pen noticed this and, one by

one, stopped riding their pigs and started to watch Victoria.

The large pig rose gently to its feet and started to carefully trot around the pen. Even the other pigs were watching at this point.

Calvin turned to Tarpa for a moment and said, "See, she's like the Beastmaster or something. Incredible, isn't it?"

Tarpa said nothing and continued to watch in amazement.

Victoria soon got bored of the walking, so she leaned forward and put her arms around the thick neck of the beast pig. She whispered something into its ear, and it suddenly began to run around the pen like mad. It started to skid all over the place and kick up the mud. The other kids ran out of the gate to get out of its way, while the other pigs went mad with fright and cowered in a far corner of the pen. Victoria was laughing and having a blast.

Tarpa looked scared for her. Calvin saw this and said, "Don't worry, she does this sometimes. I'll take care of it."

He then cupped his hands around his mouth and yelled, "Easy there, Victoria. You're making Mr. Piggy very tired."

Victoria heard this and stroked the side of the pig a few times with her hand, and it instantly settled down. She tapped it again and the pig reared back on its hind legs while Victoria held one arm up to the sky in a very surreal parody of the Lone Ranger.

There was a large crowd building up around the pen now, which cheered when they saw this.

The pig went back onto all fours and Victoria, egged on by the cheering crowd, stood up on its back while it cautiously walked around the perimeter of the fence.

The pig stopped right in front of Calvin and Tarpa, who were standing just outside the pen. Calvin lifted Victoria off the pig and set her down on the ground outside the fence.

"Well done, sweetie! Let's get you some cotton candy now, OK?"

"Hooray!" shouted Victoria.

Tarpa was still staring at the pig. It had gone back to normal now and was trying to eat the fencing. Tarpa shook her head and looked first at Victoria and then at Calvin. She said, "Well, that was... surprising."

With that excitement behind them, the three of them rejoined the throng of the fair in search of cotton candy. Calvin was happy to see that everyone seemed to be enjoying themselves. Although, it must be said, that there had been some unanticipated side effects of giving Ariel an incarnate body.

Most of the men, and a surprising number of women, had asked Ariel to remain visible to them. Every person had their own copy of Ariel that only they could see, although some groups (such as families) shared an Ariel out of expediency.

This resulted in an awful lot of people talking to thin air. Ariel would usually place herself away from others to avoid misunderstanding, but it did not always work out well when the crowds got too thick.

Calvin cringed when he heard one man say, "I hope you don't mind me sayin', but you're right pretty."

The man next to him looked stunned, and then angry.

Ariel quickly made herself visible to the angry man and said, "I'm terribly sorry. He was talking to me. He meant no offense." She winked at him and vanished, at least as far as the angry man was concerned. Then she turned back to the first man, put her finger up to her lips for a second, and said, "Shhh. Just whisper. I can hear you."

The angry man seemed satisfied and continued on his way.

Calvin had been able to witness all of this because he had asked Ariel in advance to allow him to see all of her copies, ostensibly so that he could study how the people would interact with her. In reality — and Calvin would never admit this — he just liked looking at her.

Calvin whispered, "Nicely handled, Ariel."

The man's version of Ariel turned to Calvin and flicked him a brief smile before returning her attention to the man. Calvin's spine tingled and he thought, I've created a monster. I wonder how many divorces this is going to cause?

Tarpa, who could also see the many copies of Ariel and who could read her husband's face quite well, said to him, "I think maybe you made her a little too captivating."

Calvin scratched his chin in thought and said, "Yes... Yes... I think you might be right. I just wanted people to have a positive image of Ariel so that they wouldn't feel weird about talking to her." Calvin shook his head. "Oh, I don't know. I'm sure it will sort itself out eventually."

Tarpa looked unconvinced.

Then, there was a sudden implosion of sparkles next to them as another copy of Ariel incarnated beside Victoria. Victoria, who had summoned this version of Ariel, giggled and tried to hug her, but stumbled as she fell straight through her.

Calvin called out to her, "Careful there, sweetie. She's not really there. She's more like an imaginary friend. You can talk to her, but you can't touch her."

Victoria looked confused and annoyed for a second, but then Ariel said something to her and she immediately cheered up.

Ariel turned to Calvin and Tarpa and said just to them, "Her father is still coming this way. It appears we must prepare. I will help you to stop them, but you must not kill anyone."

Tarpa and Calvin nodded, then Ariel turned her attention back to Victoria.

Calvin read the time in his display. He still had several hours before he would have to do anything about the invaders. It would be nice to enjoy the fair a little while longer.

Tarpa looked at him, as if understanding, and the two of them caught up with Victoria and Ariel. Calvin asked Ariel to turn off the other copies of her as they were somewhat distracting. For Calvin's eyes only, Ariel made them appear as if they had all burst into glitter. The glitter then swirled together and spiraled upward into the sky where it disappeared from sight.

"Show off," he murmured.

Their copy of Ariel turned to him and gave him another wink. He was really going to have to tone her down a bit, he thought to himself as the goosebumps on his arm subsided.

On the way to the cotton candy booth, they stopped at a face painting booth where an older man with amazingly steady hands painted Victoria's face to look like a bunny rabbit to match the bunny ears of her Guide. Calvin and Tarpa refused to have their faces painted, no matter how much the man tried to goad them into it.

Ariel, however, now had bunny ears and a puffy white tail, and her dress had turned pink to match Victoria's. This was not helping with Calvin's unhealthy infatuation with her. At this point, he decided, she was just messing with him.

Finally at the cotton candy booth, Victoria was in a blissed-out haze of delight as she ate some. It was even better than she had hoped it would be. She ran over to Uncle Calvin and gave his legs a big hug, leaving them somewhat sticky. Then she did the same to Aunt Tarpa, which seemed to surprise her.

Tarpa texted to Calvin:

Tarpa: She really is an adorable thing, isn't she?

Calvin nodded.

They let Victoria try the dunking booth next, but she was unfortunately not strong enough to throw the ball with enough power to trigger the mechanism, even though she was able to hit the target two out of four times. She did laugh, however, when Tarpa had dunked the clown on the first try. Then she laughed even harder after the clown climbed back up into the seat and challenged Tarpa to do it again, because she did — three more times.

They carefully steered Victoria away from the pony ride, bringing her instead to a haunted house. Victoria was scared at first, but Aunt Tarpa made her laugh when she sneaked behind one of the monsters and scared the hell out of it.

Then they watched a juggling show, and this time it was Uncle Calvin's turn to show off.

The juggler had asked for a volunteer from the crowd. Calvin raised his hand and was chosen. The juggler started to juggle three bowling pins. He explained to Calvin that he would throw him one, and then Calvin should throw it back to him when he said so.

They did this a few times and the crowd applauded. Then, to the surprise of the juggler, Calvin told him to throw him all three. The juggler passed them to Calvin with some reluctance, and was astonished to see that Calvin could juggle just as well as he. Victoria clapped. Then Calvin lit the bottoms of the pins on fire with short bursts from his arm while seamlessly continuing to juggle them. Even the juggler was impressed. Then Calvin blew them out one-by-one and passed them back to the juggler, who started to juggle them again, but this time with little tricks like letting one balance on the top of his head for a second before letting it fall back into the pattern.

The crowd clapped again. The juggler took a bow, letting one of the pins comically hit him on the back of the head. Victoria loved it. She had never realized that adults could be so fun. Apart from the occasional barn dance, people in her village had never acted so silly.

A little way behind them, Ariel slowly faded away, sensing that she was no longer required. The other three were having so much fun together that they did not notice her departure. In fact, she was surreptitiously removing her other copies whenever an occasion presented itself. She understood as well as Calvin the effect she was having on the humans and was trying to correct for the oversight.

Calvin returned to the group and noticed that Ariel was missing, but said nothing. He asked Victoria what she wanted to do next and got a cute little, "I don't know," with her arms raised upward and her hands pointed outward.

He turned to Tarpa. "OK, what about you?"

"I don't know," she mimicked with the same gesture.

Calvin laughed. "You two are so cute."

In the end, they decided to get something to eat. They found a booth selling roast turkey legs. Calvin and Tarpa ate theirs on the bone like a couple of Neanderthals, but they thoughtfully cut the meat off of Victoria's so she could eat it easier.

They rejoined the fair after their late lunch and discovered a woman who drew caricature portraits. She drew one of the three of them together and then gave it to Victoria as a souvenir.

In the picture, Calvin looked pretty much the same because, dressed the way he was, he was already quite a character. Tarpa's display lenses were drawn to look like bulging bug eyes, and there was a hint of wings behind her. Victoria was in between them, and her wavy hair flowed outward and wrapped around the other two like a hug. It was a strange drawing, but also somehow charming.

As they turned to leave, Calvin heard someone say, "Hey, boss!"

Calvin finished turning around and started to say, "Hey, Jethro," but all that came out of his mouth was, "Hey..." because standing next to Jethro, arm-in-arm, was Calvin's receptionist.

Suzette noticed his surprise and smiled at him.

Calvin recovered and asked, "So... how are you two enjoying the fair?"

Jethro gave him a hard pat on the back and said, "I haven't had this much fun since our goat ate my brother's pants."

Calvin coughed. "As much fun as that, eh? Great. Well, it's all thanks to you and the rest of the gang for working so hard."

He then looked around him and added in a more serious tone, "Just between us, if there is anything else you want to do, you have about one more hour to do it in. I think we may be ending the fair early. I'm afraid trouble is brewing."

"Trouble, boss?"

"Yes, but keep it to yourself, OK? I'll fill everyone in on it later. Actually, if you happen to see Doc and Arnold, you can tell them too. Ask them to meet me in the trailer by the gate at four o'clock for a strategy meeting. You are welcome to come too, if you'd like. And remember, don't say a word to anyone, alright?"

Jethro seemed to smarten up a bit and said, "Yes, sir. You can count on me, sir."

"Thanks, Jethro. Um... at ease."

Jethro and Suzette excused themselves and went back to the fair. When they were out of earshot, Tarpa asked Calvin, "Was that wise? You don't think he's going to blab to everyone he comes across?"

Calvin smirked and answered, "Of course he is. What better way to get information out? I figure that this way, it won't come as such a shock to everyone when I make the actual announcement."

Tarpa shook her head and said, "You know, that's why I love you. On the surface you're just a carefree doofus, but inside your head, there are all these wheels spinning at a hundred miles an hour like a room filled with hamster wheels being powered by hamsters on cocaine."

Calvin laughed and said. "Well, there's a visual I won't soon forget. I'll, uh, take that as a compliment... with one point deducted for doofus."

"He's a silver-tongued devil," added Victoria, who wasn't sure what they were talking about but wanted to contribute anyway.

"Don't you start with me too, little girl, just because you smell blood in the water," teased Calvin.

Victoria scrunched up her bunny nose at the imagined smell of blood.

"Come on, you two," said Calvin while putting a hand around each of them, "I hear there is a booth around here where you get to throw rotten fruit at each other, and I think me and Aunt Tarpa are going to give it a try."

Twenty minutes later, when the swelling had subsided and Calvin finally regained consciousness, he realized his mistake too late. He was sticky from head to toe, and had welts all over his body the shape of peach pits.

He took a brief shower and got back into his costume, which at least he had been smart enough to remove before the food fight. He left the trailer behind the makeshift arena and found the girls still watching the matches and cheering the contestants.

"I really thought I could keep up with you," said Calvin as he approached them.

Tarpa just shook her head and smiled.

Victoria said, "Aunt Tarpa is strong. You're a doofus."

"You told her to say that, didn't you?" asked Calvin, accusingly.

Tarpa shrugged and continued to smirk.

Calvin noted the time and frowned. He looked at Victoria and debated what to do with her. Things were going to get serious pretty soon.

He said to Tarpa, "It's about that time."

She nodded and then looked at Victoria.

In answer to her unspoken question, Calvin said, "We'll bring her with us to the trailer for now. Then I'll have Doc and Arnold bring her and the other children to our house. It's a castle after all, so they should be safe there."

Tarpa nodded again in agreement, then they made their way to the trailer where Jethro, Doc, Arnold, Cletus, and Darryl where already waiting for them.

The small trailer had been too cramped for all of them to fit, so they had decided to stay outside the trailer while they waited.

After Calvin had arrived, they all stood and waited for him to speak. Calvin was quiet for a moment while he gathered his thoughts, and then he addressed Victoria first.

"Victoria."

"Yes, Uncle Calvin?"

"I'm about to say something that might upset you, but I want you to know that none of this is your fault. It has nothing to do with you coming to the fair today."

Victoria looked worried. "What's not my fault?"

"Your father and lots of men from the village are headed this way. We think they want to fight with us."

"No! Why?" she whaled. She looked like she wanted to say more but didn't have the words. Instead, she burst into tears.

Calvin hugged her. "It's going to be OK. Trust Uncle Calvin. No one is going to hurt your pa, and he won't hurt us. I have a plan. It will be OK."

Victoria continued to cry. Calvin picked her up and carried her into the trailer. He set her down in the chair and kissed her forehead. "Just wait here for a little while, OK? Ariel will keep you company and you can watch a movie together, alright?"

Suddenly there was a rush of sparkles, and Ariel was in the room with them. She was kneeling down in front of Victoria and smiling at her. Victoria's crying eventually abated and she smiled back at Ariel.

Calvin thanked Ariel and went back outside. He cracked his knuckles and addressed the others. "OK, so here is the deal. We've got a few hundred Trads headed our way on foot. Most of them have pitchforks, but somehow I doubt they are coming here to muck out our barns. So this is what we are going to do..."

He explained his plan, and with only a few minor modifications, the others agreed to it. He read the time again. It was nearly five o'clock. Time to address the crowd. This should be... fun.

Calvin walked several hundred feet away from the others and paced back and forth in the empty field for a while. Finally, he worked up his nerve and asked Ariel to patch him into everyone's Guides (since calling out one's battle plans over a loud speaker would have gone down in the history of warfare as one of the stupidest things ever).

"Excuse me, everyone. Can I have your attention? This is Calvin Jones, the guy in the crazy outfit from this morning. I'm terribly sorry to interrupt your fun, but I'm afraid I have some bad news."

Calvin paused for a moment to let this much sink in, then he continued, "There is no easy way of saying this, so I'll come right out and say it. There are several hundred Trads heading this way by foot. They've got torches and pitchforks, so I don't reckon they are coming to the fair to get their faces painted."

Calvin examined their current positions on a live map and corrected himself, "Actually, Ariel is showing me that they just passed the road that forks off to the fairgrounds, so I'm guessing the sneaky little bastards are planning to wreck our city while most of us are here."

Ariel showed the map to everyone else.

Calvin continued, "As you can see, we have one great advantage, and that is Ariel. She can show us exactly where the Trads are at all times. And if you all keep your Guides on, we can also see in the dark and talk to each other at any time. Plus, we have the element of surprise, which is nothing to sneeze at.

"I imagine right now your blood is boiling. You're probably saying to yourself that you want to kill those sneaky bastards. How dare they try to destroy our homes and our shops? Believe me, I'm right there with you. They piss me off too, excuse my language. But no one is killing anyone tonight. Do you hear me? No one is killing anyone tonight. Ariel has agreed to help us, but only as long as we promise not to kill anyone. If we do, she'll leave us that instant.

"But that is not the reason why I'm asking for restraint from you. I'm asking for restraint because I know just about every one of you, and you are some of the most honorable people I've ever met. You're just plain good folk, and I'd never forgive myself for turning any one of you into a murderer. If that were going to be the case, I'd sooner fight the Trads alone.

"Do you know why the Trads are attacking us today? They are afraid of us. They're scared of our technology, our cars, our electricity, our whole way of life. They don't understand it. They don't like it. They know that we could wipe them out if we wished. So they feel that the only way to ensure their own safety is to attack us first in the hopes of catching us off guard.

"But they won't catch us off guard — not now, not ever. Not as long as we have Ariel on our side. I have no doubt that we'll drive them back home tonight. That doesn't worry me. I'm not afraid of that. What I'm afraid of is just how scared they will be of us after we do."

Calvin paused again to let his words sink in.

"Listen, everyone. Be careful tonight. And try not to lose your compassion. Please don't lose your humanity. I think one day it will be possible to make peace with the Trads, but it will never, ever happen if we go overboard tonight.

"Anyway, I think I've beat that horse enough, so I'll get on to the plan. First, I want everyone with children to bring them up to the front gate right now. A number of my men are going to escort them to my house where they will be safe. My house is that big, gaudy castle that I know some of you have complained about, but tonight I think you will find it useful. Any women who want to join them are welcome to, but I know half of you ladies can punch harder and spit further that any man, so I won't insult you by asking you not to fight. It's your town too, and I welcome your help in defending it."

Calvin then took the next ten minutes to describe the battle plan and to teach his rag-tag militia the most effective way of using Ariel as a communication hub. He was no general, they were no army, and no one had a clue what they were doing, but Calvin was still confident that they could win.

The residents of Big City soon started to filter into the field. Most of the men (and a large number of women, Calvin was pleased to see) gathered around Calvin, shook his hand, and offered their services.

Calvin started to organize them into squads while Tarpa, Doc and Arnold gathered up the children. The three of them escorted the children very quietly to the castle. They took a smaller path through the woods which circumvented the main road and kept them well away from the intruders.

When they arrived at the castle, Tarpa briefly showed them around and then left to join the fight. She locked the doors as she left and activated the bridge control, which rotated the entirety of the bridge ninety degrees about the center support, leaving no way to cross the moat without a catapult.

Meanwhile, Calvin sent the various squads into the woods to take their positions. He assigned each squad an Ariel to show them the way. These versions of Ariel wore pink camouflaged fatigues and a pink helmet. She stood out like a sore thumb in the woods, but that was sort of the point since she was a guide, and the invaders could not see her after all.

Back on the dirt road, Reverend Smelcheck and his men were walking as stealthily as they could. They had been walking for nearly thirteen hours now and were very fatigued. The sun had set, but they had only lit a single torch for fear of discovery. They held onto each other's coat tails and followed the reverend's torch the best they could.

With no moon on Evionia, the nights were definitively dark. Even the stars were dim that evening. The wind was still, and all that could be heard was the crunching of the dirt below them, and an occasional rusting in the woods that put everyone on edge.

In the dark, tired, and surrounded by unknown woodland animals that were surely stalking them, the group's nerves frayed as they came closer and closer to the enemy's territory.

Suddenly, they heard a voice in front of them. The voice was soft at first, almost conversational.

"Not a speck of light is showing, so the danger must be growing."

The men froze and peered into the darkness but could see nothing. The voice continued, this time louder and with some menace.

"Are the fires of hell a-glowing? Is the grisly reaper mowing?"

Someone in the group urinated in his trousers.

"YES!" shouted the voice as a giant fireball mushroomed into the air in front of them. Two more men wet their trousers.

The voice continued in a tortured scream that made every man shake.

"The danger must be growing, for the rowers keep on rowing, and they're certainly not showing, any signs that they are slowing!"

And then silence.

Shivering, the men were about to turn and run when the voice said loudly, "Throw the rocks!"

Now they were being pelted with rocks from both sides of the forest. They let go of each other's coat tales and scrambled this way and that while trying to hide behind each other.

Suddenly, another voice, the very authoritative voice of Brother Grimm, commanded them to light their torches. With some difficulty, they followed the command.

Now, things weren't so scary. The road ahead was clear except for one man. Just a man, not a demon. Reverend Smelcheck recognized the man and shouted, "That's him! That's the devil boy! Get him!"

Calvin was suddenly being charged by hundreds of men with torches and pitchforks.

"Help!" he yelped and leapt backward.

This was not how things were supposed to go. This was not the plan. This was not the plan at all. If they charged him, he was supposed to drive them back with his flame, but they were already too close. Reverend Smelcheck was right out in front. If he used his flame now, he'd barbeque the man alive. How would he ever explain that to Victoria?

Tarpa, who had been stealthily tracking the group from behind, said, "Oh my fucking god."

She had Ariel patch her through to her stupid husband. "Help? Help? What kind of battle cry is help? What kind of leader yelps like a little girl at the first sign of trouble? Help? Really, Calvin? Really?"

Tarpa started to plow her way straight through the group of invaders, forming a "V" of flying bodies as she went.

The invaders began to reach Calvin as he answered back, "I panicked, alright! What do you want me to say? I didn't expect them to turn on me so fast. Ouch! Who just stabbed me? Which one of you fuckers was it? You? You?"

Tarpa could hear blunt thuds as Calvin beat the stuffing out of a few men with his cane.

Tarpa answered back, "I told you to be on your guard, didn't I? You lost focus, and now look what happened."

Calvin could hear screaming in the background. It was so loud that he also heard it without his Guide.

"We aren't killing anyone tonight, are we, dear?" he asked sarcastically. "Ouch. Did someone just bite me? Seriously? What the fuck is wrong with you people?"

Calvin jabbed at a few men with the point of his cane, then spun it around and whacked a few more on the head with the heavy, metal ball.

Tarpa answered back, "No, I'm not a doofus like you. I'm just incapacitating them."

And indeed, that was what she was doing. The men that ran toward her unarmed found themselves being redirected through the air and into the forest, where the other residents would tie them to trees. Anyone stupid enough to come at her with a pitchfork found the pitchfork redirected through their foot with such force that they were unable to pull it out of the ground.

Meanwhile, at the front of the mob, several people had emerged from the forest to help Calvin. This was good, because the invaders were starting to flank Calvin now, and he was getting genuinely nervous about it.

Suddenly, Reverend Smelcheck came at him with a glass dagger, which Calvin neatly deflected by grabbing the reverend's wrist and giving it a twist in the wrong direction. He then grabbed the reverend and pushed him into the woods.

"Tie him up but don't hurt him," he shouted to the men in the woods.

Just then, a man in a white robe appeared behind Calvin with a mean-looking sword. He pulled back and was just about to cut Calvin's head off when a heavy log came crashing down on his head. The man, his sword, and the log all tumbled to the ground in a heap.

Cletus came up beside Calvin and gave him a cheery thumbs up. Calvin, not understanding what had just happened, gave him a thumbs up in return and went back to fighting. When Cletus turned around, the man in the white robe had vanished. At that point, Cletus decided that he probably had drank enough for the night.

After another minute, Tarpa finally made her way beside

Calvin and gave him a quick kiss. "Hello, sport. Still alive, I see."

"For the time being," he answered while kicking a man in the stomach.

"Got a plan yet?" she asked.

"I think so," he answered. Tarpa grabbed a pitchfork from a man, hit him in the forehead with the handle, and then handed it back to him. The man looked at it, looked at her, and then fell backward.

Calvin asked aloud, "Ariel, who's the leader here? Is it that cheeky little bastard who told them to light the torches?"

Ariel poofed into existence over the crowd. She was lying on her side as if she were lounging on a couch. She casually pointed down to one of the men and said, "Yes. This one."

The man was about thirty feet back in the thick of the crowd. Apparently, he was bravely leading from behind. Calvin pointed to him and said, "Could you just get that man and bring him here for me, dear?"

Tarpa said, "OK," and then literally jumped on top of the crowd. She did hand springs and flips off of random shoulders and landed neatly next to Brother Grimm. She punched him hard in the face and then quickly tied his hands behind his back while he was still dazed.

Calvin turned to a goggle-eyed Cletus beside him and said, "She's just loving this. She doesn't often get a chance to do this sort of thing anymore."

Calvin asked Ariel to patch him through to everyone and said, "Everyone, form up in the roadway right now, just ahead of us. We're going for a show of strength." Besides, he added to himself, I can't help but notice that we are out of rocks.

People suddenly started to pour out of the woods from both sides of the road and quickly blocked the way to town.

Tarpa came charging back through the crowd of invaders, using Brother Grimm like a shield while she made her way to Calvin. Once there, she handed the dazed man to her husband.

Calvin passed the man over to Cletus to hold and shouted, "We have both of your leaders. Turn around now and we'll let them go. Otherwise... things might get messy. Go! Now!"

Brother Grimm suddenly called out, "Everyone, do as he says. We are done here. We lost this battle, but we will live to fight another day."

"Well done, sir. Very sensible," whispered Calvin to Grimm.

The next scene played out in such a way that everyone

remembered it in slow motion because so many things happened at once.

A man from the crowd screamed, "You let go of Brother Grimm, you spawn of Satan!" and hurled a pitchfork with all of his might at Calvin.

At the same time, a small girl in a puffy pink dress, wavy blonde hair, and a face painted up like a bunny rabbit yelled, "Uncle Calvin! Uncle Calvin!" and ran up to hug him.

A split second after that, Tarpa leapt behind the girl.

A split second after that, there was a horribly meaty sound as the pitchfork's tines entered Tarpa's back.

Two seconds after that, the pitchfork dislodged from Tarpa's back and dropped to the ground with a clang. It was covered with blood.

And then there was silence.

And then there was rage.

Time suddenly returned to normal. Calvin stepped quickly around a very stunned Victoria and rushed over to Tarpa, who was kneeling on the ground. She saw the hate in his eyes and said to him, "I'm OK, Cal. Please don't kill anyone."

Calvin crouched down beside her and held his hand to her face for a few seconds. Then he suddenly stood back up with the pitchfork in his hand and roared, "Ariel, which one of these motherfuckers just threw this? Which one of these motherfuckers just stabbed my wife? Which one of these stupid motherfuckers almost killed a sweet little girl?"

Ariel lit the man up for Calvin without fuss. Even she knew it was no time for twinkly fairy dust.

Calvin started walking straight for the man, pitchfork in hand and shaking with rage. The entirety of the crowd started to back away, and the man quickly found himself alone.

Calvin was within five feet of him when the man dropped to the ground and held his hands up in defense. He was as scared as any man would be facing a husband with a pitchfork in his hands and revenge in his heart.

"Please, no. Don't! I'm sorry! Don't!"

Calvin stood over him with the pitchfork held high, shaking with adrenalin and hatred.

Then Ariel whispered to Calvin, "Victoria is watching you, Calvin. And more than that, your wife says she forbids you from killing by the authority of your marriage vows."

Calvin almost howled. His eyes started to tear up. He was

still so angry he couldn't contain it. He breathed hard a few times but it was just no use. He couldn't stop the rage.

With a scream, Calvin thrust the pitchfork down with all of his strength.

The man on the ground left a large puddle of urine on the ground, but no blood. Calvin had not harmed him. The pitchfork was in the ground just beside him.

"We're done here!" Shouted Calvin at the invaders. "Go the fuck home!" He shot a stream of fire above their heads to reinforce his point. As one, the invaders turned and fled, except for the ones that were staked to the ground by their feet or tied to a tree.

The man who had thrown the pitchfork was still on the ground in front of Calvin, too terrified to move.

Calvin bent down and whispered in the man's ear, "Remember that I let you live."

Then Calvin stood up and started to walk away, but something was still nagging at him. He turned back around and kicked the man hard in the testicles because damn it, he was still so angry.

After the man doubled over in pain, Calvin said to him, "Sorry, but I couldn't live in a world where you weren't in pain right now. Things would be... out of balance."

Now at least partially satisfied, Calvin went to check on Tarpa, who was mercifully able to walk. The tines had luckily missed her spine, and her toughened skin had kept the damage down to a minimum. She would be OK.

Victoria was beside her, hugging her and crying. Calvin hugged Victoria and Tarpa together and told Victoria that everything would be OK, which of course was a lie.

The residents of Big City were still milling around without direction. Calvin, infinitely weary with the weight of the world and pretty much disgusted with everyone in it, told them all in so many words to go the hell home too.

Calvin: Ariel, please lead my employees to the wounded on both sides and walk them through any first aid that can be done. Give priority to the more seriously injured.

Ariel: OK.

"Yo, Darryl," Called out Calvin to his nearby friend.
"Yes, your lordship?"

"Could you and Cletus unstake those men over there," asked Calvin while pointing to a row of about twenty men leaning dizzily on their pitchforks and sweating from the exertion of trying to pull them out of the ground, and from blood loss. "Get some bandages from Doc's group. Splash a little shine on their feet, then bandage them up. I'll pay you back for what you use."

"You got it, brother."

Now the question arose as to what to do with Victoria. Her father should be around here somewhere, thought Calvin. Oh, there he is, down the road a ways, tied to a tree.

Calvin held his hand out to Victoria and said, "Come on, sweetie, let's go find your dad."

Victoria looked at Tarpa, who nodded. Then she said to Calvin, "He's going to be really mad."

"Oh yes," agreed Calvin. "But you can handle this. Just give him a big hug and look up at him with those sad, blue eyes of yours. He'll turn to putty, believe me."

Victoria said nothing and took his hand. They walked a few hundred feet up the road where the Reverend was sitting with his back against a tree. He was bound to it with rope, and he was gagged.

Victoria ran up to her father and yelled, "Papa!" and gave him a huge hug.

The reverend looked wide-eyed at Calvin and tried to speak.

Calvin said, "Hold on a minute. Let me remove your gag."

"Get away from my daughter, devil boy. Did you kidnap her? Are you really that despicable? If you hurt her, I swear I'll kill you with my own bare hands."

Calvin quickly shoved the gag back into the reverend's mouth and said, "Oh, shut up already. Victoria is fine, no thanks to you and your men. She came to the fair on her own. You should have come too. But instead, you tried to burn our city while we were out having fun. I'm sorry, Reverend, but you are the devil in this story."

"Mmmmm mmm mmmmm mmmmm..." argued the reverend.

Calvin sighed. He turned to Victoria and asked, "Can I use your Guide for a moment, sweetie? I'll give it right back to you, I promise."

Victoria nodded.

Calvin pulled the Guide off her head and placed it onto the reverend's. The reverend squirmed as Calvin forced the pink, bunny-eared glasses onto his head. It was a tight fit and they bent with the strain.

Calvin removed the gag again and put his hands on the reverend's shoulders. "Just calm down. I want you to see what kind of people we really are. Ariel, show him highlights of the fair through Victoria's eyes, right up until the present time."

"Who are you talking to, devil boy? Who is Ariel? Is that... Oh my..." The reverend went silent and watched.

He watched through his daughter's eyes as she ran to Calvin and gave him a hug at the gate. He watched as she went nervously up to Tarpa for the first time and was greeted with a smile. He watched some of Ariel's strange performance. He watched as the three of them made their way through the fair, joking, laughing, and smiling the whole time.

He started to tear up as he watched. He could not remember the last time Victoria looked so happy. The three of them almost looked like family together. Now he felt like he was losing her in a different way. He wanted to vent his frustration at this, but he was too captivated by what he was seeing. He continued to watch.

He watched as the mood of events suddenly turned dark. He saw the fear and panic in people's faces as they found out about the attackers — his men. He listened to Calvin's speech and was amazed to hear him urge for understanding and for no killing. He saw that they had left Victoria safely in the trailer.

He watched as this fairy person, Ariel, pleaded with Victoria to remain in the trailer. He cried when he heard her say, "I have to help Uncle Calvin and Aunt Tarpa to stop the bad men who are coming."

And then he went absolutely silent when he saw her running up to Calvin. Out of the corner of her eye she had seen one of his men throwing a pitchfork right at her. But instantly, Tarpa was right beside her as a shield. He heard the horrible meaty sound as the forks jabbed into her back, and saw through his daughter's eyes the pain on Tarpa's face that she bore to protect her.

His head sagged, and he started to cry. Calvin said nothing.

Victoria redoubled her hug around her father. "Don't cry, Papa," she said. "Everything is OK now. Uncle Calvin protected us." This only made him cry more.

Calvin pulled the silly bunny ears off of the reverend's head and handed them back to Victoria. "Sorry, they are a little stretched. I'll get you another pair later on, OK?"

Victoria took them anyway. Calvin then cut the reverend's bindings. The reverend timidly said, "Thank you," and massaged his wrists.

There was a moment while everyone collected their thoughts and no one spoke. Finally, it was the reverend who broke the silence. He stood up and held out his hand to Calvin.

Calvin, surprised, looked at it for a moment like it was a dead fish. The reverend interpreted this as a sign of refusal and started to lower his hand, but Calvin quickly called out, "Wait!" and shook it.

The reverend was unusually at a loss for words. Instead, Calvin filled the silence by saying, "I hope we can be friends from here on out. But if not, I hope we can at least work toward a peaceful understanding with each other. I'm sorry that I let your little girl come so close to harm. I should have left a real person with her. It was a stupid oversight. I hope you can forgive me."

The reverend shook his head. "No, it's not your fault. I'm her father; I should have been watching her. And honestly, it looks like I was the cause of the danger. No, it's not your fault. I too hope that we can work for peace. I see now that I've misjudged you."

Calvin smirked. "It took you long enough."

Then reverend ignored this and looked around while asking, "Where is your wife? I owe her an apology too — and a sincere thank you."

Calvin answered, "She's gone home to get her wounds treated properly. Actually, Why don't you and Victoria come to our place and stay the night? There is no way you two are going to make a thirteen hour walk back home — you're both exhausted."

The reverend considered this for a moment and then said, "That is more than generous, but no, I think we'll pass on the offer. My men left their supplies in a clearing not far from here. They will be camping out there tonight, and I think it's important that I be there. My second in command is even more pigheaded than me. He's probably already planning the next attack. I need to try to make them all see some sense, just like you've done for me."

Calvin gave him a lopsided shrug. "Alright, well, if you change your mind, the offer is open."

"Thank you," said the reverend again, "and tell your wife

how grateful I am, and how sorry I am."

"I will."

The two men shook hands once more. Calvin crouched down and gave Victoria a goodbye hug. "See you later, sweetie. I'll come and visit soon, OK?"

Victoria nodded and hugged him back. Calvin stood back up and watched as she and her father walked away into the darkness of the roadway and faded from sight.

What a day, he thought. All he wanted to do now was to crumble to the ground and lie there in a sad, tired heap, but a greater desire held him together while he walked home to take care of his wounded wife.

CHAPTER 23

Alarms blasted a sharp warning throughout the Bobcorp3 complex. Scientists scurried around like ants while collecting valuables and running for the exits.

Unfortunately, beyond the doors was the vacuum of space, so the poor scientists had no choice but to cram into the scant few rovers and head for the airport.

The rovers' canopies were mirrored to reflect the sun's unfiltered radiation away from the occupants, but if an outside observer could have viewed into one of these rovers, she would have seen a solid mass of white lab coats with arms, legs, and heads poking out in strange and unpredictable angles. They were not happy scientists.

There were three more unhappy scientists inside the Bobford3 Lunar Collider, mostly because of the basketball-sized puncture in the outside wall.

They each had enough air in which to either evacuate or attempt to fix the puncture, but not both. Stupidly or bravely, they had chosen to stay and mend the hole.

This had been Brody's idea, of course, since this was his idea of a good time. The other two had only stayed out of guilt, since Brody would likely not make the repair in time without their help.

The exchange that had led to the decision had gone as follows:

Brody: "I'm staying and fixing it."

Mike: "For fuck's sake, why?"

Brody: "The air vents for this place are connected to the ones in the lab. People will suffocate."

Mike: "What a fucking stupid design! Can't they evacuate?"

Brody: "Only slightly more than half. Three quarters if they really cram into the rovers. A few more can put on emergency suits, but their air will not last the walk to the airport."

Mike: "Oh for fuck's sake. OK, I'll help."

Sarah: "If we remove the lower-right panel from section 3C, we can place it over the hole and secure it with... something."

Mike: "I saw a roll of duct tape in the... um... second cabinet to the right on the far wall of the control center. I think."

Brody: "Sarah, go find the tape. Mike, help me remove the panel. We'll meet up at the puncture. Go!"

Sarah moved with surprising speed as she sprinted down the corridor. Brody grabbed his tool box and he and Mike hustled to fetch the panel in section 3C.

Section 3C, as it turned out, was nearly two kilometers away. This was annoying to Mike and Brody, but given that the farthest point of the facility was more than 135 kilometers away, they counted their blessings. This was especially true because, as these things always seem to go, the puncture had severed the power lines to the tram system.

Meanwhile, yet another scientist sat alone in the kitchen of the fourteenth floor feeling very sorry for himself. He was getting cold, his ears kept popping, and he was beginning to feel dizzy.

He was nibbling on his very last kitten sandwich while he contemplated whether or not to compose his final words and send them to Ariel for safe keeping. But what would they be? He found it too hard to think about, but if he had been pressed on the matter, he supposed they would be something like: "What the hell did you guys do to my laboratory?"

Still, in the end, he had been heroic. That was something for the Bobford line to be proud of. If he had one regret, it was that he had always been too busy to spawn a Bobford clone of his own.

Now the Bobford line would end with him. There had been one original and three clones, and what did they have to show for it? Some potentially lethal fast food and a slacker from the stupid ages that will likely live forever. If only the alchemy project had worked, then he could have died a fulfilled man.

Bobford3 thought about the last half hour and frowned. He

could have saved his own skin. He had had every right to leave first. Except, down in his heart, he knew that he did not. Deep down he knew the truth — that any one of the lowest level scientists in his lab were far better people than he — far more intelligent, far more creative, and far younger as well.

So he had done the noble but stupid thing and used his time to organize the evacuation as best he could. In the end, only five people could not be saved out of several dozen. Not a bad effort.

He took another feeble bite of his sandwich and started to cry.

And then the ventilation system started to pump air back into the lab. The pressure slowly started to return, and the temperature steadily rose to normal.

A cheerful voice spoke to Bobford3 through his PC. It said, "Hey, Bob-dude. You with us, bro? We totally fixed the puncture. I'm, uh, sorry about that. It was totally my fault. I wasn't paying attention. I forgot that we had set the units for the centrifuge's speed control to rotations per second, not rotations per minute. We totally over spun the two kilogram sample by a factor of sixty. You should have seen it! It totally obliterated the wall. Loudest thing I ever heard, even behind the thick walls of the control center. Oh, wait. Shit. I'll have to get back to you — the duct tape is letting go."

Bobford3 set his sandwich down and looked thoughtfully at the ceiling. Then, after a moment of contemplation, he finally answered back in a cheery tone. He said, "I really hate you guys."

CHAPTER 24

The weather on Evionia was surprisingly routine, but every once in a while a rogue system strutted around the continent of Dirt like it owned the place. Today was such a day.

The drizzle fell on Calvin as he walked to work. He was still dead tired from the day before, but he felt that he had a duty to show up for work. No doubt his employees would be anxious to know what plans he had for dealing with the Trads — like it was his responsibility or something. Sometimes he had the feeling that they thought of him as the unofficial mayor of the city, much to his dismay.

Big City had no official government. The city had formed over time as specialty groups began trading with each other. Commerce, therefore, was the only rule of the land.

Christians rule themselves by asking, "What would Jesus do?" and then they try to emulate their vision of a benevolent, selfless human. Big City folks ruled themselves by asking, "What was good for business?" and then acted accordingly.

On the surface these two philosophies appear to be radically different, but surprisingly, there is a large overlap between them, with the latter having the added benefit of being less subjective.

As it turns out, respect for private property and personal liberty is good for business. Not getting murdered is good for business. Telling the truth is good for business. Respecting the environment is good for business.

No merchant wants to live in a city where he constantly fears for his life, or fears that his merchandise may be easily taken from him. And in turn, at least in the scope of the small and ironically named Big City, no merchant could stay in business for long if he gained a reputation for cheating his customers or for destroying the land and air in which they lived.

As for more personal affairs, such as how a man treated his wife, the citizens of Big City more or less had a policy of minding their own business.

However, there existed in the zeitgeist a collective trigger mechanism that sprung into action whenever enough was enough. Perhaps one day a group of men would notice that Mrs. Barley had yet another fresh bruise on her face, and then one of them would look at her, look at his friends, and nod. And then one or two more would nod until eventually they were all nodding in silent agreement. And that's when the "rough music" would begin.

That night, Mr. Barley might just suddenly wake up to the sound of raucous noise outside his home. He may hear songs being chanted that recounted his crime in graphic detail. Looking out of the window, he may see an effigy of himself hanging from a tree branch. After all that, he may just mend his ways, or even leave town. Failing that, he might just find himself dead the next night, if enough people were suitably outraged.

This system of trader's law was certainly imperfect, as any system of governing humans by humans certainly is. But it had served Big City well and made for a very pleasurable place to live. It worked so well, in fact, that Calvin had been hesitant at first to disrupt it by introducing the Ariel system.

As usual, it had been Tarpa who had talked some sense into him. She had explained that the current system would surely fail as the city continued to expand and a nation was born. The only hope of maintaining the peace and order of Big City as it grew was to convert it to the Ariel system, which operated on pretty much the same principles. The only important difference was that with the Ariel system, the mechanism of judgment was taken out of the hands of the people and given to an impartial arbiter.

Calvin's daydream about the running of Big City ended as he approached his company. He looked at the front of the Cal Tech building and sighed. Someone, presumably a stray Trad from the previous night, had written "GO AWAY BASTERDS" in big, red letters. Calvin shook his head and went inside.

Applause broke out as he entered. Big, burly men from the machine shop smacked him heartily on the back. Women kissed him on the cheek. Jethro grabbed his shoulder for a moment and said, "Good on you, boss." Calvin was bewildered.

"What's all this about?" he asked.

Suzette was the first to answer. She said, "What do you mean, what is all this about? It's only about our awesome boss saving the whole damn city. When you jabbed that pitchfork down with all of your might and shouted, 'We're done here!' well, it made my girly parts a little juicy, I don't mind saying."

"Suzette," answered Calvin with a sigh, "You really should mind saying stuff like that. You really should."

He then turned to the group at large and said, "Look, everyone, thanks for all of this. I'm flattered. But honestly, I just happened to be the one in a position to organize things. Any one of you would have done the same." He glanced at Suzette and added, "It's nothing to get... juicy about, I assure you. And nothing has really been resolved. If anything, the Trads are even more fired up than before."

Someone from the crowd asked, "Yeah, what are we going to do about them Trads? You got any ideas, boss?"

Shit, thought Calvin, I walked right into that one. Out loud he said, "It's not my decision, I know that. We should have a town meeting tonight and figure it out together."

Calvin heard variations of, "Sounds good, boss," returning from the crowd.

"Good, then you slackers get back to work until then. The Guides were a huge hit last night, so I think we are going to be very busy from now on."

Most of the crowd hesitantly returned to their posts, but a few smart asses first threw the remaining bits of confetti in the air before they went. Suzette gave Calvin a very suggestive wink and returned, a few feet away, to her receptionist station. Calvin tried to think of beans and poison ivy and goats and other non-sexy things as he walked quickly past her.

He was a few feet away when a thought struck him. He turned back around and returned to her desk. Then he said, "Suzette, could you do me a favor?"

"Of course."

"Could you find someone to take care of that misspelled graffiti on the front of the building?"

Suzette smiled. "Consider it done. I'll handle it personally."

"Great. Thanks. I appreciate it."

Calvin then went searching for his right-hand man. He eventually found him in the chief case designer's office. Dan, the chief case designer, had actually been the only case designer up until recently, but he had always been called the chief case designer because the title made him feel important.

Dan and Doc were sitting side-by-side in front of a drafting table with their backs to the door. The wall in front of them was covered with pictures of bears, both real bears and stuffed teddy bears. Many of the photos featured only the bears' ears. Calvin watched them quietly for a moment as they worked.

Dan said, "No, no. You see that curly part there. That's in most of the pictures. I think we need that curly part."

Doc shook his head. "Nah, I don't think that's a good idea. It makes the design too busy. Plus you have to think of the molding issues. That curly part has a negative angle. You can't mold that without silicone — which doesn't last for very many cycles. Or you have to use a very complicated multi-part metal jobber — which is a bitch to make, let me tell you."

Dan studied a few of the pictures again with fierce concentration. After a long while he said, "No, I'm sorry, but I'm standing firm on the curly part."

Doc frowned and nibbled the eraser of his pencil. Then he started to sketch something on a piece of paper. He made a mistake and tried to erase it with the soggy eraser, which only smeared the graphite around the paper. He cursed, scribbled it out, and started again next to it. After a short moment, he showed it to his colleague and said, "How about something like this? It's still got the curly part, but I've softened the contours to make it less busy and more producible."

Dan studied it for a long while, turning it this way and that while occasionally going, "Hmm."

Calvin laughed internally when he realized that both he and Doc were holding their breath.

Finally, Dan smacked the sketch down onto the drafting table and stuck his hand out for Doc to shake. "You've got yourself a deal."

They shook hands, and Calvin cleared his throat.

Doc noticed him first. "Oh, hey there, sir. Well done, yesterday. We really showed those Trads a thing or two, eh?"

Calvin diverted the conversation as quickly as he could.

"Thanks. So, what are you two working on? We aren't making Guides for bears now, are we?"

Doc answered seriously, "Oh no, we aren't doing that. That would be silly. No, we just finalized another design for the children-sized Guides. The bunny ears went over so well at the fair that we thought we would try some other animals." He gestured at the photos pinned to another wall.

Calvin had not noticed earlier, but there were hundreds of pictures of dozens of different animals — or at least their ears — pinned to another wall of the office.

Calvin looked back at his two employees and said, "I love it. But for now, let's stick with a handful of designs. We wouldn't want to flood the market all at once, right? Always leave them wanting more. I'm sure I read that somewhere. For now, let's stick with the basics — dog, cat, rabbit, and bear. Then maybe in a month or two we will consider some of the more exotic ones like..." he glanced at the wall again "...meerkats."

The two nodded in agreement and Calvin left the office to do his usual lap around the manufacturing facility. Mercifully, all was well today and the line was clicking away like clockwork.

Hours later, Calvin left work a little early to prepare for the meeting later that night. He knew that somehow he was going to wind up being the calm voice of reason. He thought, if these people only knew that I was the sort of person to skip out of work on a whim and go to the beach with my girlfriend, then maybe they wouldn't be putting so much trust in my judgment. It's a very sad day when I'm forced to be the adult in the room.

As he left the building, he glanced behind him to check that the graffiti had been properly cleaned. It had not.

Instead, someone had carefully drawn an "X" over the erroneous "E" in "BASTERDS" and wrote an "A" above it. "That's what I get for asking a secretary to take care of something like this," Calvin muttered to himself. He thought about taking care of it personally, and then he thought, nah, I'll leave it. It makes a statement.

CHAPTER 25

"Let's burn their crummy little village to the ground!"

"Yeah!"

"Let's salt their fields!"

"Yeah!"

"Let's free all of their beasts!"

"Yeah!"

"Let's broadcast the sound of crying children at them every night for a month!"

"Yeah!"

"Let's kidnap the leader and tattoo '666' on his forehead!"

"Yeah!"

"Let's set traps all along their roads!"

"Yeah!"

"Let's talk to them and work things out!"

"Yeah!"

"Wait, what?"

Suddenly, everyone in the square was looking at Calvin. As he had been afraid of, it was now up to him to be the calm voice of reason.

"Attacking the Trads is only going to make things worse. It's only going to provoke them into more attacks. I think I have the reverend on our side. Now I only have to persuade his second in command."

A man called out from the crowd, "That guy's a bastard. He'll never change his mind. We have to take care of them here and now."

A few "Yeahs" of agreement burbled from the crowd.

"So what, then?" asked Calvin. "What do we do? We ruin their crops? We release their animals? Let's not mince words — we are talking about starving them to death. Or shall we be more humane about it and simply slit their throats in their sleep?"

"If it comes to that," answered a familiar voice from the crowd.

Calvin pointed him out. "You, sir, come up front here, will you?"

The man, suddenly nervous without the anonymity of the crowd, reluctantly stepped forward.

Calvin asked him, "So, you'd slaughter the whole lot of them, is that what you're saying?"

The man looked around for support, and then finally answered, "Well, it's better them than us, ain't it?"

"Unfortunately, sir, the Trads are thinking the same thing right now — wipe them out before they wipe us out. Is that smart of them? Are you saying they made the right choice last night?" asked Calvin.

The man looked around again for support from the others, but found none. "Well, no. But them bastards started it so I reckon it's OK for us to finish it."

Calvin thought about this. The man sort of had a point. Finally, he said, "Point taken, sir. There is a certain logic to that. But do you really think it's OK to kill them all? Does that sit well with you, sir?"

"Maybe yes and maybe no," answered the man, cryptically. "But it's a matter of survival of the fittest, ain't it? We are much stronger than them, so I say we take care of this here and now. Then all our worries are gone. If we act weak, then they will just attack us again. I, for one, don't want to worry every night that one of those buggers is going to sneak into my house at night, slit my throat, and rape my wife."

"So we should attack them now because we are sure to win?" asked Calvin. "Might makes right, is that it?"

"Now you're catching on," answered the man.

"Tell me," said Calvin, "Did you get to see me fight last night?"

"You bet I did," answered the man. "You really showed them a thing or two, didn't you?"

Calvin ignored the question and continued, "You're Mike the

butcher, aren't you? You have that nice house on the hill? I'm a big fan of your shop, by the way — the best selection around."

"Yes, sir. Thank you, sir." answered Mike the Butcher, not knowing where this was all going.

Calvin continued, "And your wife is very pretty."

The man suddenly looked a little agitated. "Where are you going with this, sir, if you don't mind me asking?"

"She's got a fine ass," continued Calvin.

Mike swung at him. Calvin caught his fist in his hand and squeezed it hard. The man buckled to his knees in pain.

Calvin said flatly. "You just attacked me first. I'm stronger than you. So now I'm going to kill you. I'll probably steal your shop and burn down your home while I'm at it. Does that sit well with you, sir?"

"No," groaned the man.

"So, you would rather talk it out, then?"

"Yes."

Calvin released his grip. "Good. Me too. I'm terribly sorry about that, Mike. You know I was just trying to prove a point. You are a good man, and the remark about your wife was completely unacceptable. Do you think you can forgive me?"

Mike opened and closed his hand a few times to work out the pain and to get the blood flowing back again. Nothing seemed broken. Then he said, "Yes, fine, point taken. And yes, we're square." A half second later he added, "Only don't expect me to go shaking your hand any time soon." He massaged his right hand in demonstration.

"Sorry about the hand. Put some ice on it tonight and it will be right as rain by tomorrow. Now, going back to our discussion, do you understand now that might doesn't make right?"

The adrenaline in Mike's system was making him just a bit more stubborn than usual, and so he answered, "Not really, sir. I mean, it doesn't make sense for us to fight, does it? I mean, we're on the same side, ain't we? We're the same sort of people. But those Trads, they ain't like us. There ain't no reasoning with them."

Calvin admired the guys spirit, but not his logic. "So, we can kill them all since they aren't like us? That's the reasoning now, is it? Let's just follow through with that idea, shall we? Let's say we wipe out those nasty little Trads. Then what? Peace in our time? I don't think so.

"No. What we get, Mike, is a pretty nasty reputation. You're a trader — you know about that sort of thing. It ain't good for business, and it ain't good for your well-being, is it? If we wipe out the Trads, then suddenly the tribes of the desert are going to hear about it, and they are not going to like it. After all, what's to stop us from wiping them out next? So they will band together and we'll have yet another enemy to face, this one bigger and more ferocious."

"Yeah, but, I reckon we can take them," replied Mike.

Calvin shook his head. "Maybe. Maybe we can. No, you're right, we could. We could take them. Half the city might be destroyed in the process, but eventually we would win, I'm sure of it. And then what? The plains folk sure aren't going to like it. You get most of your meat from them, don't you? And the Jungle Empire? What of them? You can call them savages, yes, but I sure as hell wouldn't want to fight them.

"What I'm getting at, Mike, is that if we act overly aggressive now, then we will make an enemy out of the entire continent. That, surely, is bad for business. But let's keep pretending, shall we? Let's say that after a decade or two we slaughter and pillage our way across the land, wiping out all those weird people who are different than us. Then what? Peace and prosperity? Bullshit.

"What happens is that we have a lot of weapons lying around that are going to waste. So some of us start saying things like, 'You know, those people that settled in the grasslands are kind of weird. They aren't really our kind of people, are they? I mean, running around with grass skirts on, what's that all about? I reckon the grasslands could be better run by us.'

"Once it starts, Mike, it will never end. Is that the future you want for your family? Constant war? Because that's where the slaughter of the Trads will take us."

Mike took a pinch of chewing tobacco out of its case and jammed it into a corner of his mouth, mainly to buy him some time to think. Eventually he answered, "You're a smart one, Mr. Jones, that's sure enough. No, I don't reckon I want to live in constant war. But what do we do, then? I'm sure we are all open to suggestions." He looked around him. The silent crowd nodded agreement and looked to Calvin for the answers.

Calvin had one of those out-of-body moments again, the sort where you see yourself steering the entire political future of an alien civilization, and you think to yourself, holy shit — I can't believe I'm doing this.

Calvin pushed down his doubts and said, "I don't pretend to

know all the answers, but..."

"Yeah, right," interrupted someone from the crowd.

Calvin laughed. "OK, so I do pretend to know all the answers, but who the hell knows if I'm right or not. But I'd like to try things peacefully first, and surely that can't be a bad thing. So give me a week. I'll go and talk to the Trads. If we all stay calm, I'm confident we can work on a peace treaty with them. Is that acceptable to everyone?"

Most people nodded or muttered agreement. Stubborn Mike did not. "That sounds good and all, but how are you going to do it?"

Calvin shrugged and asked, "What brought you all together here in Big City? You all used to stick to yourselves, right? What changed? Commerce. Trade. That's what glues us together. Tell me Mike, do you own a car?"

Mike looked proud and said, "Yes. Yes, I do. A real beaut. I busted my ass to afford her, but she's my pride and joy."

"Except when it rains, am I right?" prompted Calvin.

Mike deflated slightly. Well, yes, you do get a little wet, what with no windows and such, but what of it?"

"The Trads make the most exquisite glass. They have crystal clear windows in their homes. They make beautiful colored glass too. And sharp cutlery — I should know, I was stabbed by it a few times last night."

This got a few laughs from the crowd.

Mike asked, "So you reckon we can work out some sort of trade agreement?"

Calvin nodded. "It's worth a try, no?"

Mike nodded back. "Very well. I don't see no harm in waiting a week. Let's see what you can do."

Mike stuck out his left hand for Calvin to shake. Calvin smiled and shook it with his left hand. Mike suddenly squeezed Calvin's hand with all of his strength. Calvin winced in pain. Mike let go, leaned toward Calvin and said, "Between you and me, your lady ain't got a bad ass on her either." He laughed and added, "Now, we're square."

CHAPTER 26

As Calvin drove slowly up the winding mountain road on his way to visit the reverend, he tried to think about what he should do when he got there. He was reasonably sure that he could forge a trade agreement with the reverend, but how much good would that ultimately do? The reverend was a persuasive man, but would he be persuasive enough to nullify all of that hatred and mistrust in a matter of days. Not likely. But Calvin had to help him try.

Calvin found a patch of woods a few miles from the Trad's village and hid his car there. He had been driving in pitch blackness with the lights out, so he was certain that he had not been seen. However, his car made a lot a noise so this was as far as he dare go with it.

He buckled on a large backpack and quietly walked the remaining way to the village. His display lenses were allowing him to see in the dark, and Ariel was giving him constant updates regarding the location of nearby patrols.

It had only been two days since the confrontation, so the Trads were still on high alert, expecting an inevitable retaliation by the Progs. The entire village was likely on a hair trigger, so Calvin had to be extremely careful.

However, the lookouts were most likely expecting a large mob to be coming, which worked to Calvin's advantage. He then thought that if he were in charge of an invasion, this is how he would do it: send in maybe four or five people under cover of night. Attach time bombs to food stores, weapons caches, and other key infrastructure. Then leave quietly and watch the chaos from afar. After a few weeks had passed and the enemy was hungry and tired from rebuilding, you attacked in force.

Lucky for the planet of Evionia that Calvin had no intention of sharing his plan. Instead, he was trying to think of a peaceful way out of this mess, which turned out to be much harder to do.

He waited for a gap in the patrols and then crept up to the reverend's door. To Calvin's surprise, it opened before he could knock.

The reverend smiled at him and said, "Hello, devil boy. Come in, quickly. Victoria told me you were here."

Calvin noticed the 'devil boy' remark, so he answered in turn by saying, "Hello Reverend Spellcheck."

The reverend shook his head and let Calvin inside. Calvin fought with the straps of his backpack for a moment and placed it gently on the floor.

The reverend then cut right to the chase. "So tell me, how bad is it?"

Calvin rubbed his hair back and forth a few times while he exhaled deeply. "Oh, pretty bad," he answered.

"So, you're going to retaliate?" asked the reverend, nervously.

"Not me, Reverend. But yes, most of the Progs are itching for payback. They don't feel safe now. They don't want to live in fear, so they figure the easiest thing to do would be to obliterate your village."

The reverend went pale.

Calvin put a reassuring hand on his shoulder and said, "Hopefully, it won't come to that. I managed to talk some sense into them. I convinced them that if they wiped you guys out, then one-by-one they would make an enemy of all the other inhabitants of Evionia. I convinced them to give me a week to form some sort of pact with you. Hopefully by then, things will have calmed down. Of course, it would help tremendously if I could bring back some sort of trade agreement. We were hoping to purchase glassware from you, in return for, well, whatever you want. The point is to make trade, not war."

The reverend softly bit the side of his closed fist while he thought. Finally, he replied, "If it were up to me, I'd do it. The problem is, there's been a major split in the congregation. Almost half of the village is still wanting to go to war with you. Brother Grimm has them worked into a frenzy. They're planning something, but I don't know what. They no longer listen to me. He has them convinced that I've been bewitched by you and your wife. Many of them no longer trust my judgment or see me as a leader."

"Great," said Calvin dejectedly. "I pretty much expected that, but I was hoping to be wrong." He then motioned to the backpack on the floor beside him and continued, "I brought along something that might help. I guess you could call it propaganda. I've brought along a projector and a video about Big City. It's not long — just under ten minutes. But I thought it would help to humanize us. Maybe if your village sees us as individual people just trying to make a go of life, much like them, then maybe they won't want to kill us all. I'd like to make one of your village to show to my people, but I'm afraid it would only show a series of doors slamming in my face, with the occasional old woman spitting on me." Calvin smirked.

The reverend smiled. "Thank you, Calvin. I appreciate your help. So... tell me... what is a projector?"

Calvin studied him for a moment to judge if he were serious or not. Yes, he looked genuinely confused.

"A projector is a box about this big that projects video — recorded images like you saw on your daughter's Guide the other night — onto a screen so that multiple people can view it at once. It has a speaker on it too, which reproduces recorded sound. If you have a white sheet somewhere, I'll show you how it works."

The reverend found a suitable sheet in a closet and presented it to Calvin, who hung it on a wall. Calvin then showed the reverend how to use the projector and explained that it ran on batteries and would therefore only work for a few hours, so he should try not to use it too much before the actual presentation.

The reverend thanked him once again and said, "I'm sure this will help, but I still don't have a lot of hope this will end without bloodshed."

"Maybe not," agreed Calvin, "but we have to try."

The reverend nodded. "I'll spread the word and hold a meeting tomorrow night. Hopefully, this video of yours will do the trick. If I can convince most of Grimm's followers to abandon their quest for war, then I will feel comfortable signing a trade agreement with you. Otherwise, I couldn't do it in good conscience knowing that it would be unenforceable."

"I can't ask for more than that," replied Calvin.

The two shook hands, and then the reverend called out over his shoulder, "OK, child, you can come on out."

"Uncle Calvin! Uncle Calvin!" said a blur of pink as it raced down the hall and attached itself to Calvin's legs.

Calvin bent down and gave it a hug.

"Hello, sweetie. Have you been a good girl?"

Victoria nodded her head.

Calvin rooted around in his backpack for a moment and then produced a Guide.

"Then, here you go — the very first of its kind." Calvin handed the Guide to her.

Victoria studied it for a moment then took off her old, stretched bunny rabbit Guide and put the new one on. Then she held her hands up above her head and went, "Grrrrrrrr!"

Calvin smiled.

The reverend knelt down beside her and examined the new Guide. He touched an ear. "Very nice work. Fine craftsmanship. It feels just like real fur. And you've even got that curly part there, which adds to the realism. Very nice." He stood back up, as did Calvin.

Calvin answered, "Thanks, Reverend. I can make a big pair for you if you'd like."

The reverend laughed. "No, thank you, that won't be necessary. Although I may take a normal pair for myself if you don't mind."

"Of course not."

"I'd also like to visit your factory one day, if things ever settle down that is."

"Sure, anytime. I'd love to show you around."

The two stood in silence for a moment, each wondering what to say next. Calvin spoke first and said, "Well, I really should be going. I'd like to get back in time for supper. It was great to see you and Victoria again. Good luck with everything tomorrow. I'm sure you will do fine."

"You won't stay for supper here?" asked the reverend.

"No, sorry. I promised Tarpa."

"OK, then. How is your wife, anyway? I hope she's healing."

Calvin waved his hand dismissively. "You don't have to worry about her. She's a tough one. She's doing just fine, but I'll tell her you were asking about her."

"Thanks," said the reverend. "Oh, before you go, Vicky has

something for you to take to Tarpa. Go get it, sweetie."

Victoria ran back to her room and retrieved the item. She ran back to Calvin and presented it to him solemnly, saying, "Please give this to Aunt Tarpa and tell her I love her."

She handed Calvin a wooden plaque. The reverend said, "Vicky made it entirely herself. I didn't even know about it until this morning."

The plaque itself was made of sanded wood. The edges had been beveled. The whole thing had been stained and varnished. It was not a half bad job. But the interesting part was what was on the front of it.

Carved on the front of the plaque was a silhouette of a woman kneeling in front of a little girl and hugging her tightly. The woman had a pitchfork stuck in her back.

Calvin was glad that he was wearing his guides because his eyes were starting to tear. He knelt back down and gave Victoria another hug. "I think Aunt Tarpa will treasure this." He sniffled and stood back up.

He swallowed hard and said, "I really do need to get going. Thank you both for everything. I hope to see you again soon. Let me know how things go, Reverend, OK?"

The reverend nodded. Victoria gave him one last hug and said, "Bye-bye, Uncle Calvin. I love you."

"I love you too, sweetie. Bye-bye."

Calvin let himself out and quickly found a dark shadow in the woods where he could remove his display lenses and dry his eyes. He really hoped that the reverend would be successful. He hated to think about going to war against them. If it came to that, he'd guard those two himself.

CHAPTER 27

It was an unusually cold night. The winds had temporarily reversed and were blowing the cold air of the mountain tops seemingly straight down the backs of the gathering masses. The people of the Trad village were huddled in groups around camp fires scattered throughout the field, trying to stay warm.

The reverend feared that this was not the best time for a meeting like this, but time was not in abundant supply, so he busily erected a makeshift screen behind his pulpit on the hill. He then set the projector on the pulpit so that it was facing the screen, and stood beside it.

Even though he had been expecting it, the reverend was saddened to see his second in command and long time friend, Brother Grimm, looking at him with skepticism from the crowd of people rather than standing proudly by his side where he belonged. With a heavy heart, the reverend began his speech.

"I thank you all for joining me on this inhospitable night. I'll try to make this as short as possible, but in light of recent events with the Progs of Big City, I thought it was important that we held a meeting and made some decisions right away. Time is not our friend right now. I'll cut to the chase — the Progs are very angry and are looking to retaliate in just a few days."

Worried inhalations of breath and nervous murmurings could be heard from the crowd. The reverend continued, "If it were not for the direct intervention of Calvin Jones, who I have callously called devil boy in the past, we would have already been attacked, and many of us would already be dead."

Someone from the crowd shouted, "You aren't siding with the devil boy, are you, Reverend? Say it ain't so!"

The reverend ignored this and continued, "We all knew it was a matter of time before they attacked us, right? Isn't that what we have been saying all along? But we were so stupid that we went and caused it to happen. You can only swat a bee hive so many times before you get stung. The people of Big City didn't want to fight us — they just wanted to be left alone. But we kept taunting them, and now they are scared. We awoke the sleeping giant, and now we await his wrath."

The crowd shifted uneasily as they contemplated a fight with Big City. The reverend continued, "However, I have a way out of this. But before I share it with you, I think it is important that we all know a little bit about our so-called enemy. First, I would like to show you the events of the other day through my little girl's eyes. She went and snuck off to the Big City fair without my permission and spent the whole day with my enemies. Can you even imagine how awful that could have turned out? But instead of my worst nightmares coming true, I'll show you what actually happened.

"And before any of you try and argue that this here is some sort of trickery, I'll have you know that my own daughter confirms everything here. And if any of you want to call my daughter a liar, you can say it to my face and I'll give you a black eye for the trouble. You all know Victoria, and you all know she is a forthright little girl."

The reverend then showed the assembled crowd similar footage to what he had been shown on the night of the fair. They watched Calvin's silly introduction to the fair through Victoria's eyes. They watched as she ran to Calvin and gave him a huge hug at the gate. They watched as she went nervously up to Tarpa for the first time and was greeted with a smile. They watched as the three of them made their way through the fair, joking, laughing, and smiling the whole time. They saw the residents of Big City having fun and enjoying themselves just like regular folk.

Then they watched as the mood suddenly turned dark. They saw the fear and panic in people's faces as they found out about the attackers — them. They listened to Calvin's speech and were surprised to hear him urge for understanding and for absolutely no killing.

The reverend paused the video at this point and said, "They

aren't exactly the soulless demons I thought they were. What do y'all think? Mr. Jones, for one, appears to be more of a man than I could hope to be. But I know some of you are hard to convince. That's fine — skepticism ain't a bad thing. However, sometimes you have to be wise enough to realize that you've been a damn fool. And it takes a brave man indeed to question his inner most beliefs. If you are still unsure about the integrity of Calvin Jones, please watch what happened to his wife later on that night."

The reverend resumed the video. The crowd watched as Calvin faced an angry mob out for his blood. They saw the shock on his face as Victoria ran up to hug him. They watched as, out of the corner of Victoria's eye, she had seen one of them throwing a pitchfork at Calvin, and by extension Victoria, with all of his might. And then suddenly there was Tarpa hugging Victoria and forming a human shield. They heard the horrible, meaty sound as the pitchfork jabbed into her back, and saw through Victoria's eyes the pain on Tarpa's face that she bore to protect her.

The reverend stopped the video again and said, "I don't want to fight these people. Never mind the fact that we would lose horribly despite whatever malarkey Brother Grimm has been telling you. The best reason not to fight is that it simply isn't moral for us to do so. Up until now, the Progs have done nothing against us apart from exist. And even now, even after the safety of their homes and businesses have been threatened, they are willing to give us one more chance. I'm pleading with you all to give this some serious thought. Let us choose the path of peace, just as our good Lord commands us to do."

The reverend waited a moment for the crowd to quiet down again and said, "We have a chance to live peacefully with the Progs, even now. All they ask of us is that we trade with them. They are particularly interested in our glassware. It seems even the fancy pants of Big City can't make a simple pane of glass. In return, they will trade for whatever we wish — iron work, food, medicine, whatever we want. They are even willing to teach us how they make their horseless carriages. All they want from us is trade. I think that is not only reasonable, but we will actually make out much better if we agree. I think this is a no-brainer.

"Unfortunately, I know there are some of us that ain't got no brains at all. There are those among us that will continue to scare you, just as I have done in the past, into hating the Progs. After all, we are all scared of the unknown, aren't we? We ask ourselves, who are these Progs, anyway? What do they want? Are they evil? All we know is, they ain't like us. They ain't like us, and we are good, so they must be bad. That's what we think, ain't it? Well, I'll tell you a little secret, here is what the Progs are really like: they're basically just like us. They just want to live in peace and enjoy life, just like us. They want their kids to be safe. They want to get along with their neighbors. They want to learn new things and make life easier for one another. That is what they are like. If that's evil, then we're evil too."

The reverend then played the next video, which was the advertising piece that Calvin had prepared for him. Suddenly, the projected image showed a satellite view of the eastern part of Dirt as it existed before Big City had come to be. A deep, announcer-like voice said, "Big City, home to thousands of traders from a hundred different trade groups, all come together for one purpose — commerce!" The crowd "ooo'ed" in surprise by the view from the sky.

The video then started to zoom in on a single area, zeroing in on a village of metal workers. The voice continued, "In the olden days, all of these groups had to make do with only the skills that they possessed." The video continued to zoom until it was following a single man as he walked through the front door of his home. He sat down in front of the fireplace and tugged off his rather bulky looking steel boots and the socks beneath them. As he warmed his feet by the fire, he said, "These iron boots are tough, but they sure are cold and heavy. I wish I could make something better."

The video now pulled back outside the man's house and zoomed out to once again show the entirety of the area. Now it zoomed again, but this time on a village of leather workers. It went through another man's door and showed him as he sat back in his chair with his feet up. He was wearing some very comfortable looking leather boots, but he was staring forlornly at a plate containing a single potato. The man said, "If only I had something really sharp and hard, then I'd be able to catch and butcher an animal. I'm getting tired of potatoes!"

The video left the house and zoomed out yet again. Then it seemed to fast-forward, and the sun could be seen rising, whizzing across the sky, and setting numerous times. The many separate villages on the ground were slowly growing and shifting in shape. Eventually, the villages started to meet and overlap until they formed the shape of the present-day Big City.

The reverend was surprised to see Brother Grimm suddenly beside him with another man. Grimm motioned for the reverend to follow him down behind the mound. The reverend nodded and followed him.

The deep voice on the video once again spoke, "Thankfully, today these groups have learned to live together and trade with each other for goods and services. Now, they can all benefit from each other's specialties. Now, every man can enjoy the benefits of many, many skills without the need for him to master them himself."

The video then zoomed in on the metal worker again. He was once again coming inside from the cold, but this time he was wearing leather boots. He patted them when he sat down by the fire and said, "I have to hand it to him, that leather worker sure knows his stuff. These boots are so warm and comfortable."

And once again, the video zoomed out and back in on the leather worker across town. He was at the table with his family enjoying a feast with many meats and vegetables. He said to himself, "I have to give it to that iron worker, he sure knows his stuff. The spears and knives he made are just incredible. I'll never go hungry again now that I have them."

Back behind the mound, Brother Grimm turned to the reverend and said, "I'm sorry to bother you in the middle of your speech, Reverend, but this is important. Brother Smith here just told me that his old mum is about to cross over and needs to be given her last rites. Please hurry, we don't have much time."

The reverend hesitated for a moment and looked behind him at the top of the hill. He contemplated running up there and telling the crowd what has happened and excusing himself, but then he worried about the extra time. The video would continue on without him, and there really wasn't anything else that needed to be said after that. It would probably be OK to just leave, he thought.

Grimm noticed his hesitation and said, "Don't worry. Brother John will explain things once your picture show ends."

The reverend looked relieved. "Thank you, Brother Grimm. I'm glad you are still my friend after all this. I'm ready, then. Let's hurry."

The three men then jogged speedily through a trail in the woods, heading in the direction of the village. Meanwhile, the video continued. It took on the look and feel of a commercial for a sought-after vacation destination.

Video snippets taken from around the city were shown in rapid succession as the deep-voiced announcer began to list the positive attributes of Big City.

"Big City citizens like to have fun, but they also work hard too. They believe in marriage and fidelity to their spouse. They don't abide stealing or murder. They believe that every man is free to do as he pleases, so long as it does not encroach on the liberties of his neighbor. They believe in fair trade, and in treating each other with respect. They don't expect any handouts but are always quick to lend a hand to those in need. They cherish their families and believe in the power of love. And best of all, Big City citizens love outsiders as long as they mean no harm and bring plenty of trade goods with them."

While the voice was giving its sales pitch, the video showed a clip of children playing tag in the park, a steel worker laboring at his forge, Market Street on a busy day, a man trying to steal an apple only to have someone trip him up and shake her head at him, a couple on their wedding day kissing for the first time as man and wife, a woman walking her dog down the street, a farmer tilling the ground with a beautiful sunrise behind him, a family shopping for clothes together, two strangers bumping into each other and then apologizing and going on their way, little Billy delivering groceries to the elderly, a couple cuddling on the beach while silhouetted by the setting sun, and finally, a visitor from the grasslands entering the city with a cart full of dried, salted meat while being greeted by a swarm of merchants all eager to trade with him.

The video ended, and the crowd seemed mostly moved by it. They eagerly awaited the reverend's return at the pulpit, but he was nowhere to be found.

Just as the crowd grew restless and was about to disperse, the projector turned on again. Ariel had patched into it and was now showing satellite imagery of the reverend and the other two men as they talked somewhere in the middle of the woods. Using her usual tricks, Ariel was able to divine sound from the image as well.

In the video, the reverend backed away from the two men with his hands out in front of him. He said, "Hold on a minute. Let's just talk about this."

Grimm shook his head and took another step toward the reverend while Brother Smith was inching his way around and behind the reverend. Grimm said, "We are past talking, I'm afraid. You've been infected by the silver-tongued devils of Big City. It hurts me to do this, old friend, but its for your own good. I'm afraid we are going to have to beat some sense into you."

Gasps of astonishment rippled through the crowd. Several people could be heard trying to work out where the reverend was at. Seemingly in answer to this, the video momentarily zoomed out to show the village and surrounding area. It paused there for a moment to allow the people to get their bearings. Then it slowly zoomed back to the reverend's location. Someone in the crowd shouted, "They're right by old Brother Hicksly's. Let's go!"

Several of the more hotblooded villagers ran off into the woods to give aid. Meanwhile, others stayed put, transfixed by the video.

They watched as the reverend argued with his attackers. "I'm not the one possessed by the devil," answered the reverend. "Look at you, about to beat up your old friend just because you can't bear to admit that you are wrong. You only know violence and hatred. I'm sorry for that, brother. I'm to blame for that. I've been preaching it for so very long. But I was wrong. Surely, you see that? Take a look at yourself, brother. You're acting like a monster."

"I'm not a monster! You're the monster!" screamed an enraged Grimm. He lunged at the reverend, who tried to jump back but was blocked by Smith. Before he knew it, the reverend was on the ground being choked by Grimm.

Suddenly, Grimm looked surprised and let go. He rolled off the reverend and clutched at his bleeding abdomen.

The reverend looked at his shaking hand — it was holding a bloody knife. He stared at it in disbelief for some time, as if not wanting to acknowledge his own actions. Beside him, Grimm moaned.

Hearing the moan, the reverend quickly dropped the knife, rolled over, and knelt beside his friend. He covered his friend's wound with his hand and shouted at Smith to go for help.

Instead, Smith picked up the glass knife from the ground and jabbed it deep into the reverend's neck while shouting, "Get away from Brother Grimm, you devil!"

The reverend dropped like a deflated balloon.

Smith then pushed away the reverend's limp body and hugged the nearly-dead body of Brother Grimm. Brother Grimm tried to speak, but only gurgling blood came out of his mouth.

Meanwhile, the crowd that had been watching all this on video went catatonic. Many of them went straight into denial, murmuring to themselves that this was some sort of trick. Others simply turned away from the screen and sobbed.

By the time help had arrived, both the reverend and Brother Grimm were dead. Brother Smith, who still had a bloody knife in his hand and was surrounded by the very evidently stabbed corpses of the two village leaders, had swift vigilante justice delivered to him in the form of a sharp spear through the heart.

CHAPTER 28

"It's OK, Calvin. Calm down," pleaded Tarpa in a placating voice.

Calvin was pacing back and forth in the living room while rubbing his head with both hands. Without stopping, he answered back, "Things are so far from OK right now. They killed him! The reverend is dead! I should have been there. I should have known this would happen. I asked too much of him. This is all my fault."

"It's not your fault..." began Tarpa, but Calvin kept on rambling.

"Everything has gone to hell, and it's all my fault. Who is going to sign a peace treaty now? The two village heads are dead!"

"I'm sure we can convince everyone here to stand down for a few more weeks in light of the situation," argued Tarpa, but she was completely ignored by Calvin.

"It's all my fault he's dead. What am I going to tell Victoria? Oh my god! Victoria! Ariel, what happened to Victoria? Is she safe?"

Ariel answered to both Calvin and Tarpa, "Victoria is safe at home. Some men from the village are just about to tell her the news. They will care for her tonight. They are trustworthy men, as far as I can ascertain."

Calvin stopped pacing. "I need to help her," he declared.

Now that Calvin had stopped pacing, Tarpa took the opportunity to hug him. She said to him kindly, "It's OK, Cal. There isn't anything you can do tonight. Things must be chaotic enough over there as it is. If you go over there tonight, you'll only make things worse."

Calvin gently pulled away from Tarpa and resumed pacing

around the room while biting his thumbnail. "I just feel so powerless. I'm responsible for all this mess — I should be there to help clean it up."

Tarpa spoke a little more forcefully now. "Calvin, knock it off. This isn't all your fault. You can't be everywhere at once. You can't quell every uprising, and you can't right every wrong. You're a great man, Cal, and I love you for it. But you aren't the reincarnation of Jesus Christ. No one could have done any better than you have. No one could have stopped the tragedy that just happened. It was bound to play out this way. If it hadn't happened tonight, it would have happened sooner or later. And at least now his death meant something. Dead men become saints, and their murderers become demons. Right now, thanks to him, there are hundreds of Trads who are completely disgusted by the violence of their fellow villagers and are eager to honor the reverend's dying wish and make peace with Big City. And besides all of that, Cal, let's not forget that you single-handedly prevented a war. You also made that wonderfully cheesy film about Big City that helped the Trads to see us as regular people. You did that, Calvin. If it hadn't been for you, most of the Trads would be dead right now — the reverend included. And many of our own friends would be dead as well. Tonight was a tragedy, but it surely doesn't lie at your feet."

Before Calvin could respond, Ariel interrupted. "I apologize for ruining the moment, you two. And for what it is worth, Calvin, I agree with Tarpa. You have performed with at least 94% effectiveness these last few days. No one could have done better. But that is not important right now. I am sorry to say that Victoria has just stormed out of her home. She undoubtedly did not take the news of her father's death well. The men lost her in the dark, but I can still track her. She appears to be cutting through the woods, heading down the steep hills that separate the road as it winds back and forth down the mountain. I think she is heading here."

Calvin stopped pacing. He and Tarpa looked at each other. Tarpa said, "You go fill up the car, and I'll get some blankets and a thermos of hot tea. It's a cold night tonight; she's going to be freezing when we find her."

Calvin hugged his wife while saying, "God, I love you." He then ran out of the front door and into the garage to get the car ready.

CHAPTER 29

Victoria was on the road to Big City. She had leaves and twigs in her hair, and her dress was dirty and torn. She had lost a shoe in the mud and had kicked the other one angrily into the dark.

She was developing a headache from crying too much. Her feet would have been sore if they were not numb from the cold. A part of her wanted to stop walking and curl up into a ball in the woods and cry herself to sleep. But a bigger part of her needed love and comfort and could only think of one place to find it. She hugged herself and shivered as a cold breeze blew past her. Despite all of this, she kept putting one foot in front of the other.

Victoria walked for another twenty minutes, but it felt like days to her. Her whole body was shaking violently from the cold. She finally realized that she could no longer possibly continue. She found a soft patch of greenery in the woods to lie down in and covered herself the best she could with leaves. She also turned out her lamp, being fearful of falling asleep and starting a fire with it.

For another five minutes, Victoria sat in the dark. She was cold and impossibly alone. Her father was gone. She could not fully get her mind around that. She wanted to see him, to talk to him, to hug him. She murmured in the darkness, "Daddy, I love you. I want to go home."

No matter what she tried, she could not warm up at all. There was just too much wind. It's a terrible thing for a seven year old to contemplate her own death, but Victoria was starting to feel so lost, hopeless, cold, and alone that she was beginning to wish for it.

As she grasped blindly around her for more foliage to pile on top of herself, she was startled by an angry roar and two dim lights approaching from down the road. The roaring quickly increased and the lights grew brighter. Victoria hid under the leaves and started to shake more from fear now than from the cold.

The roaring stopped just beside her and settled into a low, unsteady burble. Victoria held her breath and tried without success to force herself to be still. She could hear something approaching from the road and was absolutely terrified.

But then she heard a familiar voice call out, "Victoria, it's me, Uncle Calvin. I've come to get you." She felt strong arms gently pick her up and hold her against a warm body. Now completely out of tears, Victoria merely whimpered with relief and continued to shake in Calvin's arms.

Calvin and Tarpa wrapped Victoria in blankets and made her comfortable in the back seat. Then they quickly found the men who were searching for Victoria and informed them that she was OK.

The men argued against them taking Victoria at first, but conceded after Calvin looked each of them in the eye and said, "You've seen the video, haven't you? If you can name anyone else who will show this little girl more love and caring right now, then I'll gladly hand her over to them."

The men each thought about what they had witnessed on the video. The taller of the two men tipped his hat to Calvin and said, "Very well, sir. As you wish. There'll be a service for the reverend tomorrow. I'd be obliged if you brought the little girl back to say goodbye to her pa."

"Of course," answered Calvin. "We aren't kidnapping her. We'll bring her back to the village tomorrow. We just want her to be safe and warm tonight, that's all."

The man looked relieved. Then, to Tarpa's surprise, the shorter man took off his hat and held it in front of him. He looked Tarpa directly in the eyes and said, "Ma'am, I just wanted to say, well, what you did for that little girl, I don't reckon even half the men I know would have done it."

He shuffled his feet in thought and added, "I guess what I'm trying to say is that you're all right in my book. God bless you, ma'am."

Tarpa glanced back at the bundled-up Victoria in the back seat and said, "I just did what felt natural."

The shorter man nodded, and both of them backed away from the car and waved as Calvin and Tarpa drove toward home. The shorter man turned to the taller one and said, "They ain't half bad folk."

The taller man shook his head. "No, I reckon they're right decent, all things considered. They talk funny, mind you, but they ain't half bad all the same."

CHAPTER 30

Mike stood up at the small breakfast table and addressed Bobford3 the moment he walked through the door of the kitchen.

He said, "As the most eloquent member of our team, Sarah will now issue our formal apology on behalf of all of us. Sarah, if you will."

Mike sat down and Sarah stood up. She softly cleared her voice and then recited the following poem:

> It was an honest mistake
> I'm sure you'll agree
> So there is no reason
> for the third degree
> We launched some sand
> into the night so starry
> and for that, Bobford3
> we are all so sorry
> It won't happen again
> you have our word
> so please don't kill us
> our boss, Mister Bobford

Bobford3 picked up the argon laser that he frequently used for cutting and toasting sandwiches and fidgeted with it absentmindedly for a few seconds while he thought.

The other three in the room suddenly looked very nervous

and tensed their muscles in preparation to dive under the table or out of the door should Bobford3 suddenly go berserk.

Mercifully, Bobford3 set the laser back on the counter. He turned to his team and said, "Somebody tell me some good news about the project. I know you were all working on it until late in the night. What's the status?"

The team members all glanced at each other, as if silently voting on who would speak. Both Sarah and Brody looked to Mike. Mike grimaced at them for a second and then answered on behalf of the team.

"Things are going well, Bob. As you know, the..." Mike cleared his throat, "...hole was permanently repaired and all systems are back online. We spent the better part of the night fixing the centrifuge. We did a couple of very slow speed tests this time and gradually worked our way up to full speed, minding the unit of measure this time around, of course." He cleared his throat again and glanced at Brody.

"We also managed to get the heating and electrostatic elements functioning perfectly. All that is left is to install the quantum entanglement generator and sync the centrifuge with the collider. I'd say it's just a matter of a week or two before we have the whole system ready for a trial run."

Bobford3 looked pleased. "Well done, you three. Carry on as planned... with all due caution of course." He eyed Brody for a second and then continued, "I'm going to be busy in the genetics lab for the next few days. If you need me for anything, I'll be there."

Bobford3 gave them all a friendly wave and left the room. Mike and Brody looked at each other. Mike said, "Well, that went better than I thought."

Brody nodded. "For sure, bro. I thought we were toast."

Mike then turned to Sarah and said, "Well done, Sarah. I think your poem softened him up. Good job."

Sarah nodded and said, "I'm glad I was helpful." She then went back to her work on the Ariel system, or, as far as the guys could tell, staring at the wall.

CHAPTER 31

Arnold stood in front of a large screen in his living room and pondered the information that it was displaying. Amusingly, Ariel (or at least her avatar as represented by Arnold's Guide) was standing beside him with a similar look of concentration on her face.

They were studying the current status of Bobford3's alchemy project. Arnold had been following their progress closely since the beginning of the project. Of course, back then, he could barely even spell 'quantum,' but thanks to Ariel's patient tutelage, he was rapidly getting up to speed.

Arnold looked at Ariel while he formed his next question to her. She was wearing a white lab coat and glasses in an effort to look the part.

Outside of the fair, Ariel was limiting her use of an avatar because the human's would sometimes get unduly attached to her. This was a phenomenon that she did not fully understand, so she felt it best to limit her avatar usage while she studied the effect on Calvin, who had been listed in her databanks as a human test subject.

Arnold, however, seemed only interested in her knowledge. He simply liked to have a body to talk to, otherwise he said he felt like a damn fool talking to himself. He had a very limited knowledge of science, but he learned fast and his mind was surprisingly sharp, so Ariel had felt that it would be worth the risk of using the avatar with Arnold if it would help to bring out the best in him.

CHAPTER 32

Funeral services were held for the three dead men the day after they had died. Out of respect for each of them, the memorials were held at separate times to give each man his proper due.

Brother Smith's and Brother Grimm's services had already been performed. Unfortunately for Smith, hardly anyone outside of his family had shown up for him. Many more had shown up to grieve for Brother Grimm. However, the entire village was now assembling to say farewell to Reverend Smelcheck.

Just as services began, three more people joined the gathering and sat at the end of the very last pew. Two of them were outsiders, although all three were dressed in the traditional mourning clothes of the village. A few of the surrounding people expressed surprise upon noticing them, but the outsiders merely nodded respectfully and gave their full attention to the ongoing eulogy.

A man was standing in front of the open casket containing Reverend Smelcheck's body while he delivered the eulogy. He had been the reverend's understudy for several years, and was working hard to hold back tears as he praised the life of his mentor.

"We are gathered here today to honor the life, and mourn the loss, of Reverend Augustus Smelcheck."

Calvin and Tarpa looked at each other and simultaneously mouthed the word "Augustus" with questioning looks. Victoria sat quietly between them and listened to the eulogy while feeling very detached, as if she were watching all of this happen to someone else.

The orator continued, "From very early in life, Reverend Smelcheck was attracted to religion. The very first book he read was the Bible, and his very first toy he had was a cross that he had made himself from two sticks and a length of vine.

"The older ones here can probably remember the young reverend running gleefully around the village with that cross in one hand, and a glass of water in the other. Oh, the joy on his face as he would jump out from behind the bushes and bless passersby with holy water, and chase away their demons with the cross."

An old lady called out from near the front of the church, "I remember that. It was hotter-n-hell that summer, and suddenly getting a glass of water dumped over your head was a blessing indeed."

The congregation laughed. The orator smiled and continued, "Later in life, Reverend Smelcheck met the love of his life, Miss Mary Grimm, sister to the recently deceased Brother Grimm, god bless his soul."

The orator made the sign of the cross and continued, "The reverend and Mary had tremendous love and respect for each other. It wasn't long after they had met that they were wed, and Mary delivered their beautiful daughter, Victoria."

The orator suddenly stopped and looked around the room. "Has anyone seen young Vicky. Is she here?"

Calvin patted Victoria on her knee and said, "It's OK, sweetie. Stand up for a moment. There's a good girl."

Victoria nervously stood up. The orator saw her, pointed her out with an outstretched arm, and said, "There you are, my dear child. We are all so very sorry about the loss of your father. I know that no one will ever fill the void in your heart left by your father's departure from this world, but the people of this village are all your family and we love you very much. We will do all we can to see that you are taken care of."

Victoria felt very self-conscious as hundreds of faces turned to look at her with pity. She tried to bear it, but eventually she had to sit down and cover her face with her hands while bending over to avoid the stares.

Calvin put a friendly arm around her. He then whispered in her ear, "I'm sorry, sweetie. I know this is all too much for you right now. Stay like that as long as you like. Everyone understands."

The orator tactfully drew the attention away from Victoria by continuing his speech. "Unfortunately for the reverend, the joy of the birth of his daughter was marred by the death of his beloved wife, who died of complications after child birth. Left to be the sole parent, the reverend made certain to show his daughter enough love for two people. And while he might have stumbled along the way, no man here can deny that he tried every day to be the best parent that he could."

Victoria heard this and started to sob into her lap. Tarpa gently rubbed her back.

"Besides raising young Victoria, in a way, the reverend raised us all. We looked to him to settle our disputes when we fought amongst ourselves like brothers and sisters. We asked his advice whenever we lost our way in life. And recently, we turned to him for guidance when faced with the ever-increasing threat to the east. The reverend warned us that the Progs were growing stronger. He warned us that we were in ever-increasing danger of being attacked."

The orator paused for effect and then added, "But then a funny thing happened." He motioned again in the direction of Victoria and said, "Twice now, the people who the reverend had thought of as his enemy have saved his daughter's life."

Most of the church turned around to look at Calvin and Tarpa. Calvin gave a weak wave and then lowered his gaze, not knowing how to respond. Tarpa continued to stare fixedly at the orator while rubbing Victoria's back.

"In this time of Victoria's greatest grief, who comforts her now but the two that we know of as 'the devil boy' and 'the witch'. It turned out that our beloved reverend, our father in spirit, had led us astray. But being the great man that he was, he was able to come to terms with his mistake and work to make it right.

"Unfortunately, some of us refuse to believe that the reverend could have made a mistake. To them, I say, how dare you expect any man to be as great as God. Reverend Smelcheck was surely a great man, but he was still a man nonetheless. Let us not disgrace him by blindly following the doctrine that he died trying to undo. Instead, let us honor him by following the example of these three people in the back row. Let us protect and love even those who we once had thought of as our enemies."

Calvin and Tarpa both teared up slightly after hearing this, but they each denied it later on. All around the church could be heard the sound of noses being blown.

The orator then walked over to the body of Reverend Smelcheck, knelt in front of it, and paid his respects. Soon after, others formed a line and did the same.

Calvin put an arm around Victoria and said, "When my grandfather was on his deathbed, he insisted that us grandkids were not to see him after he died. He wanted us to remember him the way he was when he was alive. Other people feel it is proper to say your final goodbyes. I didn't know your father well enough to know his wishes, so I will leave the choice up to you. Do you want to say goodbye to your father?"

Victoria nodded.

Calvin nodded back and said, "OK, then." He stood up and took Victoria's hand. Tarpa contemplated for a second whether or not to join them. She really had nothing to say to the reverend — she had hardly known him after all. On the other hand, she thought that it was important right now to project a loving family image, so she stood up as well and followed Calvin and Victoria to the end of the queue.

To Calvin's surprise, several people made it a point to come over to them and either shake their hands or pat them on the shoulder while saying, "Bless you." Most of them would then kneel down in front of Victoria and give her a hug. It was really very touching.

When it was their turn to see the reverend, Calvin encouraged Victoria to go first. She nodded and hesitantly walked up to the casket. She had never seen a dead person before and did not know what to expect. It all seemed a little creepy to her.

She approached the casket and cautiously peered inside. The man inside the casket looked a little like her father, but it was not him. In fact, what was in there no longer looked like a real person to her at all. Whatever part of it that had been her father was clearly missing. Still, it was obvious that the adults expected her to do something now, so she closed her eyes and said in the privacy of her own mind, "Goodbye, Daddy. You were a good daddy. I will miss you forever."

When she opened her eyelids, several tears spilled down her cheeks. She made the sign of the cross like she had seen the adults do and walked back to Calvin and Tarpa. Tarpa took her hand while Calvin said his final goodbyes.

Calvin knelt down in front of the reverend and said in his own head, "I'm sorry, Reverend. I fucked up. I should have stayed and helped you. I'm sorry. But I promise you that I will keep Victoria safe for you. And I will do my best to see our plan through to the end. If there really is life after death, feel free to pull some strings for me, would you? I could use all the help I can get. Anyway, I'm holding up the line. There are so many people here who loved you and want to say goodbye. Take care, my friend."

Calvin stood up and gave one last nod to the reverend before rejoining Victoria and his wife. As one unit, they silently slipped through the crowd and left the church.

CHAPTER 33

Kevin6 pulled into a parking space at Myst Village and said, "OK, ladies, we're here. Thanks for taking the ride with me today. I hope we can all have fun together."

In fact, Myst Village had not been Kevin6's first choice today, or even his second. He had really wanted to let off some steam in downtown Newark, but Ariel had absolutely forbidden him from going. She had also flatly denied his request to race cars at Racetrax. So now it was down to Myst Village.

Kevin6 and the girls installed their display lenses. The girls' lenses snapped into their eye sockets while Kevin6's were more old fashioned and looked like the sort of sunglasses the secret service are popularly portrayed as wearing. They connected to the PC behind his ear via a curly length of wire, which added to the effect.

Today, Kevin6 was wearing tan shorts and a white t-shirt. The women were also wearing shorts and t-shirts, but their shirts were the familiar red and blue colors that they had become known for.

They walked for about a mile until they found a small building. It looked to be a temple of some sort and had a puzzle on the door consisting of several shapes that needed to be slid around the door into a special pattern before the door would unlock.

Sharon tried the puzzle first. She took her time and moved the pieces around with care and forethought. After two minutes of this, Lucinda nudged her aside and said, "This is going to take all day. Let me do it."

Sharon protested, "but I nearly had it. I was two moves away." Unfortunately, Lucinda was already flicking the shapes around the door with reckless abandon. Sharon shook her head and took a step back.

After a minute of futility, Lucinda became visibly annoyed. Kevin6 noticed this and said, "Lucinda, dear, I think I see the answer now. If you could just stop for a minute, I think we can work this out together."

Lucinda stopped her assault on the puzzle and took a step back. She glanced at Kevin6 and said, "No need, Mr. Bacon. I've had training in lateral thinking. The goal is to gain access into this shrine, am I right?"

"Yes..." answered Kevin6 hesitantly, suspecting what was about to happen.

Lucinda nodded and looked back at the door. With a graceful spin and a kick, the stone door shattered inward and fell off the hinges. Lucinda picked up the largest piece of it and threw it aside as if it were made from paper mache. She dusted off her hands and said, "There you go — job done." She had a very smug look on her face.

"Oh, very good," snapped Sharon. "You just broke the game. Well done, you ape."

Lucinda inhaled in preparation to deliver a stream of obscenities. Kevin6 quickly moved between them and said, "Tut tut tut tut," in order to head off the inevitable tirade. He held his hands out to each side, palms out, and said, "OK, enough, you two. Sharon, apologize to Lucinda right now."

Sharon muttered, "I'm sorry I called you an ape."

"What was that?" asked Lucinda while cupping her hand around her ear dramatically.

"I said, I'm sorry for calling you an ape, you fucking pig!"

"Who are you calling a pig, you sappy little bitch!?!"

"Enough!" shouted Kevin6.

"Sorry, Mr. Bacon," said the two in unison.

Kevin6 shook his head. "Maybe we should just call it a day."

"No, Mr. Bacon. I'm sorry. I'll behave," pleaded Sharon.

"Don't do that sir. We'll watch ourselves from here on out," added Lucinda.

Kevin6 thought in silence for a moment while the other two held their breath. Finally, he said, "OK, let's keep going."

He pushed aside some rubble and found a map inside the

shrine. It showed the way to the next puzzle. He held it up and said, "OK, let's follow this for a bit."

They walked some way until they encountered a bridge that spanned a deep ravine. They were just about to cross it when a short, shaggy, old man seemingly sprang out of thin air and blocked their path. There was a sudden mist and a surge of lightning. Kevin6 was knocked unconscious.

When he awoke several minutes later, the mist was gone, and so was the old man. The two angels were kneeling beside him while he lay flat on the ground. They both looked very worried.

Lucinda was the first to speak. "I am so sorry, Mr. Bacon. He just sprang out of nowhere. How was I to know he was only a hologram?"

"I'm sorry too, sir. I didn't mean to gas you like that. It was just reflex."

Kevin6 sniffed. "Do you smell that? It's like... burnt hair?"

Lucinda looked down at the ground and said, "Um, sorry sir... that's your hair, I'm afraid. I sort of, well, electrocuted you by mistake. I'm terribly sorry."

Kevin6 felt his hair. It was mostly still there, but slightly crispy along the edges. Then he said, "You know what? I think I'm done playing this game for today."

CHAPTER 34

Victoria was chasing a butterfly around the garden while Tarpa and Calvin unpacked lunch. It had been nearly two weeks since her father's funeral, and while she was not completely back to her old self, she was at least getting more cheerful by the day.

So far, things were also peaceful between the Trads and the Progs. Calvin had been able to convince the community leaders of Big City that changes were taking place among the Trads, and that they were definitely not planning any more attacks.

Along these lines, Calvin had decided to ride the current wave of peace and good will by sponsoring another fair. His stated reason for doing so had been to make up for the previous one that had inadvertently been cut short. This was true, of course, but he also saw it as an opportunity to invite a dozen or two key Trads and expose them to Ariel and the Guides. With any luck, he would soon have several ambassadors to help spread the gospel of Ariel among the Trads.

Calvin watched as Victoria finally captured the butterfly between cupped hands. She held it captive for a few seconds and then slowly opened her hands to let it out.

The butterfly twitched its wings experimentally but remained on Victoria's hand for several more seconds. Victoria used the opportunity to give it a closer inspection. When she did, the butterfly hopped onto her nose and made her stumble backwards into a melon patch.

Victoria giggled as she stood back up. The butterfly was a few feet away, as if taunting her to play another game of tag.

Calvin was pleased to see that Victoria was not the least bit upset and had no thought of hurting the butterfly, only to play with it and admire it. She really was a good girl.

This was fortunate, because as near as Calvin could work out, he and Tarpa were now her legal guardians. Of course, there was no cohesive legal system on Evionia, so maybe the correct way to put it is that they were now her guardians, and no one else seemed to have a problem with that.

Calvin and Tarpa had never intended for this to happen, at least not consciously, but on the day that they were meant to take her back to the village, it had been clear that neither Calvin nor Tarpa had wanted to give her up. So when Victoria herself had thrown a tantrum at the idea of parting ways, that was all it had taken for Calvin and Tarpa to nod knowingly at each other and put away their coats.

Tarpa finished setting the plates and called Victoria over to eat lunch. Calvin watched her with mild annoyance as she approached the table with a bird perched on her shoulder. He had always disliked birds for some reason and thought of them as dim-witted pooping machines. He gestured toward the bird and said, "I think he's got his own food. Maybe he can go play somewhere else while we eat."

Victoria took the hint and whispered a word to the bird, which pecked her lightly on the cheek and then flew lazily away in the direction of Calvin's recently washed car.

Calvin never ceased to be impressed by Victoria's amazing power over animals. But he had really been surprised when Victoria was first introduced to the garden.

That day, Victoria had stridden straight up to the perimeter while shrugging off the flurry of warnings that both Calvin and Tarpa had been calling out. And to their collective amazement, the plants had parted ways for her in the same way that they would for Tarpa, but without the benefit of her special bio-engineered perfume.

Calvin's current theory was that Victoria could somehow control anything with a dim intelligence, which seemed to include Tarpa's carnivorous plant life. He wondered how far up the food chain something had to be before she could no longer control it. He then briefly thought about how surprisingly fond he and Tarpa were of her, but quickly dismissed that thought as silly. Victoria was kind, well-mannered, and cute — there was no need for mind control when it came to loving her. Besides that, her ability seemed to be rooted more in basic communication than it did in control.

The three of them sat quietly and ate lunch while enjoying the weather. Like many of the days in Big City, today was a beautiful, sunny day with mild temperatures and just enough of a breeze to keep the air fresh.

Calvin chewed thoughtfully, swallowed, and asked, "So, what do you girls want to do today?"

The two girls shrugged and continued eating. As far as they were both concerned, sitting in the garden while sipping tea was among the best things that life had to offer and neither one was eager to do anything else at the moment.

Calvin, however, was rapidly growing into the role of father-figure, which meant that he now somehow felt that it was his responsibility to schedule every minute of the family's free time. With this goal in mind, he said brightly, "How about we go to the park? We could feed the ducks and play some Frisbee?"

Tarpa and Victoria looked at each other and rolled their eyes. Tarpa sent Victoria the following message:

Tarpa: Oh brother.

Victoria giggled but could not write back secretly using her bear-eared Guide since it required her to dictate the message.

Tarpa then wrote:

Tarpa: He's cute, though, isn't he? How about we humor him and go to the park? You could make the ducks chase him around. That would be fun, wouldn't it?

Victoria laughed again and nodded.

Calvin asked, "What are you two conspiring about now?"

Tarpa smiled and said, "Nothing."

Victoria smiled too and said, "We can go to the park later, Uncle Calvin."

Tarpa added, "It's a good idea, sport, but let's take things easy today. For now, how about we just eat lunch and enjoy the garden?"

"Yes, dear," answered Calvin automatically.

"Good boy," said Victoria. She looked at Tarpa and giggled.

Calvin also looked at Tarpa. "You told her to say that, didn't you?" he asked.

Tarpa merely smiled in return.

CHAPTER 35

"You sure are dressed all spiffy today, devil boy," said a random stranger to Calvin as he walked through the fairgrounds.

Calvin stopped and studied the stranger. Judging by her plain and rather drab clothing, Calvin correctly guessed that she was one of the visiting Trads, so he gave her some extra attention.

Calvin took a step back, held his arms out to his sides, and spun around once to show off his outfit. He put his arms back down and said, "You like it? It's actually a copy of something I saw in a movie long ago. Oh, and you can call me Calvin."

The woman looked confused. Suddenly, Ariel incarnated from specs of dust in the air and addressed her.

"Movies are moving picture shows similar to the one that the reverend played for you a month ago. They tell a story by the use of actors who pretend to be characters from the story."

"Like a play?" asked the woman.

"Very similar," replied Ariel.

"Thank you, Ariel. You're a gem," said the woman, who then pointed to Calvin and asked, "So who is he meant to be, then, in that fancy getup of his?"

Ariel pretended to look Calvin up and down and said, "The owner of a chocolate factory, I believe."

The woman studied Calvin's appearance again. After a moment of reflection she shook her head and walked away, muttering, "Strange folks in these parts."

Calvin turned to Ariel and said, "I think that went well, how about you?"

Ariel replied, "She did not spit on you, so I would call that a win." She smiled at him and then disappeared into a whirling cloud of sparkles.

"I think you rather enjoy being incarnate, don't you?" asked Calvin to the empty air.

Ariel reassembled in the exact reverse of the way she had just disappeared and replied, "I have no emotions, so I do not enjoy it, but I do find it interesting. People treat me differently when they are addressing this avatar."

Calvin looked again at the representation of Ariel that he had helped to create — a graceful fairytale princess with the beauty of a model and the grace of a queen — and replied, "Yes, well, to most people your avatar is sort of..." he searched for the right words "...awe inspiring. You, I mean this persona you are simulating, it's... I don't know how to explain it. It's like, looking at you, people think of royalty, wisdom, grace, and beauty. They are instantly enamored with you."

Ariel smiled and replied, "Is that why you had me appear with fairy wings and dance around the garden the other day? Are you enamored with me, Calvin?"

Calvin looked around nervously and said, "That was just a test, alright? Let's say no more about it."

"As you wish," replied Ariel.

"Anyway," continued Calvin, "I think it's for the best that you don't get too flirty with everyone. You should try to impress them with your brain and not your body."

Ariel looked back at him with a slightly tilted head and said, "OK, Calvin, I will try your suggestion and report back to you with the results." She blew him a kiss and once again burst into sparkles.

Calvin shook his head and continued walking the fairgrounds. The girls were off having fun together somewhere else, most likely riding the pigs. They had agreed to give him a few hours alone so that he could try to build up a rapport with the visiting Trads.

Calvin was glad that the two were getting along so well, but a little part of him was just a bit jealous — he wanted Victoria to be a daddy's girl after all. Still, it made him smile to see his two girls so happy together. A loving home was obviously good for Victoria, but Calvin suspected that Tarpa was also benefiting positively from the new arrangement.

Calvin walked on until he arrived at one of a handful of

booths that were being manned by a Trad. He was selling glassware, and his booth was populated with dozens of shelves filled with the most beautiful items.

One side of the booth had useful things like knives, forks, spoons, plates, cups, vases, window glass, etc. The other side of the booth, and the surprisingly more popular one, had decorative items such as dolphins made of a rich, blue glass that caught the light in such a way that the dolphins almost glowed. There were also delicate crystal fairies that were so lovely that they almost made Ariel's avatar look plain, and large birds with sweeping wings that made Calvin think of Native American artwork.

Calvin stood on his toes from behind the large crowd and peered into the booth. He saw a youngish man hustling back and forth between customers. The man had a young boy with him, most likely his son, who was collecting the payments from the customers and running them over to the large wagon parked outside.

The wagon was about ten feet long and six or seven feet wide. It was rapidly filling up with completely random items from Big City — everything from toilet paper to video machines. Calvin saw this and thought to himself, I need to get Ariel fully in place very soon because this barter business is going to become rather burdensome. I wonder how on Earth I'm going to convince everyone to give up money and barter? Hmm. Well, that's a problem for another time.

For now, Calvin was pleased that the Trads seemed to have gotten the hang of using the Guides with a minimum of fuss. He had half expected shouts of "Witchcraft!" when Ariel had started her little show for them that morning, but instead they had acted much the same as the citizen's of Big City had — in awe, but without a trace of fear.

He could only guess that the avatar he had created for Ariel was serving its purpose. This was certainly true, but what he did not know was that the Trads, who had spent years imagining all the strange and wonderful things that the heathens of Big City could create, felt that a magical fairy girl was pretty much par for the course.

As Calvin turned to leave the booth, an older man approached him with an outstretched arm. The man said, "I'm Reverend Thompson. We never formally met, but we saw each other at the funeral for Reverend Smelcheck."

Calvin smiled at him and shook his hand. "Yes, I remember

you — you gave the eulogy, correct?"

Thompson nodded.

Calvin continued, "That was a fantastic speech, Reverend. I think Reverend Smelcheck would be very proud of you. And personally, I have to give you my thanks and my respect as well. You helped to make all this possible." Calvin gestured first toward the glass maker selling his wares, and then to a cluster of four teenage kids — two Trads and two Progs — who were chatting amiably as they walked together around the fair while pointing out interesting booths to one another.

The reverend nodded appreciatively.

Calvin then asked, "So, how are things going in the village? Are things starting to quiet down?"

"Oh yes," replied the reverend. "Things are mostly back to normal. There's still a few thick heads running around, but you'll get that anywhere, don't you know."

"Very true," agreed Calvin. "Well, I look forward to working with you. Hopefully between the two of us, we can keep the thick heads to a minimum."

"Agreed. I'm happy to make your acquaintance, Mr. Jones, and I look forward to working with you as well. Give my regards to the misses."

"I'll do that," agreed Calvin.

The two men shook hands and parted ways. As Thompson disappeared among the crowd, Ariel appeared again in an implosion of sparkles.

"That was great, Calvin. No spit yet again. Well done."

Calvin stuck his tongue out at her.

"I have the results of my experiment, would you like to hear them?" asked Ariel.

"Experiment?" questioned Calvin.

Ariel gave a delicate nod. "Yes, you said that I should try to impress people with my brains and not my body. To that end, I picked a random sample of twenty people of mixed age and gender. I then picked an additional twenty people with approximately the same demographics. To the first group, I tried to teach them the basics of quantum mechanics, while to the other, I simply smiled and winked at them. I'm afraid, Calvin, that you were wrong — the second group was much more receptive to me."

Before Calvin could argue, Ariel suddenly sprouted fairy wings and flew away. As Calvin watched her open-mouthed, Ariel glanced back at him, and with a gleam in her eye she said, "See."

Calvin watched her fly away and said, "Oh my god, what have I created?"

"What are you staring at?" asked Tarpa from behind him.

Calvin jumped. "Hey, what? Me? Oh. Uh. Nothing. Nothing at all. Just thinking."

"OK, well, don't hurt yourself, sport."

"Ha-ha," replied Calvin. "So, are you two enjoying the fair so far?"

"Oh yes," replied Tarpa. She put her hand on Victoria's back and said, "Victoria, here, got the sheep to dance in a chorus line. You should have seen it." She tapped the side of her display lenses and said, "I recorded it for you so you can watch it later."

"Thanks, babe," replied Calvin as he looked around at the growing darkness. "It's almost time for the fireworks to start. Come along, you two — I have the perfect spot reserved."

Victoria asked, "What are fireworks?"

Calvin was about to answer when Ariel appeared in front of them with her usual flourish. She raised her hands up skyward and a few seconds of fireworks erupted in the night sky, at least in the eyes of Calvin, Tarpa, and Victoria. Ariel then said, "They are like that, Victoria, only with smoke and noise."

Victoria's face lit up. "I want to see the fireworks!"

"OK, then. Follow me," urged Calvin.

And because, to Calvin at least, Ariel had appeared with fairy wings, he silently texted to her:

Calvin: OK, knock it off with the wings, OK? You've made your point.

Ariel: As you wish, Calvin.

He watched as her wings shrunk down and disappeared. Surprisingly though, the rest of her had not. Instead, she walked along with them like a member of the family. Calvin was secretly suspicious as to why, but said nothing since the other two didn't seem to mind.

They made their way quickly to Calvin's secret spot, which turned out to be the top of the clock tower. He had three comfortable lawn chairs already arranged for them to lie on. Amusingly, Ariel made her own chair and lounged to the left of Calvin, while Tarpa and Victoria were off to his right.

Calvin motioned in her direction and asked, "Does anyone

else see her?"

Tarpa looked over at Ariel and said, "Yes, I do. She's not hurting anyone, and Victoria enjoys her company, so just leave her be."

Calvin thought about pointing out that Ariel would, in fact, be watching the fireworks from hundreds of Guides and several satellites simultaneously, and therefore did not, strictly speaking, have to be visible to do so. But then he thought the better of it and kept his mouth shut.

As if reading his thoughts, Ariel smiled at him and made a show of making herself comfortable on the chair.

Sure, he thought, let's all ride the bus to Crazy Town together.

Out loud, however, he said, "OK, then. Well, make yourself comfortable, Ariel, and, um, welcome to the family, I suppose."

Ariel answered, "Thank you, Calvin. Tell me, am I your sister, your daughter, your mistress, or perhaps..." she winked at him "...your fairy godmother?"

"You're my invisible friend who won't stay invisible," answered Calvin, coldly.

Tarpa interrupted, saying, "Are you sure you aren't cheating on me, Calvin? You two are bantering back and forth like an old married couple."

Calvin replied defensively, "I think she's using me as a guinea pig to learn what buttons to push."

Tarpa replied, "Well if you know that, then stop reacting to her." Tarpa then looked past Calvin at Ariel and said, "And you, Ariel, just so you know, Calvin's buttons are all mine, so if you don't want me to shoot down all of your satellites, then I suggest you turn the flirting down a notch, OK?"

Arial answered smoothly, "As you wish, Tarpa."

Tarpa nodded and sat back in her chair in anticipation of the fireworks that were due to start at any second.

Then, to Calvin's utter surprise, once Tarpa was no longer looking at her, Ariel made a face and stuck her tongue out at Tarpa.

Calvin chuckled despite himself. Fortunately for both of them, his laughter was masked by the first few pops of the fireworks.

CHAPTER 36

Bobford3 cautiously immersed his hand into the two pounds of ultra-fine powder that had just been presented to him by his three juniors. He grasped a handful of it and examined it closely. After a moment he said, "It's moon dust. What of it?"

Mike shook his head and said, "Guess again."

Bobford3 looked at it again as he rubbed it between his fingers. Eventually he said, "I'm sorry, but it looks like moon dust to me."

Mike and Brody looked at each other, and then Mike waved his hand for Bobford3 to follow him while saying, "I'll show you. Come with us."

They walked into a nearby lab where Mike carefully spooned a few grams of the powder into a regular, lab-grade crucible and turned on the heater beneath it. After a few minutes, the powder melted and pooled together into a silvery liquid. At that point, Mike turned off the heater and turned on the cooler. A few minutes after that, Mike presented Bobford3 with the result.

Bobford3 took the silvery blob in his hand and hefted it a few times while trying to judge the weight. Then a smile crept across his face and he said, "No way."

Brody said, "Way."

Mike said, "Way."

Sarah said, "It's aluminum. We got the transmuter to work."

Bobford3 asked, "Why is it in powder form? I thought the process took place at melting temperatures."

Mike pointed a thumb at Sarah and said, "Miss Random

Thoughts over here realized that the moon dust was fine enough to act as a fluid on its own, so there was no need to waste the extra energy to heat it to the melting point."

Bobford3 looked at each of them in turn and said, "I love you guys."

CHAPTER 37

Calvin, Tarpa, and Victoria arrived home from a secret trip to the remote island where there shuttle was hidden. However, they had not gone to use the shuttle but rather to pick up some supplies that had been delivered by probe from Earth the night before.

Among these supplies were a breakfast cereal that Calvin was fond of, some shampoo for Tarpa, and several varieties of plants — also for Tarpa.

Calvin opened the trunk of his car and grabbed a handful of potted plants. He turned to Tarpa and asked, "Where do you want these?"

"Just put them in the shed for now. Vicky and I will plant them in the garden tomorrow."

"OK."

Now with a destination in mind, Calvin carried the plants around to the back of the house and into the shed. As he placed the last plant on the floor, a robed figure appeared behind him. It picked up a nearby ax and hefted it menacingly above its head.

Still bent over, Calvin blindly kicked behind him with brutal force. He spun around in time to see the robed figure fly out of the shed and land on his back with a very solid thud. Calvin immediately grabbed the ax and held it up for the figure to see.

"Start talking or I start chopping," said Calvin with a grin. "Let's start with who the fuck you are, and then move on to why the fuck you are trying to kill me. And if you're feeling lucky, you can finish with why the fuck I shouldn't kill you right now."

The robed figure cautiously moved his hands up to his hood and pulled it back. Calvin said, "Oh my fucking god."

The man, who looked very much like Jesus Christ to Calvin, said, "Do not blaspheme in front of your God."

Calvin said, "Go on, pull the other one — it's got bells on."

The man claiming to be Jesus sat up. "I do not take you for a fool. I am the son of God."

"Yeah, well I'm an atheist," replied Calvin.

"But the proof is right before you," protested the man.

"All I see before me," argued Calvin, "is a disheveled man in a robe that, frankly, could use a shower, a shave, and a haircut."

The man frowned and then held his hands in front of him about a foot apart. With a look of concentration on his face, sparks started to jump back and forth between the hands.

"Oh, very nice," said Calvin, "but as Arthur C. Clarke used to say, any sufficiently advanced technology is indistinguishable from magic. The Trads don't understand how I can shoot fire from my arm, but you don't see me claiming to be the son of Satan. What else do you got?"

The man looked annoyed. "What do you want from me — a miracle?"

Calvin laughed. "Well, yes, in fact."

The man thought for a moment. While he was thinking, Tarpa came around the corner of the house carrying a potted plant. She stopped cold when she saw the two of them.

"What the hell is going on here?" she asked.

Calvin answered brightly, "Oh, honey, come over here and meet someone."

Tarpa walked over and stood beside her husband. Calvin continued, "Let me do the introductions. Tarpa, this is Jesus. Jesus can make sparks between his hands. And Jesus, this is Tarpa. She can make sparks between her..."

Calvin was cut short by a sharp nudge in the ribs by Tarpa's elbow.

Calvin groaned and continued, "Anyway, this shady looking guy is the person who has been trying to kill me these last several weeks."

-SMASH-

The vision of the man claiming to be Jesus suddenly went dark. Pottery shards lay scattered around him, and a clump of soil rested on his head with two purple flowers protruding from it.

The sight put Calvin in mind of a cartoon, and he half expected to see birds circling around the man's head. He turned, awestruck, to Tarpa and asked, "Did you really just knock out Jesus with a bowl of petunias?"

CHAPTER 38

Kevin6 stood in front of the wall-length window that spanned the dining room of his cruise ship. He gazed upon the moon's reflection as it undulated on the surface of the Alaskan waters. In the distance, he could just make out the snow-capped peaks of a craggy landscape.

He was once again wearing his white tux, and his two female companions were each wearing very elegant evening dresses in their respective blue and red.

It had been a few weeks since their last outing together. In the intermediate time, Kevin6 had busied himself with books and television. But not wishing to become a couch potato, he had decided to give his two escorts another try.

While shopping around for a destination, Ariel had suggested an Alaskan cruise. Kevin6 had thought this was a wonderful idea and had asked Ariel to arrange matters for him.

In the interest of security, Ariel had arranged for a very special voyage on a ship without a captain, staff, or any other guests. The ship would be fully automated.

Kevin6 had felt sure that this arrangement would be the perfect formula for relaxation — after all, there would be no one to guard him from, and nothing to compete for, so his two Dark Angels would surely be able to relax and get along. That had been his hope, at least. But he had been wrong.

To his right, Lucinda was leaning behind him while addressing Sharon thusly:

"Why don't you wander off to bed now, Sharon. You look as

if you could use some beauty sleep."

To his left, Sharon was leaning behind him while answering Lucinda thusly:

"Eat shit, you pig."

Kevin6 pinched the bridge of his nose and said in exasperation, "Ladies, we've been over this a hundred times. Your constant arguing is killing my good mood. In fact, I'm so annoyed right now that I'm about to order you both off the ship. I apologize for losing my temper, but can you two please knock it the fuck off already?"

To this, Lucinda said, "I'm sure that Sharon is sorry, Mr. Bacon. You know how crabby she gets when it's past her bedtime. She's like a big baby, really."

Sharon, now enraged, replied, "OK, I've had enough of your shit — let's do this!"

Kevin6 never had a chance to say anything before the room was filled with poison, electricity, missiles, bullets, piano wire, flying cutlery, flying glassware, flying chairs, flying tables, flying people, and over two hundred angry wasps, which were also flying.

When two Alaskan fishermen sifted through the wreckage of the washed-up cruise ship the next morning, they found three heavily mutilated bodies dressed in red, white, and blue.

CHAPTER 39

Jesus, or at least the man claiming to be so, woke up with a bad headache. He was not happy about that. He was also bound by his hands and feet to a tree, which he was definitely not happy about.

As his eyes began to focus, the first thing he saw was Calvin's concerned face peering at him from a few feet away. His focus then shifted further into the background where it settled on Tarpa, who was smiling and waving at him while she held a flower pot in the other hand with surprising menace.

His focus snapped back onto Calvin as he said, "I'm sorry about the ropes. Still, it could be worse." He pointed a thumb over his shoulder and added, "She wanted to put you on a cross."

Tarpa gave the man another friendly wave and a smile.

Calvin then asked politely, "OK, mister, let's hear what you have to say. Why are you trying to kill me?"

The man considered his options. He was well aware of Tarpa and her capabilities, but he also knew that his own powers were considerable and he could most definitely defeat her. However, there was something about the way she was smiling at him that planted a rather large seed of doubt in the soil of his mind. In the end, he decided to talk.

"Whether or not you believe me is irrelevant. I am Jesus, the son of God. It was my father who has sent me on this rather peculiar errand..."

"Hold on a minute," interrupted Calvin. "Are you telling me

that God — the big guy upstairs — sent you personally to come here and kill me? Is this, in fact, what you are telling me?"

"I am afraid so," replied the man.

"Why?" asked Calvin in a hurt tone. "What did I do that was so horrible?"

The man thought for a moment and then said, "It isn't so much what you have done, but what you are going to do in the future that God is worried about. But an even simpler explanation is this: you are an anomaly. You do not belong here, in this time. Furthermore, you are artificially extending your lifetime, which means that you will continue to be a disturbance to the balance of the universe well into the future." The man looked at Tarpa and added, "You and your wife."

"Wait, what? Me?" questioned Calvin frantically. "What are you... I mean, how am I..."

"I think what he's trying to ask is, what the hell are you talking about?" clarified Tarpa.

The man took a deep breath and said, "It's really very simple. Because of your extended longevity, your prodigious power, and your expanding influence, you two are going to cause untold damage to the human race. As you may know, my father and I try to maintain a hands-off policy when it comes to meddling with human affairs, but since you were due to die nearly three hundred years ago, God sees this as a no-brainer — return you back to the grave, save the human race, job done."

Calvin sat down on the lawn while he let all this seep in. He struck a pose that resembled "The Thinker" as he stared at the man and pondered.

After a long five seconds, Calvin suddenly sprang to his feet, pointed at the man, and shouted, "You're a terminator!"

Tarpa called out from the background, "You want me to dismantle him for you, Cal?"

"No, honey. Give me a few more minutes, OK?" replied Calvin.

The man shook his head and innerly wept for the future of the human race. Then he said, "Calvin, I am not a terminator. I am Jesus Christ, son of God. But since I am a creature outside of time, and I'm here to kill you on behalf of the future of mankind, I suppose, in a very loose way, you could call me that."

Calvin twisted around to look at Tarpa for a moment and said, "See there, honey — I knew it! That explains the zappy hand trick. Besides, if God really wanted me dead, he could have just snapped his fingers or something."

Before Tarpa could respond, the man said, "It does not work like that, I'm afraid. OK, yes, technically speaking, God could wipe you out of existence just by forgetting about you. Poof. But when he created this universe, he set it up with some basic rules and does not wish to alter them midstream. There are no miracles. Not here. Just science."

Calvin gaped at him and said, "This is some serious next-level shit you're laying on me, here."

"I wish you would not curse in front of me. It makes me sad inside," replied the man.

Calvin shook his head for a moment and said, "OK, let's just back up here a bit. You said that Tarpa and I have all this power and control, but we don't. I mean, OK, we have a few body modifications, but so do thousands of others on Earth. I still don't get what you mean."

The man looked quizzically up in the sky for a moment, as if his eyes were linking with one of the satellites, and said simply, "You'll understand in about five minutes."

Calvin glanced in the same direction but saw nothing. He then looked at Tarpa, who merely shrugged.

Calvin said, "Um, OK. Very ominous. So... in the mean time, do you mind telling me more about that bit where God forgets about me and I disappear? What's that all about?"

The man replied, "Before I answer that, do you mind answering something for me?"

Calvin gave a half shrug. "Sure, why not?"

"How did you know that I was behind you in the shed? I am sure that I did not make a sound nor cast a shadow."

Calvin smiled. "Well, Mister Clever, I had already figured out that you could somehow mask yourself from Ariel."

The man tilted his head slightly and said, "Yes, so?"

Calvin gave a small chuckle and said, "But you were still leaving footprints."

The man's head drooped.

Calvin continued, "After I figured out that you were masking your presence, I had Ariel watch out for those sorts of anomalies. She warned me by text."

Tarpa called out from the background, "That was very clever, Cal."

"Thanks, honey," answered Calvin.

The man rolled his eyes.

Calvin asked him, "So, how did you hide from Ariel, anyway?"

The man looked around conspiratorially. Then he gestured toward his white robe with his head and said, "It's a robe of invisibility. Just between us, it's from your future time."

"Very cool," admired Calvin.

"Thank you," replied the man.

"Geeks," muttered Tarpa in the background.

Calvin then said to the man, "OK, anyway, about that thing..." but trailed off as he started to read an urgent text from Ariel. Tarpa received a copy and read it as well.

After about a minute, they had both finished the text but said nothing for a few seconds more. Finally, trembling and pale, Calvin said, "Jesus fucking Christ."

The man who claimed to be Jesus sighed and said, "Must you continually blaspheme right in front of me?"

Calvin looked at him distantly and said, "Oh, sorry."

Calvin then read the text aloud, partly so that the strange man could hear it, but also to help Calvin wrap his mind around what it had said. The text read as follows:

Ariel: **Calvin, I am sorry to interrupt, but I have urgent news to relay to you. Kevin6 Bacon is now deceased. He was caught in the crossfire between his two guards as they fought between themselves. Fortunately, mechanisms are in place for dealing with this contingency. Prior to his death, Kevin6 had created a formal succession plan. With that in mind, I have a text to deliver to you from Kevin6. It was to be delivered to you in the event of his death. Here is the text:**

Kevin6: **Hi there, Calvin. How are you? I am sure you are doing better than I am right now, since if you are reading this, I am dead. I really hope that I died in a cool way and not in some hospital bed smelling of my own urine. But anyway, on to the point of this letter. I will cut right to the chase. Calvin, I have named you as my successor. Now, if I know you (and god help us all if I do not), you probably just went catatonic. That is perfectly understandable. But listen, I know it sounds like a really big deal, and of course in some ways it is, but it is not as scary as you might think. Firstly, unlike me, you will not have**

to stay in cold storage — isn't that nice? You are essentially immortal after all, and your wife is the most capable Angel I have ever met. The job itself, as you know, entails fixing the little niggly problems that crop up every decade or so when some clever chap decides to have a poke around the Ariel system. The most difficult part of the job is to not become that clever chap. You must never use your access to manipulate Ariel, only to restore her. Do you understand? I hope you do, because if you start mucking around with her, I swear to God, Calvin, I will haunt you from the grave. I will turn all of your dreams into nightmares. I will whisper hateful words in the ears of all those around you and turn them against you. I will fill your pants with chiggers. I think you get my point. Well, good luck my friend. I left some notes for you in my desk drawer, other than that, you are on your own. Cheers, Kevin6 Bacon.

Calvin finished reading and went silent once again.

The man who claimed to be Jesus looked at him and said, "And thus the prophecy begins."

Calvin furrowed his brow at him. "You knew about this, didn't you? This is the power and control you were talking about, wasn't it? How do you know all this?"

The man looked at Calvin like a disappointed father and answered, "I am the son of God. God sees all."

"OK, fine, don't tell me," huffed Calvin in annoyance. "Anyway, the future isn't written in stone, is it? Don't I have a say in this? Surely, now that I know this information, I will be careful not to mess things up in the future?"

The man looked at the sky again for a few seconds and said, "The future is fluid, yes, but I'm afraid that as of this second, nothing has changed. The deed will still be done."

Calvin started to pace around in a circle. Every so often, he would go "Hmm." Tarpa and the man both watched this with interest. They caught each other's eyes and shrugged in unison.

"Ah-ha!" shouted Calvin suddenly. To his annoyance, no one shouted back "What?" with interest. He carried on regardless. "Jesus — and I'm just calling you that as a name, mind you, and not as acknowledgment of any sort of godliness — since you are also an immortal like us, or at the very least some sort of time

207

traveler, then surely you could pop in once in a while and keep me on the correct path? Surely you know that I am a decent man at heart. Rather than kill me now, can't you let me live and be a force for good? Already I have quelled a potential war here on Evionia. Ariel thinks that I am more valuable alive than dead. What does God think?"

The man looked up at the sky again for a moment and then said, "God agrees to your terms and will continue to monitor you with interest. As for me, you will be seeing me around."

Tarpa raised the flower pot in her hand. The man quickly added, "Not as an assassin, only as a guide."

Calvin nodded and took a step toward the man, but Tarpa stopped him by asking, "You don't really believe that nutter, do you Cal? You're not going to let him run loose again, knowing that he could attack you again at any moment?"

Calvin looked at the man. The man said, "You have my word that I will not."

Calvin replied to Tarpa, "I believe him. I'm letting him go."

The man said flatly, "No need. I'll do it myself."

There was a sudden crackle of electricity around the man's hands and feet, and the ropes instantly turned to smoke. The man stood there, unbound, but did not look smug. This somehow annoyed Calvin more than if he had.

The man held his hands up and showed them to Calvin while saying, "Healing hands — they have the power to right any wrong." He flipped his hood over his head and added, "Thank you for being kind to me, my son. May you stay on the path of righteousness. Goodbye, for now."

A mist rose up from the ground around the man and enveloped him. After it had subsided a few seconds later, the man was gone.

Calvin turned back to Tarpa and said, "Look, I know he's a looney, but you can't go around calling crazy people crazy to their faces. They tend to go really mental when you do that. Besides, in an odd sort of way, I think he could be right. We do have quite a bit of power now. I think it might do us good to have someone to keep us in check."

Tarpa considered this and said, "Alright. Fine. I'll trust your judgment for now. But Ariel and I are going to keep our guards up. I'll kill that raggedy bastard if he even looks at you funny."

Calvin smiled. "Thank you, honey. You're the greatest."

CHAPTER 40

Calvin, Tarpa, and Victoria carried their suitcases from the car, through the woods, and to the hidden spot on the east coast of Dirt where Calvin kept a motor boat for use in going to and from the unknown island that contained their shuttle.

They were doing this under the cover of darkness, more out of habit than out of prudence. Now that so many people had come online with Ariel, such things as Calvin and Tarpa's true origin had more or less become public knowledge. Just the same, Calvin and Tarpa preferred to remain as inconspicuous as possible — no need to flaunt a flashy spaceship.

Calvin and Tarpa loaded the luggage onto the boat while Victoria practically vibrated with nervous anticipation. Ever since she had met Calvin, her horizons had been continually expanded. Right now, she felt as if she were going to burst from it all. It had not been long ago when her entire world consisted of the Trad village and the sand pits to the south. Now, her world also contained an amazing city filled with weird and exciting things, and weird and exciting people. Soon, it would contain a whole other planet. Thinking about it made her feel like she needed to pee.

Calvin squatted down beside her and gave her a one-armed hug. "I know this is a lot for you, but you'll be fine. The people on Earth are pretty much the same as they are in Big City, except there are lots more of them. Besides, I think you're really going to like Newark. It's just unfortunate that we are going there for another funeral, but I won't drag you to this one.

Tarpa is going to show you around the city instead. We'll probably spend a week or two on Earth, as long as you are OK with it. I think you will be fine, but we won't stay any longer than you are comfortable with, OK?"

Victoria nodded and answered, "OK, Uncle Calvin."

"You're such a good girl, Victoria. I'm very proud of you. You're much braver than I was when I was your age."

Victoria squinted. "But you're the bravest man in the whole, wide world, Uncle Calvin. All the kids at school say so."

"Really?" asked Calvin, genuinely surprised.

"Uh huh," replied Victoria with a nod. "They say that anyone who would marry Aunt Tarpa must be the bravest man in the world."

Calvin almost choked. "That's probably true, but do me a favor and never, ever tell Aunt Tarpa that. I don't think it will go well for your classmates if you do."

Victoria pressed on. "Billy said he saw her throw a knife so hard at a man's leg that it went in one side and out the other." She smiled as if this was a fact to be proud of.

Calvin squirmed a little and answered, "Yes, well, Aunt Tarpa was raised with a very strong sense of justice. She doesn't take kindly to people taking things that don't belong to them. I'll tell you what, though, there is nobody else in the entire universe that will protect you better than Aunt Tarpa. So don't worry about visiting the Earth. The Earth is no match for Aunt Tarpa."

Tarpa, who had been listening to the entire conversation, walked up behind Calvin and flicked his earlobe.

"Ow!"

"Would you stop filling her head with weird ideas, you goofball?" asked Tarpa, jovially. Then she turned to Victoria and said, "Victoria, sweetie, it's true that I would defend you against the whole Earth, but it really isn't going to come to that. The Earth is a very friendly place — you'll see."

Tarpa looked around at the surrounding woodland and then asked, "So, where is our other passenger?"

A cloud of sparkles appeared in the distance, streamed single-file to a spot about three feet away from Tarpa, and rapidly assembled themselves into Ariel's avatar. Amusingly, she was carrying her luggage."

"Oh god," said Calvin, "She's not coming with us, is she?"

"Calvin," answered Ariel while tapping a finger behind her

right ear, "I'm always with you."

"You know what I mean," he huffed.

Ariel ignored this and said to Tarpa, "Arnold will be here momentarily and sends his apologies. He had some last-minute problems finding someone to watch his pigs while he is away."

As promised, a moment later, Arnold emerged from the woods hefting a suitcase and panting like a dog. He set it down beside the others and said, "Sorry I'm a runnin' late. I got to thanky again, old friend, fer keepin' yer promise."

"No problem — a deal is a deal," replied Calvin, sagely. "You helped us to get established here, after all. It would have been so much harder without you. Now it's time for our end of the bargain."

"I have to say, I'm so darn excited. I been up all night talking to Ariel about things to see on Earth."

Arnold then sidled up next to Calvin and whispered to him behind a cupped hand, "Ariel said ya might want to accompany me to a certain museum while we're there." He waggled his eyebrows to drive home the point.

Calvin nodded subtly and winked.

Tarpa, who had bionic hearing, rolled her eyes and loaded Arnold's luggage onto the boat.

The other three then joined her on the boat, and within minutes they were motoring to the unnamed island in the middle of Just Ocean.

While they were traveling, Calvin happened to look behind them and saw that, inexplicably, Ariel was pretending to water ski behind the boat. She took one hand off of the handle and waved to him. Calvin wondered whether this was the sort of glitch he was meant to fix now that he was Ariel's maintainer. He waved back and then ignored her for the remainder of the brief voyage.

Calvin was relieved that Victoria showed no signs of seasickness. He knew that the shuttle ride was coming up next, and even he had yet to fully get used to it — at least the takeoffs and landings.

Once on the island, they transferred to the shuttle. Victoria had never seen anything like it and wanted to ride on top, but Uncle Calvin said no.

Tarpa, Arnold, and a slightly pouty Victoria boarded the shuttle while Calvin pulled the refilling hose out of the ocean and stowed it in its special compartment on the side of the shuttle.

Somehow, the shuttle could refuel itself with ocean water and sunlight. Calvin asked Ariel how it worked, but then after a minute, his eyes glazed over and he suddenly said, "Yeah, OK. Magic. Got it," and walked away to board the shuttle.

Ariel shook her virtual head at his retreating back and said, "Another loss for brains versus beauty."

Inside the shuttle, Calvin helped Victoria into one of the travel compartments and explained to her about the virtual view, which would let her feel as if she were sitting on top of the shuttle without actually dying of asphyxiation. He also explained about the all-important pressure blanket, which would squeeze her down to keep her held in place during the takeoff and landing.

Calvin flashed back to when he had first met Victoria — she had ridden on top of a great, thundering beast while urging it to go faster and faster. He patted her hand and said, "You'll be fine."

Victoria's whoops and yells of excitement during the takeoff proved him right. Arnold, however, did not fare quite as well and spent the majority of the trip hiding under his blanket while the other three left their compartments and played games in the zero gravity.

CHAPTER 41

"Welcome back, Cal. How was the funeral?" asked Tarpa as Calvin walked through the door.

Calvin gave her a hug and said, "Eh, very strange, if I'm honest. I mean, the poor guy really didn't have any family or friends, so the whole event was more like a show for the world. It struck me more like the opening ceremonies of the Olympics than a funeral. We probably could have brought Victoria, actually. It was surprisingly entertaining. I think Kevin6 would have been pleased. It was more like a celebration of his life than the mourning of his death. Anyway, how did you three fare today?"

Tarpa answered, "Well, Arnold went off to do his own thing. He'll be fine, since he is already so accustomed to using Ariel. Vicky and I did the usual touristy things around Newark. She had a great time and had no trouble adjusting to the Earth, apart from finding it weird that the gravity stayed the same all day. Oh, and you should have seen her playing Hide Zack's Shoes. I don't think that poor kid will ever find them."

Calvin chuckled. "They're still playing that old game, huh?"

Tarpa replied, "Well, we've only been gone a couple of years, and the classics never get old."

Calvin thought about this and said, "You know, it's really weird to be back here. I mean, so much has happened to us in these few years that it feels like we've been gone for decades."

He looked around the apartment, which was in a different room from the one he used to live but had been decorated by

Ariel to look identical. He said, "There was a time when I had felt like Newark was my home town, but now I sort of feel like a visiting stranger."

"I think I know what you mean," agreed Tarpa. "Apart from checking in to make sure everything is still sound, I really don't have any desire to visit my California home."

"You know," said Calvin without much enthusiasm, "I inherited Kevin6's estate. It's not compulsory, but we are welcome to stay there if we want."

Tarpa made a face. "I don't know, I think I'd sooner live in my own home if I had to choose. His place is a bit too... old man, if you know what I mean. Plus the weather is better in California."

"No, I agree," said Calvin. "I was just throwing it out there. At least we have options."

Tarpa looked suddenly serious. "Does this mean we have to live on Earth again?"

Calvin looked a little surprised and answered, "Well, no, I don't think so. I mean, it would probably be a good idea for us to visit often — you know, to check up on things — but no one has said anything to me about having to actually live here. So wait, does this mean you actually prefer Evionia now?"

Tarpa looked slightly embarrassed, which was cute. She answered, "I suppose I do. It's like, I don't know, a closer community up there or something. Plus, I have my garden up there. I love my garden. And it's Vicky's home, after all. I'd hate to make her move now that she's just made all new friends at school."

Calvin nodded a few times and said, "OK." He hugged her and said, "We'll stay on Evionia."

Tarpa kissed him and said, "I'm so glad that I met you."

To Calvin's surprise, he almost teared up after hearing it. A little hoarsely, he said back, "I'm so glad I met you too."

Victoria, who had been waiting patiently beside them, made a face and said, "OK, enough of the kissy faces. What are we going to do next?"

They both laughed and Calvin said, "Well, if it's OK with you two, I'd like to stop by Kevin6's place. He said he had some notes for me. Plus, I want to make sure everything is in a fit state. And we should probably stop somewhere on the way and get some flowers for Gladas."

Victoria and Tarpa looked at each other for a moment and

then Tarpa said, "I think we're fine with that. Who's Gladas, by the way?"

"The tour guide at Kevin6's place. I think she was rather sweet on him. I'm sure she is crushed."

Tarpa smiled and said, "Plus, if we butter her up, we can convince her to stay there and mind the place in our absence, right?"

Victoria shook her head and said, "You're devious, Uncle Calvin."

"Me?" exclaimed Calvin with mock innocence. He pointed at Tarpa and added, "She's the one who said it."

Victoria replied, "Yeah, but you were thinking it, weren't you Uncle Calvin?"

"Was not," protested Calvin. "Mind you, I'll admit that it does work in our favor, though, to be kind to the old biddy."

"Uncle Calvin," scolded Victoria.

Calvin raised his hands in surrender. "Only joking. Anyway, for whatever reason, how about we get going?"

The girls agreed. They all loaded into a packet and took ODIN to the K6B museum, which had doubled as Kevin6's home and personal cryogenics facility.

As they approached the house, Calvin pointed to a section of the front wall and said, "They did a good job of patching up the hole — you'd never know it had been there."

Tarpa glanced at the wall without interest and nodded.

Calvin rang the doorbell. After a short while, it was answered by Gladas. After seeing Calvin, she said, "Oh, Mr. Cow Fin! What a wonderful surprise. Come on in, deary."

Calvin and the others entered the foyer. Calvin stood still for a moment while he stared vacantly at a seemingly random spot on the floor.

Victoria noticed this and asked, "Are you OK, Uncle Calvin?"

Tarpa replied quietly, "Just give him a moment, sweetie. Something really bad happened here. Uncle Calvin is just remembering it, is all."

Quietly, Victoria walked over to Calvin and hugged his legs.

Calvin slowly emerged from his memories and focused on Victoria. He patted her on the top of the head and said, "Thank you sweetie, I needed that."

Gladas said, "Come along, Cow Fin. I'll make some tea."

Calvin corrected her. "It's Calvin, actually. Oh, and these are for you. We're very sorry about your loss." He handed her a bouquet of flowers.

Gladas took the flowers. "Suit yourself, deary. Oh my, these are very nice. It's just dreadful what happened to Mr. Bacon, isn't it? Just dreadful. I told him not to go gallivanting around with those floozies. You can't trust those Dark Angels, I said. They're all wacko in the head. I told him he needed to settle down with a good woman more his age. Damn fool." She began to tear up.

Tarpa graciously ignored the remark about the Dark Angels. Calvin helped Gladas over to a chair.

"I think we're just going to have a look around, if you don't mind, Gladas," said Calvin to the teary-eyed woman. "You take a little time and collect yourself."

Victoria stood beside her chair and pattered her arm. "It will be alright, Miss Gladas. Do you want to talk about it?"

Calvin and Tarpa looked at each other in surprise. Calvin texted to her:

Calvin: She grew up watching her father comfort the whole village, remember? This is probably second nature to her.

Tarpa mouthed back, "Wow."

Calvin then said, "Victoria, you can stay here with Gladas if you'd like. We are just going to be downstairs if you need us."

"OK, Uncle Calvin."

Once downstairs, Calvin said, "She's something, huh?"

Tarpa nodded. "Yes, definitely. She's a great little girl. I hope we don't fuck her up."

Calvin chuckled. "I know what you mean. I think it will be alright. Probably. Well, we'll just do our best, at any rate."

They walked further into the den. Calvin found Kevin6's writing desk and retrieved a notebook from inside of it. It read "Zero Calvin" on the front cover. Calvin held it up for Tarpa to see and said, "Everyone's a comedian."

They each took a moment to look around the room. After a while, Calvin said, "That was quite a day, wasn't it?"

Tarpa continued to look around and answered, "It sure was, Zero."

They looked around for just a few more seconds and then Calvin asked suddenly, "Do you want to get the hell out of here?"

"I sure do," Tarpa quickly replied.

As one, they turned and walked back upstairs. They found Gladas in the kitchen with Victoria, making tea.

They had a seat at the kitchen table. Calvin asked Gladas, "How long have you lived here, Gladas?"

Gladas turned off the stove and lifted the kettle while she thought. "Oh, I'd say nearly thirty years. How time flies."

"It must have been lonely here, all alone," interjected Tarpa. "I mean, since Kevin6 was frozen for most of the time."

"Oh, yes," replied Gladas. "Well, there were the guards, of course, but they were about as much fun as watching a cat puke up a hairball." Gladas then looked around as if she were about to share a secret and then added, "Just between us... about twice a year I'd thaw out Mr. Bacon and we'd play scrabble together, watch movies, or read to each other. We never told Ariel — she would've pitched a fit."

Calvin chuckled and said, "Good old Kevin6."

Tarpa said, "Tell me, Gladas, how would you like to continue to live here? As you probably know, Calvin and I inherited this place. But we've decided to continue to live elsewhere. It would help us out tremendously if we had someone to stay here and look after the place. I imagine people will still have an interest in visiting here, especially now. You are welcome to keep it open to the public or make it private — your choice. And of course, you don't have to stay here at all, if you don't want to."

Gladas looked delighted. "Oh, deary, that is so kind of you. I'd love to stay. I've lived here for so long, I don't know where else I could go. Oh, this is wonderful."

"Excellent," said Calvin rubbing his hands together. How about that tea, then?"

Gladas looked down with surprise — she was still holding the tea kettle. She quickly filled some cups and served her guests.

Victoria sat down at the table and took a few sips of her tea. She was rapidly getting bored, but tried not to fidget. After a few more minutes, however, she could no longer stand it. She asked, "What else are we going to do, today?"

Calvin thought about this. "Hmm, I don't know. It's getting late. Maybe we'll call it a day, go home, have some pizza, and watch a movie or two. Sound good?"

Victoria said, "I love pizza, Uncle Calvin."

"Great. Then that's settled. Maybe tomorrow we'll take a day trip to the moon. You can meet the mad scientist that brought Uncle Calvin back to life."

"Back to life?" asked Gladas with concern that she might have inadvertently invited the undead into her home.

"It's a long story, Gladas. I wasn't really dead, just mostly dead."

"Oh, that's alright, then," answered Gladas in relief.

"What's the moon?" asked Victoria.

Calvin glanced at the window. It was already nighttime. "Come outside," he said. "I'll show you."

Once outside, Victoria stared in fascination at the gibbous moon, which was just shy of being full. "Is that like a very dim sun?" she asked.

Calvin shook his head a little and answered, "No, it's just a lifeless hunk of rock. It's smaller than the Earth's sun but much closer, so it looks about the same size. The light you see is reflected sunlight."

Victoria continued to study it and asked, "A lifeless rock?"

Calvin shrugged. "Yeah, there's not much up there, I'm afraid. There is really no air to breathe, so you have to stay in a special suit or in a special vehicle to be on the surface. But the gravity is a lot less than what it is here, so you can jump really, really high."

"Cool," enthused Victoria.

"About the only thing on the moon is the laboratory that we are visiting," added Calvin.

"Why is it on the moon?" asked Victoria.

"Well," said Calvin, "if you believe the owner of the lab, it's to give his employees a new perspective in which to view the world."

"And the real reason?" asked Victoria, perceptively.

Calvin chuckled. "That's my little skeptic. The real reason, I suspect, is because he is always doing stupid stuff that is way too dangerous to be done in populated areas."

"He sounds fun," observed Victoria.

Calvin looked up in thought and said, "Eh, for a given value of fun, I suppose so. Just promise me to never, ever be in the kitchen when he's making sandwiches."

CHAPTER 42

Calvin, Tarpa, Victoria, and Arnold were all crowded into a single moon rover, which Calvin was driving from the airport to the lab. The infamous crater was fast approaching. Calvin glanced at Arnold, who was turning green, and made a last-minute decision to go around it.

Calvin struck up a conversation with Arnold to help take his mind off of the journey. "So, Arnold, what did you do yesterday? Anything interesting?"

Arnold opened his eyes and focused on Calvin while trying not to look at anything outside the rover. He wiped a bead of sweat off of his forehead and said, "Oh, yessir. I went to that there museum without ya. Sorry about that. I reckon I can be talked into going again, if ya wanna go together."

"That's OK," said Calvin, flatly.

"And then... and then I went to this place, Calvin. Oh my goodness." Arnold made the sign of the cross. "Oh boy. I mean, Calvin this place. It was like..." he shook his head "...it was like being in Sodom and Gomorrah. My..." he glanced at Victoria and modified what he was about to say, "my frank and beans will never be the same, I reckon. I mean, Calvin, they had electrics there. Down there!"

"Where did you go?!?" asked Calvin, already suspecting the answer.

Arnold wiped more sweat from his forehead and answered, "It were called the Screaming Skelington, or some such thing."

"You went there alone?!?" asked Calvin and Tarpa in tandem.

Arnold looked from one to the other and then answered, "Well, yeah. I sure as shootin' weren't gonna bring you along, Calvin. My ship don't sail that way, if ya catch my meaning."

Calvin wisely did not bother to answer. Fortunately, they had just arrived at the lab and were now going through the incremental pressure locks. As he drove, he said, "Arnold, Victoria, your ears may pop a few times like they did in the shuttle, but there is nothing to worry about. It helps if you keep swallowing."

Once in the parking garage, they all got out of the rover and stretched. They waited for Arnold to look a more natural color and then took the elevator up to floor 14, Bobford3's usual stomping ground.

When the elevator doors opened, a paper party horn unrolled and blew a sour note at them. Bobford3 removed it from his lips and said, "Welcome back, you two."

Before he had even formed the "W", Tarpa had already stepped protectively in front of the others and had her arm-knife at the ready.

Bobford3 smiled at Tarpa while she retracted her blade. He said, "Tarpa, dear, how I missed your psychotic outbursts." He rubbed his neck. "Even the scars around my neck have healed."

"You want some new ones?" asked Tarpa with a smile.

Bobford3 ignored this and said to Calvin, "Hey there, ice-pop. Nice to see you again."

"Hey Bob. Good to see you again, you crazy bastard," replied Calvin, and then shook Bob's hand.

Calvin then gestured toward Victoria and said, "I'd like you to meet our adopted daughter, Victoria." He noticed Bobford3's surprise and added, "It's a long story."

Bobford3 squatted down to Victoria's height and said, "Nice to meet you, Victoria. I'm Bobford3, but you can call me Bob. Welcome to my laboratory. Just remember, buttons aren't toys, OK?"

Victoria looked at him quizzically and said, "OK, Mr. Bob."

Bobford3 then stood up and looked at the seemingly out-of-place Arnold.

Calvin said in explanation, "This here is Arnold. He's a native of Evionia. He's just here on holiday."

Bobford3 gave Arnold a nod and said to him, "Nice to meet you, Arnold. Welcome to my lab. And the same thing goes for you — buttons aren't toys, OK?"

Arnold looked at Calvin for a second, as if wanting a translation, and then finally said, "Thanky Mr. Bob, sir. I'll surely remember it."

"Oh," said Bobford3 suddenly, as if just remembering something, "I forgot to congratulate you two. Married, huh? Wow! It's a crazy old world, isn't it?" He reached down beside him, picked up an aluminum briefcase, and handed it to Tarpa. "A belated wedding present for you guys. Go ahead, open it. It won't explode, I promise."

Tarpa opened it facing Bobford3 just in case it did explode. When it did not, she spun it around and showed the contents to Calvin.

The case contained a large container of orange powder and two stoppered test tubes filled with gray powder.

"You folks ain't drug addicts, are ya?" asked Arnold, nervously.

"That there," explained Bobford3 for everyone's benefit, "is the elixir of eternal life. Calvin, Tarpa, I've improved the nano-rebuilders for you. One gram of these little buggers will now see you through the better part of a year. There's enough here to last each of you, say, two hundred years. The other stuff is just Tang powder. You'll need to make more of that, of course, but that's easy enough."

Bobford3 smiled at Tarpa's surprised expression and said to her, "You noticed that I said each of you, I see. Congratulations, your last test came out positive. You're now a mutant just like Zero Calvin over there."

Tarpa carefully closed the case and held it by the handle. She looked at Bobford3 and said, "Seriously, Bob, thank you. This is actually a very wonderful gift."

"Yeah, Bob. You rule!" added Calvin beside her.

"I'm glad you both like it," replied Bobford3 with a slight bow. "Now, come along. I want you to meet someone very special."

With a shrug, the others followed Bobford3 to Lab 4.

Of all the things that they had expected to find there, a nursery had not been one of them. Calvin and Tarpa stared with their mouth's slightly open as Bobford3 lifted a baby from a very fancy crib and said, "Everyone, I'd like you to meet Bobford4."

Tarpa started to say something and then stopped. Calvin, too, was at a loss for words. Victoria, however, said brightly, "So you made a clone of yourself, Mr. Bob?"

Bobford3 said cheerily, "My, you are a smart one, aren't you? It's definitely clear to me that you were adopted."

Victoria shrugged and said, "I just learned yesterday that Mr. Bacon was a clone, and I learned what the Bacon number is. You have a Bacon number, so that means you are a clone."

Calvin finally found a voice and said, "Wow, Bob. I guess congratulations are in order. What brought this on?"

Bobford3 shrugged. "I just figured it was time."

He placed the baby back into the crib, being careful not to get him tangled in the mobile of stars and rocket ships. He then ushered them all out of the room and said, "Alright, now it's time to meet my new crew."

"I'd surely like to do that," said Arnold, excitedly.

Bobford3 asked with some surprise, "You know of them?"

"Oh yessir," replied Arnold. "I'm a big fan. I've been watching your progress through Ariel. Right impressive work, it is."

Calvin, Tarpa, and Bobford3 all exchanged glances and shrugs. Bobford3 said, "Alright then... uh, well, step this way."

Bobford3 walked them through the tunnels that led to the BLC collider, and into one of the control rooms where Bobford3's new staff were twiddling with knobs and trying to look busy.

Just before they went through the door, Bobford3 looked at both Arnold and Victoria and asked, "You remember what I told you?"

Arnold shook his head and said no.

Victoria said, "Buttons aren't toys."

Bobford3 patted her on the head and said, "Good girl." He then pointed at Arnold and added, "You keep an eye on him for me, OK?"

"OK," agreed Victoria.

Everyone shuffled into the room, and then Bobford3 did the introductions. "OK, old staff, meet the new staff. New staff, meet the old staff — well, these two at least. This is Tarpa, my former nurse. This is Calvin, a former patient. This is their rather brilliant daughter, Victoria. And their friend, Arnold, from Evionia, who I'm led to believe is a fan of our work. Now on this side, we have Brody, our mechanical engineer; Sarah, our researcher; and Mike, our chemist."

Arnold took off his hat in respect and practically dove across the room to shake the new team's hands. He clenched his hat close to his chest and said, "It's a right honor to meet y'all. I'm a big fan of your work." He walked over to Brody and said, "You can build damn near anything, can't ya, son?"

Brody smiled and said, "I do my best, bro."

Arnold then took a few steps to the left and said, "And you, miss, you're right smart — a damn genius if I'm any judge. You're also right perdy, if ya don't mind me sayin' so."

Sarah remained silently staring into oblivion.

Mike said, "Don't feel bad, tiger. She does that sometimes. Your compliments were probably just too much for her. Sometimes she blows a fuse — she'll reset in a few minutes."

Arnold took a few more sideward steps and stood in front of Mike. "And you, Mike, you're the funny one."

Mike made a face. "That's it? That's my contribution to the team? I'm the funny one?"

Arnold laughed and swatted Mike with his hat. "I'm just bustin' ya balls, son." He then remembered that he was in the company of women and added, "Excuse my language, ladies."

Bobford3 interrupted, "OK, so anyway, guys, this is my latest project... a transmutation device. Right now we've got the facility dialed in so it's turning lunar dust into aluminum. Oh, that reminds me, I've got a couple of commemorative rings for you guys." He fished in his pocket and pulled out a pair of aluminum rings. He blew the lint off of them and handed one to Calvin and one to Tarpa.

Calvin studied his. It was just aluminum, but he had to guess that it had been lunar dust in its past life. Pretty cool, he thought. The ring had Bobcorp3 Laboratories engraved on it. Calvin tried it on.

Mike coughed and said, "Um, those are still sort of fresh, so they might still be slightly radioactive. I'd give it another week before wearing it, if I were you."

Calvin hurriedly took the ring off and placed it far away from him on the counter. Tarpa glanced at hers and put it into a padded, shielded compartment in her left arm.

Bobford3 said, "We've got this puppy making over two hundred kilograms a day, atom by atom."

"Impressive," said Calvin, who felt obligated to say something.

Arnold took off his hat again, clenched it close to his chest, and said, "I knows I'm just a simple pig farmer, so y'all have to excuse me if I'm speaking out of turn. But I've been studyin' yer design and talkin' it over with Ariel, and it seems to me that if y'all use resonance to build up the speed of the particles instead of using that there linear accelerator, then you could probably reduce your machine to somethin' like the size of, I don't know, maybe an oven. Maybe smaller if Brody gets clever."

Mike and Brody looked at each other. Brody asked, "Can that really work?"

Mike shrugged.

Sarah's head suddenly made a quick, sharp movement that pointed her face directly at Arnold, but she said nothing.

Arnold, in turn, looked back. Suddenly he said, "Yes. Uh huh. No, I was thinkin' wave harmonics. No, probably not. Hey, yes, that could work! Just a little bit, though. Exactly — just like a molten salt reactor. No, I weren't kidding about you being perdy."

Then, Sarah finally spoke. She said, "Particles bouncing between spinning seas, gaining strength for the final release. They crash into the sandy shore, where they set free so many more. Will you have dinner with me tonight? I promise you, I do not bite."

CHAPTER 43

"Doc, we are going to make so much money," said Calvin while putting his arm around the bewildered man's shoulder.

Doc ducked out of Calvin's hold and asked, "How so, boss?"

Calvin grinned. "We're starting a whole new company, Doc — Alchemy Motorworks. Check out these plans." Calvin had Ariel display the plans on the wall.

Doc studied them for a while and then said, "It looks buildable. Whoever drew these plans was a mechanical genius. I have no idea what it is or if it will work, mind you, but I know I can get the lads in the shop to build the parts, and I think the assemblers should be able to put all the parts together in the right order."

"Excellent. Good man," said Calvin. "Get someone to slap up another building out back. We'll leave the machining here, but I'd like you to set up a new assembly line for these motors. Take some of the more experienced people and transfer them to the new line. Feel free to hire more people to back-fill for the Guide's assembly line as needed."

Doc, trying hard to keep up, said, "Sure, boss. I can do that. But first, do you mind telling me what the heck this new motor does?"

Calvin sighed. "Sorry, Doc. I went into hyper-active boss mode again, didn't I? Um, the motor is a very special sort. It really does run on alchemy. Actually, it runs on sand, well, silicon to be more exact. The sand has to be preprocessed for now. Maybe in a later revision, we will address that. But anyway, it basically shaves a hydrogen atom off the silicon — don't ask me how — which leaves you with aluminum as a byproduct. The hydrogen is burnt as the fuel for the motor. Since it is being consumed more or less as it is being created, there is no chance of any explosion from a hydrogen leak. The system only stores a tiny bit at a time."

"And that works?" asked Doc, doubtfully. "Wouldn't it take more energy to split the silicon than you would get from burning the hydrogen? Or, at least the same amount?"

"I'm not sure. It's basically a really small nuclear fission reactor, and it is capable of safely reprocessing anything radioactive that it may inadvertently create from a faulty split — at least that's what they tell me. And since other nuclear reactors also make energy from matter, I don't see why our motors couldn't work. Anyway, they are building a prototype on the Earth's moon as we speak, so we will see soon enough. Actually, come to think about it, let's hold up on the new building for now. This is a Bobford3 project after all. Let's make sure the prototype works first."

"Good idea, boss," agreed Doc. "Oh, and boss, what do we do with all the leftover aluminum?"

Calvin pointed a finger at the ceiling. "Ah, a good point. Well, we don't do anything with it — the Trads will take care of it. I'm thinking that since they control the sand pits, we will sell them the motors. We'll help them to build an automobile plant."

"Why would we do that?" asked Doc, without thinking it through.

Calvin smirked. "So that we can sell them more motors, of course. They will also have to set up refueling stations. I imagine it will be a simple matter of pulling out a compartment of aluminum powder and replacing it with a fresh one full of silicon powder. They can use the aluminum to make more cars, or sell off the excess. Supposedly, the design can be tweaked to accept aluminum and spit out magnesium. Maybe we can make a hybrid unit — I'll have to look into that. We would probably be smart to stop there, though."

"Why is that?" asked Doc, dutifully.

"Because magnesium would be reduced to sodium, which reacts violently with water and explodes."

Doc nodded. "Yes, I can see there being safety issues with that. He thought for a moment and then added, "Although, since it is being made in small quantities, couldn't we just purposefully introduce the sodium to water in some part of the engine? Like a sort of afterburner?"

"Doc, you're a damn genius," said Calvin brightly.

Doc smiled.

"Except, of course, that the byproduct of that is sodium hydroxide, or lye as it is commonly called. Very caustic. Very nasty."

Doc stopped smiling.

Calvin added, "But I like that you're thinking outside the box. Good work. Keep that up."

Doc smiled again. "Thanks, boss."

CHAPTER 44

Victoria was at school, so Calvin and Tarpa were taking the opportunity to spend some quality time together. Calvin was sitting at the picnic table in the garden. Tarpa was standing beside the table while holding a plate of sandwiches. She was wearing furry bunny ears, a fuzzy bunny tail, and nothing else.

She set the plate of sandwiches down and said, "I still don't see why you are making me wear this?"

Calvin raised his hands up and said, "Listen, my hands are tied here. You were the one that started this. You were the one that chose the nuclear option by invoking the mutually assured destruction clause of our marriage agreement. You forced me not to kill that Trad bastard. Now, I'm afraid, that there must be consequences."

Tarpa furrowed her brow at him and said, "Yes, but Calvin, you agree that it was the right choice, right? I mean, otherwise you would have started a war."

"Oh, for sure," agreed Calvin. "But that's not the point. The point is that you chose the option, so you must pay. Those are the rules. Otherwise, you might be tempted to take the power for granted later on."

Tarpa put her hands on her hips and asked, "And this isn't taking the power for granted?"

Calvin gave a half shrug. "It's the only thing I could think of that would bother you."

It was now Tarpa's turn to shrug. "It doesn't really bother me."

Calvin smacked her on the butt and said, "Good, then shut up and get me some tea."

Tarpa's arm-knife extended a few inches and then retracted.

Calvin smiled. "But that bothers you, doesn't it?"

Tarpa poured a cup of tea over Calvin's head and said, "Yes, it does. It bothers me if you act like a douche. And you know I don't take orders from anyone, even from you."

Calvin did his best not to react to the tea. He raised an eyebrow and answered back, "You'll take orders if I invoke our marriage clause, though, won't you?"

Tarpa reached for another cup of tea.

Calvin raised his hands in surrender and said, "OK, fine. I take it back." He gestured to an empty chair and said, "Have a seat. Only if you want to, of course. It's not an order." He grinned.

Tarpa sat down and stared at him.

Calvin said, "What? Oh don't look at me like that. Oh, alright. I admit it. I just wanted to see you naked in bunny ears, is that so wrong?"

Tarpa shook her head and grinned. "Oh no, Calvin. I'm not mad at that. I told you, I don't mind this at all. I'm just trying to decide what I'm going to make you wear tomorrow."

"Oh god, help me," said Calvin as he imagined the possibilities.

Tarpa hushed him and said, "Don't say that — do you want Jesus to come and crash our party?"

Calvin laughed. "No, not at all. Anyway, it's hard to imagine that we are doing anything right now that could possibly destroy civilization."

Tarpa shrugged. "Collapsing its moral standards?" she suggested.

Calvin nodded. "Could be. Not a bad way to go, though, when you think about it — surrounded by bunny girls."

Tarpa rubbed her chin and said, "Hmm, maybe I'll make you a gladiator tomorrow."

Calvin thought about this and said, "How about a vampire, instead? More realistic."

"True," agreed Tarpa. "Speaking of which, I'm on the pill now, as it were. I took some of Bobford3's rebuilders yesterday. They seem to work. I cut my leg shaving this morning, and it healed right up."

Calvin smiled and said enthusiastically, "Cool! So we are both immortal now, more or less. Just you and me against the world, eh? Two stones wading the endless seas of time together. How cool is that?"

"You know," said Tarpa with a smirk, "I think maybe I'll stop taking the pills after all."

"Ha-ha," replied Calvin. "Seriously, though. I wonder how Victoria is going to handle having ageless parents?"

Tarpa replied, "Well, seeing as her real parents are both dead, I think she'll be thrilled to have ones made from tougher stock."

Calvin tilted his head and said, "I never thought of it that way. So, do you think we should make her immortal as well?"

Tarpa wrinkled up her nose and said, "Well, not until she's older or that would just be weird. But, when the time comes, we'll let her choose. It's not like she can't change her mind afterward, anyway. It doesn't have to be forever."

Calvin nodded. "Yeah, right, of course. I wasn't saying we should keep her a kid forever. Although, she is a little cutey-pie right now, I must admit. I wonder what she's going to be like when she's older? I mean, I'm basically just a slacker, and you, well, I think you will make a good mother, don't get me wrong, but I don't really picture you nurturing Victoria to be a woman so much as training her as a disciple."

Tarpa thought about this. "You might be right, sport. But that's not so bad, is it? For her to have your people skills and compassion, and my cunning and situational awareness? I think she'll be rather awesome, actually."

Calvin thought about how much he enjoyed being with Tarpa and smiled. "I really love you, you know. I'm glad that we are both immortal, because a lifetime is not long enough to spend with you."

Tarpa pointed at Calvin and said, "You see, if Victoria turns out to be a smooth talker like you, she might be glad that she learned from me the twenty-three ways to incapacitate someone with a spoon. You boys can get overheated sometimes, you know."

Tarpa then stood up from the table and walked over to Calvin. She took him gently by the hand and said, "Now, come with me. Since I'm dressed like a bunny, I'll show you what bunnies like to do."

Calvin was then led into a secluded spot of the garden — a spot that he later nicknamed bunny heaven.

CHAPTER 45

Sarah and Arnold were sitting side-by-side on the couch in her living room, staring at the wall together. They were each wearing the latest model of display lenses, a gift from Bobford3.

They did this for over an hour, barely speaking to each other in the real world, but instead, leading each other through wild fields of data, frolicking in random connections, and otherwise having a geeky time together.

Suddenly, Sarah turned to Arnold and recited the following poem:

At last I've found my soul mate
Arnold is the one for me
I'm having a great first date
I've never been so happy
Let's leave this digital world
of bits, bytes, octal, and hex
Come over here my Arnold
It's time to have some sex

www.ingramcontent.com/pod-product-compliance
Lightning Source LLC
Chambersburg PA
CBHW070930180626
46817CB00003B/1229